FOUL
SHOT

FOUL SHOT

...

DOUG HORNIG

CHARLES SCRIBNER'S SONS

NEW YORK

Copyright © 1984 Doug Hornig

Library of Congress Cataloging in Publication Data

Hornig, Doug.
    Foul Shot.
    I. Title.
PS3558.068785F6   1984   813'.54   84-10594
ISBN 0-684-18187-8

1 3 5 7 9 11 13 15 17 19   F/C   20 18 16 14 12 10 8 6 4 2

Printed in the United States of America.

AUTHOR'S NOTE: I'm indebted to my editor, Betsy Rapoport,
for helping to guide me through the process of first publication.

For Frankie

FOUL
SHOT

· 1 ·

Clementine quit on me shortly after I'd turned west off of U.S. 29. She bucked and wobbled for a moment, as if hit by a sniper's bullet, then, with a final, shuddering spasm, ceased to function.

No, I thought. Not now, of all possible times.

But it *was* now. Here and now and no two ways about it.

With a sigh, I pulled the emergency blinker button and coasted to a stop on the narrow road's shoulder—what there was of it. Which was about as much as there was on the adolescent Twiggy.

For a while I just sat, my hands folded on top of the steering wheel, my forehead resting against them. A posture not unlike prayer, though the closest I'd been to a church in the past twenty years was when I was hired by the Baptist minister's wife. He was cheating on her, of course, but my having confirmed that wasn't going to help me now. You apparently don't get any brownie points with the Lord for exposing His shepherds as philanderers. More's the pity; I could have used some divine intervention. It was damp, chilly December, and my automobile's heart had stopped beating. The temperature inside the old Volkswagen was falling at an alarming rate, and it hadn't been all that warm to begin with. The Krauts never did manage to make an efficient heater.

I spoke to the car softly, with the easy intimacy that develops over a long-term relationship.

"Clementine," I said, "we've come quite a ways together, you and I. Over ten years now. The fat years and the lean. Mostly the lean. And just when I get a call from some serious money, you conk out on me. Now why would you want to do that, old friend?" She

1

didn't answer. But then her unwillingness to move any farther forward was an answer of sorts.

Shrugging to no one in particular, I got out. The pavement was still slick from the thaw of the previous night's black ice. Without much in the way of expectation, I buttoned my coat, trooped to the back of the Bug, and propped open the engine compartment. It was all there in front of me: '72 was the last year Volkswagen made an engine that was comprehensible to someone who hadn't been to automotive engineering school. By '75 my mechanic could challenge me to peer into the innards of the current model and offer me five bucks if I could tell him how to get the spark plugs out. I never collected.

Clementine was making the normal cooling-off sounds. Groans and pings and whatnot. I studied the situation.

I'm not much of a mechanic, which is one of the reasons I've held onto the "People's Car" for so long. I stopped paying attention about the time they invented fuel injection, and I wouldn't know an overhead cam from a canned ham. But I've learned to maintain my Volkswagen and to cope with minor emergencies. I studied the situation some more.

Suddenly, in a bug-sized version of enlightenment, I saw it, staring me in the face. I was looking at the fuel line. Just before it heads into the carburetor, it passes through a tiny plastic gas filter. I hadn't changed the thing in years, being in fact less than acutely aware of its existence. It was obviously an important piece of equipment, though, and the continued functioning of the engine depended on it. At the moment, it had been reduced to a few shards of plastic clinging to the gas line. Its age and the recent unseasonable cold snap must have conspired to make it exceptionally brittle, and what with my banging over the marginal back roads of Albemarle County, it eventually just shattered like Ella Fitzgerald's wineglass.

Since I didn't have a spare filter in my pocket, it was time to face some facts.

Fact one: the car was not going to run without an uninterrupted fuel line.

Fact two: I had a meeting scheduled with John Majors in a few minutes, and it was a meeting I'd rather not miss, since it held out the delightful and timely prospect of my converting some of his considerable cash into mine.

Fact three: I was on a secondary road with little traffic. There was a substantial highway a mile back, but the cars on it were headed north and south.

Fact four: the Majors place was still a couple of miles west.

Fact five: it was cold.

To my credit, and in spite of my predicament, I didn't swear a lot. If you don't develop a little patience and resignation to the inevitable as you grow older, you probably haven't lived properly.

I swore. For fifteen seconds I cussed and yelled and kicked at the gravel under foot.

Then I calmly closed the engine compartment and started trudging along the shoulder of S.R. 666.

The road was lined with locust trees in various stages of dying. Something—a fungus, a pest, chemicals in the air—was killing off the locust trees in central Virginia. Maybe it was happening everywhere; I didn't know. Maybe the locust was committing species suicide to call our attention to the deteriorating quality of the environment. Whatever, it was very bad news for Virginians who valued sturdy, rot-resistant fence posts and for those who planned to heat with wood in the future. The idea that species were becoming extinct all around us depressed me. I liked the locust trees, with their eccentric growth patterns and their deeply gullied bark and their strange yellow heartwood, and I didn't want them to go the way of the American chestnut. I picked up a rock and threw it at the nearest tree, as if I could somehow frighten off the shadowy demon that was raping the landscape.

There was a slight rise in the road. From the top I could see all the way to the ridge line that marked the eastern boundary of the Shenandoah Valley. Dark gray clouds were scudding across its crest. Snow clouds, with my luck. Today or tomorrow we were going to get some. I hunched down into my coat and quickened my pace.

The way sloped steadily downward now. All around me was gently rolling farmland. Prime horse country. Several thousand of these acres would belong to the Majors family, living proof that you *can* make a fortune in real estate if only you're ruthless enough.

I wondered idly why they'd called me. Probably because I was the only private investigator in the Charlottesville phone book. It was an advantage, but it also accurately reflected the frequency of demand for my services.

I heard her from a long way off. It had to have been a long way, considering how fast she was driving and how long it took her to get to me. At a distance, the engine sounded like a junkyard dog who's about to take on the intruder.

The car topped the rise, becoming airborne for an instant. It was an old Mustang, one of the originals, lime green and apparently in mint condition. The bulge in the hood suggested a nonstock engine, and the rear end was jacked up over extra-wide tires. A very distinctive automobile. At the moment, this very distinctive automobile was behaving as if there weren't quite enough room hereabouts for both me and it. I stepped well back on the shoulder and stuck out my thumb. The Mustang fishtailed to a stop on the slippery road and waited, the engine blatting ominously. I wasn't at all sure that I wanted to get in the thing.

She settled matters by leaning on the horn. It was one of those designed to deafen anyone who dares to offend you. I got the message.

Cautiously, my ears ringing, I went over to the car and opened the passenger's side door.

A beautiful girl of about eighteen said, "Well, get in, turkey."

I got in.

Before my door was fully closed, she'd popped the clutch, the fat rear tires had squealed in protest and then caught, and we were off. She drove recklessly but, I had to admit, with skill.

I wet my lips and asked how far she was going. It still sounded like "How furrer y'gwun?" They didn't make girls like this in my day.

"Another mile and a half," she said.

"Good. Do you know the Majors place?"

She glanced sideways at me, then laughed.

"You must be Swift," she said. "That your car broke down back there?"

"The VW?"

"Only one I saw."

"Yeah, it's mine. But how do you know me?"

"Don't you suppose I'd know what goes on around my own house?"

"Uh, I guess so."

"Well, I do. I know *everything*. I make it my . . . business." She smiled as if locking away a childhood secret.

4

"Oh," I said. She didn't look like she was going to offer anything further, so I continued, "Well, I'm Swift. You can call me Swift." It's not a bad lead-in line, but she didn't take it. Maybe it *is* a bad lead-in line."And you are?"

"Melissa Majors."

"Oh."

She'd said her name as if it terminated our conversation, such as it was. I settled back and studied her as nonchalantly as I could.

She was striking. A long face with high cheekbones, patrician nose, and deep black eyes. Straight hair black as Nixon's heart. A slender body that would probably be quite tall when she uncoiled it from the driver's seat. She was wearing a dark green wool car coat, belted and hooded, that looked very expensive and reached to mid-thigh. Without peeking, I bet myself that she was the sort who would have on knee-high leather boots. I checked. She had on knee-high leather boots. Her appearance reminded me that there's just no substitute for a moneyed upbringing.

At the same moment I realized that she was also studying me. Quite frankly. Why women hate it when we do it to them I'll never know; I love it when they do it to me. I tried my best not to look over thirty.

The girl finished her scrutiny and returned her eyes to the road. There was a smile that might have been a smirk on her lips. I wasn't sure I'd passed the test.

She spun the steering wheel sharply to the right and did a nice controlled drift into a paved driveway. We pulled up before a huge wrought-iron gate. I wondered what kind of vehicle needed something so wide and decided that these people might occasionally have visitors who arrived in a carriage behind horses hitched eight abreast.

"Home sweet home," Melissa said. Honest.

She punched a button on the dash, and the massive gate divided in the middle and swung open. We jolted up the drive as it closed behind us, sealing the world out and us in.

The driveway was little more than half a mile long. It was lined the whole way with what looked to be Japanese cherry trees. In April they would make a spectacular archway, but right now they were just bare trees like any others.

Melissa took the drive with a studied aplomb, at about sixty. She didn't slow down until we reached the end, a cobblestone circle with a fountain in its center that probably spouted multicolored plumes of water in the warmer months. If you were seriously into fountains as your life's work, then you might conceivably miss the house it stood in front of, an all-brick affair that was like three connected boxes, the center box having an extra story of height over the other two, plus a dome. Turretlike structures at the corners gave it somewhat the air of a nineteenth-century Southern military academy, while the sizable all-glass conservatory off the east wing argued that these people loved flowers, not war.

My escort left an inch or so of her oversized tires on the cobblestones as we made our landing, and I got out, not in the least reluctantly. A man in a blue uniform appeared, to transfer the car safely to the garage, a hundred feet away to the left. The garage stood at right angles to the house, connected by a covered walkway. It was open and also of brick. Perhaps a former stable. In it were a black Mercedes sedan, one of those extra-long ones that either seat nine comfortably or have a full wet bar inside; a white Aston Martin convertible; and a dull red Ford pickup truck, shiny as new but dating from about 1950. With the Mustang they made quite a quartet; it would be fun guessing which belonged to whom. The remaining stalls of the garage were empty, awaiting the arrival of guests or the family's other ten cars, whichever came first.

At right angles to the house, on the other side of the courtyard, was a long, detached two-story building. Brick, of course. The construction material of choice on old plantations. These would be quarters for the slaves, later called servants, nowadays called housekeeper, kitchen manager, grounds maintenance specialist, and so on. By whatever name, in this part of the country they were usually black.

I returned my attention to the main house itself. It actually wasn't that impressive. If you wanted to fit the L.A. Coliseum inside, there was at least a fifty-fifty chance you'd have to use the big shoehorn.

Melissa grabbed my hand and yanked me toward the three dozen or so pink marble steps in front of me.

"C'mon," she yelled. "John doesn't like to be kept waiting, you know." Nor would she. This one didn't do anything halfway.

And I was willingly led. More than a decade had slipped by since an eighteen-year-old girl last held my hand. I reminded myself that girls her age can easily make men my age look very foolish, especially when you're short of breath after climbing some steps and they're not. I also reminded myself that fantasies are basically harmless.

The door was solid oak—what else?—with a polished brass knocker, fancy carved scrollwork, and buffed leather hinges that didn't do anything. Although it outweighed the two of us put together, it swung open noiselessly at the slightest touch. Counterweights, somewhere out of sight. The door closed with a muffled thud.

I was surprised not to find myself in the grand entrance hall, watching Miss Scarlett sweep down the double staircase. Instead, it was a small wood-paneled foyer, with plush carpet and muted lighting. Its quiet was abruptly shattered.

"Deya!" Melissa yelled, or at least that's what it sounded like. Then *"Deya!"* in a near-hysterical impatient scream. It made her ugly. The impetuous, seductive child-woman of a few minutes earlier had been replaced by the petulant brat who inhabited the same body. I almost expected her to stamp her foot, too. My fantasy was blown.

Fortunately, Deya appeared before things got out of hand. She was a graceful black woman in a satiny black outfit and seemed unperturbed by the girl's behavior.

Melissa eyed her coldly.

"Take this man to Mr. Majors," she commanded. "He's expected."

Just to play the role, I handed Deya one of my cards. All that's on them is "Swift Investigations" and my phone number. Clever, eh?

Deya checked the card out, failing to note the cleverness, then looked back at me and inclined her head slightly to the right. I followed her through the nearest door.

We left Melissa in the middle of the foyer, watching after us with arms akimbo and a face that looked like it was being pinched by an invisible hand.

• • •

The maid moved lithely, which I think means with a kind of oozy sexiness. After a couple of turns she led me down a corridor with ten-foot ceilings, which I guessed to be the main artery in the east wing. It terminated at the conservatory, behind whose faraway misted glass I could make out only some hangy green things.

About halfway along, Deya opened a door to our left and motioned me in.

The room would have been suitable for the Elks Club New Year's Eve party. The north wall was floor-to-ceiling glass around a walk-in fireplace, with a view across some miles of pasture and woodland. Exposed rough eight-by-eights that might have been genuine chestnut defined the space overhead and contrasted nicely with the polished maple parquet floor. There was a bar at the far end with enough quantity and variety to make even the Elks happy.

Roughly in the center of the room was an intimate furniture grouping for a dozen or so. Within it, I spotted my clients-to-be. I stayed by the door, holding my imaginative detective's hat over my privates, as Deya trotted over to her employers. I noted that she had abandoned the slip-sliding hips and was all well-starched efficiency now.

While I waited, I nonchalantly inspected a large glass trophy case that stood next to the door I'd entered by. In it were quite a number of trophies with little guns on them. Awards for marksmanship. The name on the plaques was Elizabeth Majors.

Deya presented my card to the gentleman. He glanced at it, then over at me with what must have been, for him, the affirmative look. He said something to Deya, and she trotted out by another door.

I took her exit as my cue. I'm sharp about these things sometimes. It was quite a trip to where they were, but I made it in under two minutes.

The lady was seated in a plush high-backed chair. The gentleman stood next to her, one hand resting on the chair and the other in his pants pocket. He hadn't looked her way since I arrived, nor she his. They projected all the native warmth and friendliness of your average bivalve.

When I'd completed my journey, the gentleman said, "Mr. Swift. I'm John Majors. This is my wife, Elizabeth." He gestured toward her without looking, then extended his hand, not bothering to grip mine as we shook. It was exactly like the scene in *The Bank Dick* where the bank president gives W. C. Fields a hearty handshake. He withdrew his hand as if it belonged to someone else.

I studied the Majors marital unit. It was like an illustration for one of those "Can This Marriage Be Saved?" articles that women's magazines used to feature.

John Majors was in his early forties, medium height, bulky, dressed in a conservative gray suit that fit him so well he hadn't bothered to learn how to wear it properly. He was dark and clean-shaven, with the haircut of a 1950's businessman, combed straight back and clipped close around the ears. His eyes never blinked except when you weren't looking.

Elizabeth was something else again. She was right at the magic Jack Benny age and would have been a very attractive woman if she hadn't been fighting it so hard. Which meant too much makeup and too self-consciously sexy a dress. It was impossible to imagine her in pants. She'd be above average height when she stood up and was as fair as her husband was dark. Her eyes were blue but not compellingly so. What really grabbed your attention was her hair. It was the color of clover honey, without a streak of gray, and there was lots of it. Fortunately, when she slopped on the makeup, she left her hair pretty much alone. She was smoking a cigarette, and I noticed a number of butts stubbed out in the ashtray by her side. I checked the pack on the coffee table. Virginia Slims.

Hers would be the Aston Martin, his the Mercedes. In this family no one would be caught dead leaving someone else's tire tracks in the snow.

Elizabeth had a small heart-shaped mouth. It moved now.

"John," she said, "perhaps Mr. Swift would like a drink."

"Jameson?" I asked.

"Of course," he said.

"Over ice, with Perrier, if you have it." What the hell, might as well play the role to the limit.

"Of course." He had it.

As John trekked to the bar, Elizabeth shot me one of those long-suffering looks that asks you to be on the person's side in some endless dispute that's never going to be resolved.

"Sit down, Mr. Swift," she said. I did, choosing the most comfortable sofa I'd ever parked my poundage in. And I do mean in.

"You can call me Swift," I said. "Everybody does. I like it, actually. Prefer it to my first name."

"Which is?"

"Loren."

She smiled, with just a hint of seductiveness. "All right . . . Swift. You really must excuse our manners here. We don't do a whole lot of . . . entertaining."

"Yes, I noticed your lack of facilities."

9

"Such a sense of humor the man has."

"Six-year-olds think it's my greatest asset."

"And what about us older ladies?" She cocked an eyebrow.

"Mixed reviews, at best." I gestured roughly in the direction of the trophy case and said, "I see you're quite a marksperson."

"John taught me, actually. He's a crack shot, though you'd never know it. He doesn't care for, ah, competitive sports of any kind. I've taught the children, of course. Knowing how to shoot is a necessary survival skill in the modern world, wouldn't you say?"

"More like an unavoidable evil."

"Much the same. But then you must be a rather good . . . shooter yourself."

There went that eyebrow again. Elizabeth did love to play the part.

Our witty repartee was interrupted by the arrival of the drinks on a silver tray, which Mr. Majors set on the beveled glass coffee table. All of the drinks looked more or less alike, so I took the bubbliest one, figuring it was mine. No one contradicted me. John hiked up his trouser legs a notch and sat in a chair next to his wife, facing the sofa.

"Thank you for coming at such short notice, Mr. Swift," he said.

"No problem. The governor can wait," I said.

"And he likes to be called Swift, dear," Elizabeth chipped in.

"Swift," John said, mouthing the word as if he'd just looked it up in the dictionary. "Well, all right, then." It must have been hell for him. He cleared his throat. "Well, you will be wondering why I called you."

"It crossed my mind."

"Right. Let me just say that I don't have much contact with people in your, ah, profession."

"Neither do I. But that's what happens when you're the only one in the phone book."

"I suppose so. That's how we found you, of course. I wouldn't know how else to . . . do it." He paused, steepling his fingers.

"My husband takes a while getting on with things," Elizabeth said.

"Okay," I supplied helpfully, "What exactly do you need me to do, Mr. Majors?"

"I'd like you to find our daughter."

"No problem. She just rode in on a green Mustang."

"Not Melissa, Mr.— Swift. Leigh."

"That's L-E-I-G-H," Elizabeth put in. "Not like the actor."

"Okay," I said, taking out my pocket notebook, "now we're getting somewhere. Leigh Majors, not the actor. And she's how old?"

"Nineteen."

"She live here?"

"No. She goes to the University—"

"In Charlottesville?"

"Yes. She lives on campus, the Lambeth complex. Do you know it?"

"Yeah." He gave me the number. "Roommate?"

"Yes, a girl named Lisa Kaslow."

"Now, you say she's missing. What exactly do you mean?"

John cleared his throat again. He had a regular frog convention in there. "I mean that no one's heard from her for several days. She's not been to classes or anything, and she didn't tell anyone where she was going. That's not like her." At this, Elizabeth raised her eyebrows. "Lisa called us to say that she was concerned."

"Have you notified the police?"

"No."

"Why not? That's what they're there for."

"I'd prefer that this were handled privately."

"What my husband's trying to say, Swift, is that if Leigh's off at an all-week party, we don't want the cops to find her loaded down with dope, not knowing where her clothes are—"

"Elizabeth!"

They exchanged looks, he glaring, she bemused. He turned back to me.

"Don't listen to her, if you please. Leigh is a very nice girl. She's never been in any trouble. She's an excellent student. We're very proud of her."

Elizabeth silently mouthed the word "we" as if it were a question.

"All right," I said, "she's the all-American girl. No bad habits? Drugs, gambling, rotten company?"

"Not that I know of."

"Not even drinking?"

"No."

I looked up. "At the University of *Virginia?*"

11

"Leigh doesn't drink."

"She went to the wrong school, then. Any boyfriends?."

"I wouldn't know."

"He doesn't *want* to know," said Elizabeth. John did his glare act again.

"Okay." I closed my notebook. "Mr. Majors, in cases like this, ninety-nine times out of a hundred there's a very simple explanation. In most of the ninety-nine the kid shows up and wonders what all the fuss was about. But if you still want me to look into it, I charge two hundred a day plus expenses." If they can afford it, I do, I could have added.

"I'll give you a check for three days," John said. "If you find her before then, you can keep the difference. Will that be satisfactory?"

"More than."

"Good." He took out a checkbook and wrote me a check. He handed it to me along with a business card. It said, "Carter Lockridge, Attorney-at-Law," with a Court Square address. "This is the name of my attorney. He's also an old and close friend of the Majors family. I'll instruct him that if you need any legal assistance, he's to give it to you. Will you require anything else?"

"A recent photo would be nice."

"Of course. How foolish of me. I'll get one." He left the room.

"Leigh's such a sweet little thing," Elizabeth said prissily.

"Is she not?"

"She's an ungrateful little bitch, is what she is. And she's done this before, as my husband failed to tell you."

"Done what?"

"Run off. It doesn't mean anything. She just pulls these grandstand plays to get his attention because she hates me so much, and he eats it up. Makes me want to puke. I think he's secretly hot for her, if he still remembers what that means. Not that he'd ever admit it to himself."

"That's a lot to say about your own daughter."

"I wish she *were* a little bit more *my* kid."

"Where does she usually go when she 'runs off'?"

"I could care less."

"Mrs. Majors, I'm not doubting you, but if Leigh does this a lot, why call me in this time?"

"Ask him."

12

John had reentered the room. He walked briskly over to me.

"There you are," he said, handing me a wallet-size color photo. "Beautiful girl, isn't she?"

I nodded. She was. The honey hair and blue eyes of her mother but an altogether softer face. A few freckles. Innocent expression. The American male's number-one dream girl. You want them to be every bit as ideal as their fathers think they are, but so seldom does it happen.

"Tell me," I said to him, "has this sort of thing ever happened before?"

"What sort of thing?"

"Leigh disappearing for a few days."

"Certainly not."

"Your wife seems to think otherwise."

He turned to glare at Elizabeth, but she was gazing disinterestedly out the great windows. He returned his attention to me.

"Mr. Swift," he said, "I'm hiring you to find my daughter. I would appreciate it if you would do that for me."

And that seemed to be that. I decided I could live with the confusion for the time being.

"All right, Mr. Majors, I'll see what I can do. I'll try to check in at least once a day. If you need to get in touch with me, call my answering service. I talk to them regularly when I'm on a case. And I'm in the book, as you know, if you lose this." I gave him a card.

"Good." He favored me with another gripless handshake. "I love my little girl," he said. "Make sure nothing's happened to her." For a moment he became almost human to me; then Deya had materialized by my side.

"I'll try," I said.

Deya led me out the door we had entered by and closed it behind us. I started back down the long corridor, but she plucked at my sleeve.

"The Colonel wants to see you," she said.

• • •

Right, I thought.

And now we go into the conservatory, and there's the flinty old buzzard. In a wheelchair, with a blanket over him in the ninety-degree heat, pale as death. And then the plot thickens.

13

But no.

Deya turned to the right before we reached the conservatory and showed me into a small, windowless room. Floor-to-ceiling bookcases stretched around three walls, filled with the sort of old hardbound books that are kept mostly for their potential value as collector's items. There was a businesslike solid oak desk and a couple of comfy-looking chairs. The room smelled like old leather that's been oiled and kneaded twice a day for about forty years, and the carpet under my feet contained maybe ten thousand bucks' worth of Middle Eastern threads.

The Colonel had his back to me. There was no wheelchair, but he was leaning on a cane. He was pretending to study the spines on the complete works of Aristophanes, or some such.

"Mr. Swift," Deya announced.

The Colonel turned slowly and looked me over. Then he nodded, and Deya melted quietly away. He watched her go with a sexually appreciative look on his face.

"You like nigger women, Swift?" he asked.

I shrugged and said, "I'm sure you didn't call me in here so we could exchange racial—"

He cut me off with something between a snort and a laugh.

"Can the crap, boy," he said. "You're as bad as my wife. Where you from, anyway?"

"Charlottesville."

"I mean before that. I know you ain't no native Virginian."

I didn't like what he was doing but decided to tell the truth. A failing of mine.

"Boston."

"Right. Up there, you'all call them Negroes. Or is it blacks now? And then you hide them away in Roxbury or someplace and throw rocks at them if they try to go to white boys' schools, ain't that so?"

"I suppose."

"Course it is. Around here, niggers is niggers, and white folks is white folks, and ever'body knows who they might be. We manage to go to the same schools without some fool judge telling us how to go about it. Any year of the world I've personally known more niggers, and known them well, than you will your whole life, so don't preach me, boy." He paused. "Besides"—he grinned with a badly misplaced sense of camaraderie—"nigger women are the best, and don't let nobody tell you different."

I sighed.

"All right, Colonel," I said. "You've made your little speech. Good for you. Now I believe we already agreed that you didn't call me in here to enlighten me with your views, such as they are, on the relative sexual attractiveness of the various races. Correct?"

He grinned again, but there was a light in his eyes such as you might see glinting off a very finely honed straight razor.

"Right you are. Sit down," he said.

I did, selecting one of the soft leather armchairs. If the people in this house were half as comfortable as their furniture, it would be a nice house indeed. If.

I studied the Colonel as he three-legged it over to a swivel chair behind the desk.

He was old but not that old. Seventy, maybe. Whether he needed the cane was a good question. He moved as though he could get around pretty well without it. I wouldn't have been surprised to find that it was one of those with a sword inside and that the Colonel had at times drawn blood with it.

Physically, he wasn't that imposing. A little above medium height. Thin, or what used to be called wiry. No hair on the top of his head. Around the sides, a white, rather long fringe, the way Friar Tuck wore it. A narrow face, deeply tanned, with furrows like a highway after a severe winterful of frost heaves. A steep straight nose, thin lips, and dark eyes that didn't give away anything.

You might have expected him to be wearing the uniform of whatever war he had fought in. Instead, he had on a blue blazer with matching slacks. Circling his throat was a peach-colored ascot of the sort that some old people think makes them look distinguished. On the Colonel it was more likely an attempt to soften his predatory appearance. If so, it was a failure. The man, according to local legend, was a ruthless son of a bitch who had parlayed an army pension and a swollen ambition into a staggering real estate empire, and he looked the part.

He sat down, swiveled his chair a couple of times, and came to rest with his chin on his folded hands. He scrutinized me as if he were going to offer me a deal. If he did, I wasn't about to take it.

"So," he said at last, "let me guess. John wants to hire you to find Leigh."

"I doubt that you ever guess about anything, Colonel," I said.

He chuckled. "Right you are. If I didn't know what went on in

15

my own house, I wouldn't have gotten very far, would I? All right, so I'm aware of the nature of your visit. And how did you like the charming young couple?"

"Romeo and Juliet they're not."

"Indeed. Nor even the early Taylor and Burton, eh? But mine own. I've raised that boy up from a pup. Scrawny, he was, always littler than the other fellows. It turned him against people, I think. But he's got brains. When he came of age, I took him right in. Handles most of my business now, and I've never regretted it for a minute." He made a brushing gesture with his hand. "Her I can do without."

He paused. When I didn't say anything, he continued. "What did they tell you?"

"Colonel," I said patiently, "as I'm sure you're aware, any communication I get from my clients is privileged."

"Ah, horse crap, boy. You're working for all of us, you know? . . . All right, *I'll* fill *you* in, then. Did you meet my other granddaughter?"

I nodded.

"Good. Everything that Melissa is, Leigh's the opposite. The younger one is just like her mother. Leigh is, well, let's just say that she's John's favorite. He loves that little girl, Swift. As do I. Couldn't either of us bear to have anything happen to her. So you make sure she's all right, hear?"

"Strangely enough, that's exactly what I'm being paid to do." I was almost terminally bored with the arrogant old man at this point, but I hung on. You never knew when these warm family chats would suddenly produce a useful nugget of information. I ventured the obvious question.

"You wouldn't have any idea where she is, would you?"

"No, I wouldn't." His eyes hurt the back of my skull.

"Okay. You mentioned your wife earlier. Does she live here?"

"No."

"Where can I find her, then?"

"Sarah Jane doesn't know anything."

"Colonel," I said patiently, "in my experience, young people often tell their grandparents things that they'd die before they let their parents find out. Now, your wife does know Leigh, doesn't she?"

"Yes."

16

"Then I'll need to speak with her. I can find out for myself where she lives, or you can save me a small but tedious bit of detective work by telling me."

I raised my eyebrows in what I hoped was a self-assured manner. Silently, he wrote out an address on a slip of paper and handed it to me. I glanced at it before putting it in my pocket. A fashionable street off of Court Square in Charlottesville. The elder Mrs. Majors would be well-to-do.

"Thank you," I said. "Is there anything else you can think of that might be of use to me?"

He'd leaned back in his chair. The slight animosity that had surfaced a moment earlier was gone, and I was being regarded with a casual tolerance again. It made me feel like a large target on the live ammo range, and I didn't care for the feeling.

"I think not," he said.

"In that case, Colonel—"

He raised his hand sharply. "Hold on, boy. Sit down, sit down. You don't think I called you in here to rehash the obvious, do you? No, I don't believe you do. I think that you are not a stupid man, Mr. Swift."

"I like to think not. Although there are those who wouldn't agree."

"No." He folded his hands over his stomach. "Not stupid. Certainly not so stupid as to fall for— Let me ask you this: did Elizabeth say that this sort of thing has happened before?"

I shrugged.

"That's right; you don't answer questions about your so-called clients, do you? Very well. I'm sure that Elizabeth did her best to poison you against her own daughter. Don't believe it for a minute, Swift. Leigh is everything that her mother might have been if she hadn't been such a bitch, and the woman hates her for it, take my word. My daughter-in-law is a devious creature, son, and you can take that as a warning if you like. It wouldn't surprise me if she hopes Leigh is gone forever. Her own daughter. I wouldn't let Elizabeth influence you in this matter if I were you. Do you know what I'm saying?"

"I'll do what I have to do, Colonel. I'm not particularly worried about what you do amongst yourselves."

"Good. That's good. If John's concerned, then there's something to be concerned about, and so am I."

17

I started to get up, but Colonel Majors held up the sit-down hand once again. Whatever he was driving at, he was getting there about as fast as my '57 Chevy, which I'd left up on blocks in a garage in South Boston. I decided that I wouldn't care to be involved in a real estate negotiation with this man. Me and a couple thousand of my neighbors.

"One more thing," he said. I put on my best anticipation face, and he continued. "I'd like to hire you."

"Your son has already done that."

"Not about Leigh. I want you to find out who my daughter-in-law is fooling around with. It's a job that needed doing years ago, but I've held off because of the children. Now that they're older, I'd like to show John just what it is he's married to. After that, well . . . who knows?"

"Sorry, Colonel, one case at a time."

"Don't be a twit, boy. You're going to be involved with the family, anyway. You probably won't even have to go out of your way. I'll pay you well."

"Sorry. I'll come see you after I find Leigh. Now if that's it—"

"Suit yourself. But keep it in mind." He rose. "Let me get Deya."

"Don't bother; I'll show myself out. I know the way."

We shook hands stiffly, and I headed back down the long corridor. I'd nearly negotiated the last turn before the foyer when I heard someone call my name.

• • •

I felt like I might never get out of the house, that I'd somehow slipped into a Twilight Zone all my own. Any moment I expected to hear Rod Serling solemnly intoning something like: "Portrait of a man on an endless time loop. To wit, Loren Swift, would-be private detective, condemned to pass eternity shuttling from Majors to Majors, one man's private vision of hell . . ." and so on.

Still, I sleuthed my way back to the name-caller.

She was in a bright room with a piano and a lot of window overlooking the front fountain. She'd changed her clothes since I last saw her and now had on a pair of those designer jeans that you can't get into unless you can suck your belly up against your backbone and a filmy top that was for all practical purposes transparent. Her stomach was as flat as a teenager's should be, and her breasts were

18

small and thrust in my direction, as if being offered on approval. I approved, but the pose was a bit too rehearsed for my taste; she'd arranged herself against the sofa, resting her hands on its back and arching her upper body. It was sexy if you liked women who got their idea of sexiness from nighttime soap operas about decadent southern families.

"Hi, Melissa," I said. "You rang?"

I gave my voice about the same level of enthusiasm that I have when I discuss the price of a six-pack with the clerk at the Seven-Eleven, and it wasn't lost on her. She must have been used to the fellows going all hoarse and sweaty when they saw her tits. She'd get over it.

She straightened up and gave me a self-conscious pouty look.

"You want a drink, Swift?" she asked, and without waiting for an answer walked over to the bar that no room in this house was complete without.

"No, thanks," I said. "Your father makes them stiff enough that I can't squeeze two into the same hour."

She mixed up something or other and came back over to stand very close to me. Her smell was raw and musky, and it did the job where her slinky posing had failed. I reminded myself that she was a bratty rich kid like any other. Maybe I even believed it. She drained half the glass in one swallow.

"So," she said after taking in enough air to make it dramatic, "dear daddy wants you to find my big sister."

Her eyes were hooded. I looked into them, trying to see past the surface. It helped me ignore the fact that a beautiful young girl was acting in what she thought was a provocative manner, for my benefit.

Suddenly, I realized there was something at work in her brain besides alcohol. Downs of some kind. Probably 'ludes. Maybe PCP, God forbid. This girl was in big trouble. Alcohol and downs was an unpredictable combination, and mixing them could get you dead very fast. Or somebody dead because of you.

It's not my problem, I told myself. If I tried to rescue every kid who was into bad drugs these days, I'd be stark raving mad before noon tomorrow.

"What're you on, Melissa?" I said. So much for my own good advice.

" 'On'?"

"Yeah, 'on.' You know. Soapers? Angel dust? What?"

"Who do you think you *are*, my *father*!"

"No, just—"

"Well, you're *old* enough to be!"

She was wild-eyed and within an inch of taking a swing at me.

"All right, forget it. Kill yourself any way you want to. Let's talk about your sister."

"Screw my sister!"

"I think that's my cue," I said, and turned to go.

"No, don't leave!" After she'd said it, she looked surprised that she had. Her mood shifted abruptly. "I mean, I'd like you to stay for a while," she said with a lame smile. "Nobody comes here anymore. There's no one to talk to most of the time."

It sounded like a poor, friendless teenager rap was on the way. Unfortunately, I'm a sucker for that kind of thing. Even if they're as whacked out as this one. I knew I'd regret it if I let her get to me.

"I warn you, I'm a boring conversationalist," I said. "All I do is ask a lot of questions."

"So ask."

"All right. Where's Leigh?"

"Do we have to talk about my sister?"

"That's what they hired me for."

An alcohol and Quaalude flush came over her.

"You know," she said suggestively, "you could be cute if you tried a little harder."

"So could you if you didn't. And the drugs don't exactly enhance your sex appeal, by the way."

Her mouth tightened.

"My sister's fine," she said between her perfect teeth. "She doesn't need you to find her."

"How do you know that?"

"Bitch," she said harshly, and I didn't think she was referring to me. She turned and walked to the windows, gulping at her drink. When she looked back, she'd gone coy again. "You'd like to know, wouldn't you?"

"If it'd save some wear on my manly footgear."

She checked out my ratty boots and giggled. "I shouldn't help you. You look like you need the money."

"And you maybe need to get to the point," I said.

"Ummmm," she said. Slurp, slurp. "No point. My big sister's a little tramp, that's all."

"What do you mean by that?"

"Just what I said, turkey. She's no good. She thinks she'll get some attention from *them* if she disappears for a while. Fat chance."

"From who?"

"You know."

"Melissa," I said, trying to keep the exasperation out of my voice, "do you have something you want to tell me?"

"Sure. My sister's no good, and she runs around."

"Runs around with whom?"

She peered over the top of her glass and giggled again. "Well, with the niggers for one." She sashayed over next to me and turned on the big grin.

Jesus, I thought, whatever happened to the New South? If this family was representative, it's in big trouble.

"Just like you-know-who," she went on, looking at some third party in the room that only she could see. Granddad, most likely. Between the two of them, they could set race relations back a hundred years.

"Is there any chance you'd like to tell me what you're talking about?"

She shook her head. "You never heard it here," she said, trying to chuck me under the chin and missing. She thought that was funny, to the extent that she exhaled a small misty cloud of liquor spit. I'd had enough.

"Look," I said, "if anything occurs to you that might help me, give me a call, will you? I'm in the book, home and office both."

"Wait," she said, "don't go." Flirty once more. She started to come toward me, but I was already backing for the door.

"Call," I said.

She stopped. The ugly, spoiled-kid look had returned.

"I hope you never find her."

"You have a nice day, too, Melissa."

Before she had a chance to say anything else, I was in the corridor and around the last turn. I pulled the foyer door shut behind me and leaned back on the knob. The foyer was quiet, reassuring. The polished wood paneling glowed in the soft lighting. Civilized people lived here.

I took a few deep breaths and stepped outside.

Then I remembered that I didn't have a functioning automobile.

Not wanting another trip round the fun house and lacking any more positive plan, I wandered over to the garage and checked out the lineup there. The various family wheels were all still in their allotted spaces. I touched the gleaming black surface of the Mercedes. It felt like any other piece of cold steel.

"May I help you, sir?" asked the blue-uniformed fellow who had materialized behind me.

I explained my plight and asked if he could give me a lift back to my car. I also requested a large straw and a roll of electrician's tape.

No problem.

He returned in short order with the items I needed, and we headed down the drive in a new but modest compact. I assumed it was either the chauffeur's own or reserved for emergencies involving the Majorses' less presentable guests. Like myself.

· 2 ·

On the way down 666, I brooded about things.

I'd just spent an hour with a thoroughly depressing collection of beings, and that wasn't good for my morale. Because lately I'd been in one of those moods where any previous period of your life looks like a better time than the one you're currently living through. For me that meant romanticizing my failed marriage, the stint in college before I flunked out, the army. All of it, even Viet Nam. The worst part was that, comparatively speaking, my life wasn't that bad. I wasn't a Jew in Russia or a socialist in Chile. Though my bank account was nearly nonexistent, I made more money in a year than a dozen average Bengalis. Interesting women occasionally looked more than once in my direction. My car ran most of the time. And I even enjoyed my work now and then, which made me a member of one of the smaller American minorities.

Still, more often than I wanted to, I found myself thinking about the long slide, the one that carries you inexorably from the place where anything seems possible to the place where nothing turns out like you'd hoped.

"Loren," Marilyn had once asked, shortly before we broke up for good, "do you *want* to save this marriage?"

"Of course," I'd said.

"Then why don't you grow up?" she'd said. "Find something useful to do with your life. All you do now is pry into a lot of stupid people's sordid little affairs as if the *Answer* were somehow there. It isn't there, Loren. The only thing that's there is the *Problem*.

23

Can't you see that? You're like a little kid who's trying to learn about sex by looking at his parents' dirty underwear, for God's sake."

"But I'm happy with this kind of work," I'd said. "Sometimes."

"That's what I mean, you idiot!" she'd said as she stormed out of the room. Marilyn liked to speak in capital letters and storm out of rooms. Once I'd loved her in spite of it.

"What's what you mean?" I'd asked the door.

From the other side I'd heard a howl of frustration.

So it goes. You start with a beautiful, erotic dream, and you end up with soggy sheets. If Boston isn't big enough for the two of you, you move to Virginia and continue to do what you do best. Then the years slip by, and you slowly realize that the dream hasn't been replaced by anything of value. That's a sure sign that you're on the long slide. The only thing surer is the growing fear that you'll never find that missing something of value, or worse, that there isn't and never has been anything worthwhile to find. When you hit that spot, you're near the bottom.

That's when you begin getting jobs from collections of lunatics like the Majors family.

Clementine came into view, and the sight of the old Volkswagen provided me with a sorely needed link to a somewhat saner reality. I thanked my nameless driver, and he acknowledged me with the obligatory head nod before driving off. I guess if the master is sufficiently superior, then the live-in slave feels himself a cut above the odd hired hand.

No matter.

It was still cold enough to warrant a trip to the glove compartment, where I keep an emergency supply of Jameson in a stainless steel flask. One of my few extravagances, Jameson. There are other and cheaper Irish whiskeys, but nothing nearly as good.

I put enough inside me to begin the warming process and got out to work on Clementine. I'd just propped open the engine compartment when a big sedan pulled over behind me. I turned. It was a dull gray Ford of some kind, and it fit on the shoulder even more poorly than Clementine. The driver got out, leaving his emergency lights flashing.

He was short and stocky, about my age, and didn't look to be in the best of condition. Not that I am, either, but I try to get to the Nautilus machines a couple of times a week. In case a job gets a little . . . physical. The guy was wearing heavy boots, a long dark overcoat, and a muted plaid scarf. He had one of those Russian-type fur hats on his head. The net result was probably warm but looked out of place for rural Virginia.

"Howdy," he said like someone unused to the word, "anything I can do?"

"Naw. Just a little fuel-line problem. I got it jerry rigged so I can get home. Thanks, anyway."

He didn't look like he was going anywhere, so I didn't go anywhere. The old unreliable sixth sense was telling me that this wasn't your random helpful passerby.

Sure enough, he said, "You're Swift Investigations, ain't you?" Score one for the occasionally reliable sixth sense.

My guard instinctively went up. I don't like being on an instant last-name basis with total strangers, though it's easier to take when the stranger is young and beautiful. Young and beautiful and bratty, I reminded myself.

"Why?" I said.

He chuckled, with something more than amusement in his eyes. "Don't get paranoid," he said, "we're sort of on the same team."

As he said it, he unbuttoned the top button and reached inside his coat. I froze, figuring that this guy was probably the smiling winged messenger of death and was going for his .357 Magnum or something else that kills no matter where it hits you. You have that kind of fantasy a lot in a business where it's so difficult to tell the good guys from the bad. If this is truly it, I thought, then it's my own damn fault for moving from a state where they have a tough law prohibiting unregistered handguns to one where they're more interested in getting tough with weekend pot smokers. I didn't have one of my own guns, of course. You never do when you're most in need, which is probably why I so seldom carry one anymore.

I was thinking of Chief Dan George in *Little Big Man* and wondering whether this was an appropriate day to die when the guy's hand finally emerged from the overcoat bearing a business card, which he passed to me. My sphincters relaxed a little.

The card said, "Continental Pacific Investigations, Sacramento, California," and had a phone number and the guy's name and rank: Harlow Brennerman, Associate Investigator. I wondered if investigating associates was big business in California these days but was too shy to ask.

Instead, I said, "You're a P.I.?" Good to see that the fear hadn't clouded my cleverness.

He smiled and bowed slightly.

"Well . . . you're a long way from home." Keep it up and I was a shoo-in for a guest shot on Griffin or Carson. My mouth was beginning to taste like a mouth again. "What're you doing in this neck of the woods?" Realizing that this wasn't what I really wanted to know, I added, "And how do you know me?"

He shrugged. "When I go into a new area, I like to work with the local talent . . . if possible. Around here, you're it."

"Does that mean that you try and find me while I try and hide?"

"Suit yourself. I'd prefer it if we could work something out."

"About what?"

He folded his arms across his chest, but his expression was more bemused than impatient.

"You think it's coincidence that we happen to meet on this road?" he said.

"I don't know. Is it?"

"Of course not."

"You've been following me?"

"Not exactly. All I know is that you've been hired by the Majors family for something or other."

"Is that so?"

"C'mon, I took deduction in school, too, y'know. Give me a little credit. Here you are, surrounded by Majors land, with your broken-down car pointed in the direction of their house. On the way in, I passed the Majorses' chauffeur, heading east. He and I have, ah, already met. It seems rather likely that he dropped you here on his way somewhere. So now I know where you were coming from. Do you see the Majorses socially?"

"It's not my place to discuss—"

"Swift," he said with exaggerated weariness, "what are you going to do, come on to me with some crock about professional ethics and all that garbage? I've heard it before, and it doesn't interest me. Here's what's happening. Right now I'm on my way to the Majors place. You just came from there, so it's safe to assume, considering your less than exalted station in life, that you're involved with them

26

professionally in some fashion. So am I, in another. How I see it is that it would likely be, ah, mutually profitable, shall we say, for us to do some pooling of information."

"What in hell are you driving at, Brennerman?"

He was a while in answering.

Finally, he said, "Okay, I believe you. So you don't know. Or rather, I know more than you do. But you've still got the local expertise. We should still strike a deal."

"Any time you want to let me in on what—"

"Money, Swift, money. Of course, What are *you* in it for, the glory?" He checked his watch. "Look, let's meet later and talk things over. I'm staying at the Mountain Vista Motel, room fourteen. Nine o'clock, okay?"

"If you bring your tongue along."

He laughed. "Deal," he said. "See you then." He climbed back into the gray sedan and headed west, toward the Majors spread.

I went to work, patching up Clementine. There wasn't much to it. With the scissors on my Swiss Army knife I snipped the plastic straw to a useful length. Then I pulled out the broken gas filter and replaced it with the straw, which fit more or less snugly. Good enough for the time being. Finally, I wrapped the line with the electrician's tape to hold it together. The gas would no longer be filtered, but it would get to the carburetor. I wasn't sure it really needed to be cleaned, anyway.

I climbed back in and cranked her over. She started up right away.

"Good girl," I said, patting the dashboard.

And then I thought, Harlow Brennerman. Another fearless P.I. in the same neighborhood. What did *that* mean? What did the Majors family want with him? Or was it the other way around: what did he want with them?

It was pointless to speculate, of course. I gave up, wheeled a tight U-turn, and headed in the opposite direction, toward Charlottesville.

• • •

Who can figure, at the time, what effect an experience will eventually have?

In my case, fifteen years ago I tried to pretend that I was college material. I chose the University of Virginia because I'd heard that it was a good party school. It was. In fact, it was so good that I never made it through my freshman year. But that's another story.

By any objective standard my college career was a disaster, and you might have thought that I'd never want to return to the scene of the crime. Yet when I needed to put some space between myself and Marilyn, memories of Charlottesville popped into my head like kernels of corn that had been waiting for a fire to turn them white and fluffy. Lacking any more attractive alternative, I came back. And have stayed.

Things have changed at Thomas Jefferson's University since the days of my misspent youth.

Among other things, they didn't admit blacks back then, and they didn't admit women. Today blacks are, if not common, at least a visible and reasonably tolerated part of the student population. And the incoming freshperson class is, for the first time, more than half women. Jefferson would croak if he hadn't already.

Less importantly, there's the matter of housing. The dormitories that I remember were more reminiscent of brick army barracks than anything else. The new ones look like garden apartments pilfered from some affluent Washington suburb, which, uncoincidentally, is where a lot of the kids come from.

I pulled off Emmet Street, into the Lambeth dormitory complex. It was definitely more garden than army. A group of three-story detached apartment clusters, scattered about like brick dice. The place radiated a palpable sense of the easy life, and for a moment I felt a twinge of jealousy. Until I remembered that if I had it to do over, going to college wouldn't be what I'd choose.

I located Leigh Majors' dorm building with a little help from one of those modern Southern coeds who appears to believe that a return to the era of genteel plantations is just around the corner. Behind my thanks, I was silently wishing her the best of luck and wondering how I could have gotten so out of step with a group whose age was not all that far from my own. Cycles, I figured. The next generation would be my kind of people again.

Lisa Kaslow, Leigh's roommate, was in. She met me downstairs. Now that schools no longer care who visits whose room, I guess I should have expected not to be invited up. More cycles.

Lisa was a slim blonde with a pert, innocent face. She'd be the hands-down winner at the Leigh Majors Look-alike Contest if they ever got around to holding one. The idea of someone else as roommate must never have crossed their respective minds.

We introduced ourselves, and I immediately asked her if she knew where Leigh was.

"Gee, I don't have any idea, Mr. Swift," she said. "That's why I called Mr. and Mrs. Majors."

I believed her. That kind of spontaneity is hard to fake.

"Does she do this a lot?" I asked. Lisa looked puzzled, so I added, "I mean, go off without telling anyone?"

"Well, Leigh's kind of a private sort of person. I'd say she likes to be by herself a lot. But no, not like this. Not for most of a week, with classes going on and all. Though Leigh doesn't have to work *that* hard." There was more than a trace of envy but no jealousy that I could detect.

"Her mother says she does it a lot."

Lisa grimaced. "Well, her mother should know."

"What do you mean by that?"

"I'd rather not say, Mr. Swift. It's always getting me in trouble, putting my two cents in."

"Her sister says she runs around a lot, too."

"Melissa." Lisa said the word with the sort of disgust usually reserved for viewing monkey vomit.

"You don't like Melissa?"

"That girl is vicious, Mr. Swift. Someone as nice as Leigh, and she'd as soon cut her up as look at her, if you ask me. She's a jealous, hateful person, and I don't say that about most. Let's don't talk about her anymore."

"All right, it's not important. Would you say that Leigh has a lot of close friends?"

"Not that many," she said, relieved at the change of subject. "Most of the kids here like to party hard when they're not studying. Leigh's not like them. I think she'd *rather* study."

"Is there anyone she confides in besides you?"

"Yeah, a couple of people. There's her grandmother—"

"Sarah Jane Majors?"

"That's her. She likes the old lady pretty much and visits her a lot."

"And?"

Lisa paused, giving the impression that she was considering something. "Well," she said finally, "I guess her best friend is probably Delmos."

"Delmos Venable?"

"You know him?"

Sure I knew him. Every basketball fan in the country knew Virginia's sensational senior point guard.

"Not personally," I said.

"He's a nice guy." She shrugged. "Not at all stuck up like you might think. Anyway, he and the Majors kids grew up together. His mother used to work for the family."

"She sees a lot of him?"

"Pretty much. What are you asking, if he's her boyfriend?"

I was trying to. It might be the early eighties, but in Virginia you still had to approach some subjects extremely tactfully. Interracial relationships, for one.

"Whatever you can tell me would be helpful," I said.

She shrugged again. "It wouldn't bother *me* if he was." Behold the New South, in the flesh. "But I honestly don't know. Leigh's a very private girl about some things, like I said."

"Okay. Any other boyfriends?"

She shrugged once again. I had to restrain myself from putting my hands on her shoulders to hold them in one place.

Instead, I said, "Where does Delmos live?"

"On the Lawn. But this time of day you can be sure to find him at U. Hall."

Of course. The team would be busily fine tuning for the Carolina game. The real Atlantic Coast Conference struggle didn't begin until February, but each year you got one ACC game in December to whet your interest. Usually, it was with some conference also-ran like Clemson. This year, for reasons unknown, the powers that be had penciled in a December clash between Virginia and North Carolina. The game had national significance, and it was set for Saturday, four days hence. The practice schedule would be heavy from now on.

"Okay," I said. "Thank you very much, Lisa. If you think of anything else that might be helpful, give me a call, will you?"

I handed her a card. She looked at it, then back at me as if to wonder whether this handsome, dashing fellow was truly the same Swift of Swift Investigations.

30

Well, maybe she did, anyway.

Since University Hall was just across the street from the Lambeth dorm complex, I decided to walk. It was still cold, and it still threatened snow. But I felt a certain warmth at the prospect of meeting one of my all-time favorite sports heroes.

Delmos was a twenty-one-year-old basketball genius whom many were already comparing to Oscar Robertson, the finest guard ever to play the game. What's more, he was entirely a local boy, having grown up in the Charlottesville area and then having chosen the University of Virginia over what must have been a hundred other schools competing for his talents. The previous season, as a junior, he'd led Virginia all the way to the national semifinals, the fabled Final Four, before losing a game, no mean feat in the tough Atlantic Coast Conference. This year, with its starting five back intact, Virginia was the favorite to cop the championship. Charlottesville had come alive with basketball madness in November; by March, you wouldn't be able to get into any bar in town on game night unless you arrived two hours before tip-off.

But there was more to Delmos Venable than his skills with a basketball. To perhaps the same degree that he delighted the crowds in U. Hall, he outraged others by his behavior off the court. Traditionally, Virginia's athletes, and especially black ones, have been expected to be as invisible as possible when not engaging an enemy team. Under no circumstances were they to have opinions on any subject outside of their sport. Delmos had broken with this tradition in a big way. He had the spotlight, and he was using it. Much of the University community was still in shock.

It must have seemed simple to him. He'd been endowed with some spectacular physical gifts that enabled him to escape the predetermined life shared by most of his fellow black Virginians. Why not, then, take advantage of this accident of fate and try to help these same people? Simple.

So Delmos had from the beginning become deeply involved in black politics at the University. He worked tirelessly to increase the number of black students being admitted and to keep them in school once they'd arrived. He was among those who lobbied the administration most heavily concerning the snail's pace at which the recruitment of black faculty was proceeding.

On the court, Delmos was the messiah. Off it, the pariah. He

31

was everything Kareem might have become if the former Alcindor hadn't been stuck with John Wooden for a coach.

The press, sensing a good story, had played up the two sides of Delmos Venable from the moment it discovered how talented he was. This publicity had more than one of the good-old-boy alumni of the University scratching his head, wondering if this kid was a gift from God or merely a cleverly disguised Antichrist. The jury was still out on that one. What was certain, and what the vast majority ended up settling for, was that the Virginia Cavaliers, familiarly known as the Wahoos, were playing a hell of a game of basketball.

Home court was in University Hall, a smallish indoor sports arena with a scalloped white dome. I entered it at the front and walked toward the practice court. There were a couple of security guards, of course. Never can tell when Carolina is going to send up some spies to try and steal the game plan. I got past them with some fast talking and the judicious use of the special deputy's badge a Boston homicide lieutenant had given me in a moment of weakness, after I'd helped him break a tough case.

Then I was courtside.

For a while, I just stood and watched like the fan that I am. The team was split into two groups. At one end of the court they were running three-on-two defensive drills. At the other, the starting five was working on an inbounds play. The inbounder would pass it to the man in the corner, who would hit Delmos circling behind a double pick for the shot. It was a play designed for the last five seconds of a close game, when the final basket decides it all. Virginia ran it exactly the way the Celtics used to do it for Havlicek. They practiced it over and over again. Each time, Venable hit nothing but net. Beautiful. A trip to the ballet for us lowbrow types.

Eventually, I collared one of the half-dozen assistant coaches that a modern college basketball team seems to need and told him why I was there. He didn't believe me. Delmos is of course the object of considerable media attention, so when anyone asks to see him, the working assumption is that the guy is a reporter of some kind. I put on my most trustworthy expression and produced a walletful of credentials. The coach studied them as if I might be Mark David Chapman in disguise with a Charter Arms .38 tucked under my coat. I don't think he was totally convinced that I wasn't, but he finally handed me back my identity and allowed me to have a seat on the floor. He promised me thirty seconds of Delmos's time at the next break.

I settled myself and waited out fifteen or twenty minutes that seemed like five.

It was the first time I'd seen Delmos Venable up close, and I felt like an afternoon TV freak would if he suddenly found himself at dinner with Luke and Laura.

As basketball players go, Delmos isn't that big. He goes maybe six-three and a rock-hard 185, which would have made a strong forward on *my* college team; now it's a small guard. Anyway, in the real world he's still pretty imposing. Compared to me, at least. One-on-one I'd be giving away five inches and ten pounds, not to mention a dozen years. Way too much.

We're also different colors, he and I, but not *all* that different. I'm a dark white man, due to a generous infusion of Mediterranean blood, and he's a fairly light black man, due to who knows what, about the shade of Muhammad Ali. Perhaps our ancestors even interbred, back when the Moors were sacking Spain.

We swapped introductions, and he shook my hand with just the right amount of familiarity. When he smiled, he reminded me of Magic Johnson before the Magic Man started making 7-Up commercials. You couldn't help but like the kid.

I gave him fifteen seconds' worth of why I was there.

"Yeah," he said, "I'm worried, too. Come and see me after practice, and we'll talk. I'll be back at my room about six." He gave me an address on the Lawn.

That was it. Delmos went back to swishing baskets, and I went out into the cold, which didn't seem so cold anymore. Sure, part of it was the cheap thrill you get from rubbing elbows with a national celebrity. But there was more to it than that. You spend a couple of minutes with someone, and you often get a crystal-clear impression as to whether they're real people or seriously full of shit. Delmos was one of the real ones. I silently thanked him for being different from the folks I'd spent the rest of my day with.

• • •

I had some time to kill before six o'clock, and I'm one of those guys who, when he's working on a case, prefers to keep working even when there's nothing obvious to be done at the moment. I decided to pay a visit to the lawyer Lockridge.

His office was in Court Square, the old center of Charlottesville, all brick buildings and fluted white columns, statues of Confederate Civil War generals and manicured lawns like putting greens. An area that looks steadfastly forward into the nineteenth century. It's also the legal hub of both the city of Charlottesville and the county of Albemarle, which makes it the spot where the big deals go down. Since the county is one of the country's ten most wealthy, some of those deals are very big indeed. If you were a lawyer on the make in Charlottesville, Court Square is where you would want your office, as much for the prestige of the address as to keep close to the action.

Lockridge had located in a two-story frame building directly across from the courthouse. I pushed through a door marked "Lockridge & Lee" and walked into his receiving room.

I almost turned and walked back out again, so hard did my stomach hit the floor.

It was an average office for this area. Paneled in a dark wood of some kind that was too highly waxed. A brown plush couch for those who can relax in lawyers' offices and some straight-back chairs for those who can't. End tables with magazines and unobtrusive lamps on them. All calculated to give you the impression that the man you were about to meet was your friend and was here to help you rather than steal your money.

In front of me was an average wood desk stained the same color as the walls. Behind it was an average legal secretary. Only she wasn't average in the slightest.

She was in her early thirties and looked it, if that can be said as a compliment to the visible strength of character that living had given her. She had long, straight auburn hair tied back with a barrette. A delicate oval face. Deep-set eyes behind oversized plastic frame glasses. A mouthful of teeth that she'd flashed when I entered the room. She had on a spruce-green business suit and a cream-colored blouse. The outfit went perfectly with her coloring. She wore no makeup and needed none. A nameplate on her desk proclaimed her to be Patricia Ryan. And except for the glasses Patricia Ryan was a ringer for my ex-wife Marilyn.

I must have looked fairly foolish, standing there with my jaw resting on my breastbone. If so, Patricia Ryan didn't let on.

"May I help you, sir?" she asked, showing the mouthful of teeth again.

"Uh, hi, Pat," I said. Never at a loss for words.

"I dislike nicknames." She managed to say it without appearing unfriendly.

"Me, too. Every Nick I've ever known took me to the cleaners one way or another."

She cocked her head at me. "Something of a local wit, are we?" I was almost at the point of turning into a small puddle of goo at her feet. It is, of course, ridiculous that we should be attracted to someone simply because they happen to remind us of someone we once loved. Completely ridiculous.

"That *is* what all the girls say."

"I'm hardly a girl, Mr.—"

"Swift. Yes, I know. That's why I'm surprised. Over the age of ten and I usually can't fool them." That got a small chuckle, maybe.

"Well, keep trying. I hear Ralph Nader is always looking for good new material."

That got a laugh from me.

"You win," I said, looking defeated. "How about lunch tomorrow?"

"I'm very busy, Mr. Swift."

"Oh. How about if I promise to show you my collection of off-color Italian hand gestures?" I tried, hoping she hadn't seen the Woody Allen movie I'd stolen the line from. She laughed as though she hadn't, so it didn't matter. Her green eyes twinkled. Yes, twinkled, damn it.

"How about if I promise *not* to show them?" I said.

"Give the man credit," she said. "He is persistent. But surely you didn't come in just to badger me for a date."

"Not that I wouldn't have." With a modest flourish, I produced one of my trusty cards for her. She glanced at it, then handed it back perfunctorily.

"I thought you said your name was Swift, Mr. Jones. I'm afraid I don't date dishonest men."

I looked at the card. It said, "State Mutual Life Insurance Corp., Barnwell Jones, Claims Investigator." In my business, it pays to have a legitimate-looking card for every occasion.

I found myself beginning to blush and fought it, although at that

35

moment a small child could have decked me with one punch. Patricia smiled as if she'd been looking through my laundry and found telltale signs of the solitary vice.

"Oh, yes," I said lamely. "A friend of mine's. I don't know how it got in there. Sorry. Now, here we go." I forked over a crisp new "Swift Investigations."

She checked it, then regarded me with exaggerated seriousness.

"So maybe you're the real Investigator Swift," she said dubiously. "So what?"

"Right. I'd like to speak to Carter Lockridge."

She shrugged. "He's a busy man. What about?"

"John Majors." I gave her a wink.

She looked at me as if to say that nobody winks anymore, but the name had gotten her attention. She picked up the phone and pushed a button. After a slight pause she said, "A Mr. Swift to see you. Concerning Mr. Majors." Another slight pause and she hung up.

"The magic words," she said. "Right through there," she added, gesturing to the door at her immediate right.

"Thanks. Now about that lunch date."

I did my best to look cool. Ronald Reagan at a meeting of the Socialist Workers' Party would have done almost as well.

"Mr. Swift—"

"You can call me Swift. It's not a nickname."

"Mr. Swift, are you accustomed to asking strange women to lunch? Is this something you do a lot?"

"Well, actually—"

"Perhaps as often as I'm accustomed to accepting such invitations."

"I don't—"

"But you think that if you're cute enough and smile winningly enough that I'll accept out of curiosity, and then you can let me see who you really are, your more serious qualities and all, is that right?"

"Well, if you put it—"

"And if I *don't* accept, it'll confirm in your mind that I really just don't have the same sense of ad*venture* as you do, won't it? And these sudden encounters *are* adventurous, aren't they?"

"Uh, I—"

"It *was* a spur-of-the-moment decision, wasn't it?"

"Yes—"

"Mr. Lockridge is waiting," she said. "I wouldn't keep him in suspense for long if I were you."

She gestured toward the door again and turned away from me. Before she did, I thought I detected a little smile that she was trying to hold in. I could always hope.

It was the wrong moment to say anything further, and I knew it. I went into Lockridge's office.

Carter Lockridge was, in a word, oily. Not oily like I am, in the sense of having inherited part-Mediterranean sweat glands. Oily in the sense of slippery, forever eluding your best grasp. A typical lawyer, I suppose. Like Nixon or John Dean.

He was also something of a gun freak, I noticed immediately. Hanging on the wall in wooden frames were several examples of classic and modern sidearms. I picked out, among others, a tiny over-and-under derringer; a Luger that looked like one of the original storm troopers had worn it; a pearl-handled nineteenth-century revolver; and a crossed pair of Colt Woodsman .22 target pistols, deadly accurate and relatively quiet, said to be a favorite with professional assassins.

The man himself was in his late forties and as youthful-looking as you can be at that age without ever being mistaken for a younger man. Tall, a couple of inches over six feet. Trim. A somewhat fleshy face but smooth. Clean-shaven, with an abundance of blond hair clinging perfectly to the contours of his head. Pale blue eyes, the kind that will look no different in death. And a pair of muttonchop sideburns, not too obtrusive, just enough to add a hint of the flamboyant.

He was dressed in impeccable taste. A gray pinstriped three-piece suit, complete with gold watch chain. Light blue shirt to match his eyes. University of Virginia school tie. Black wing tips.

This was the sort of man that women are attracted to in droves. In fact, he had the air of someone who has never failed to obtain *anything* that he really wanted. I envisioned him in bed with Patricia Ryan and hated him for it. But then he was extending his hand.

"Mr. Swift, so good to meet you." My friend, the good old boy.

"Likewise. John Majors has told you about me, then?"

"Yes. I handle all of the Majorses' legal business. If there's anything I can do—"

"Do you know a man named Harlow Brennerman?" I gave it to him quickly, before we'd had a chance to develop the give-and-take of conversation. In my experience that's the best way to get a fix on whether someone is lying about a key question.

Lockridge was good. He hesitated, but only for an instant. He might have recognized the name, or he might have been confused by the suddenness of the question. I couldn't tell for sure.

"I'm afraid not," he said. "Should I?"

I was a little disappointed. It was really the only question I wanted to ask Lockridge. If anyone would know about Brennerman, he would. I'd hoped he'd be able to tell me why I met a California P.I. my first day on this job, and one who was also working for (or possibly against) the Majors family. Lacking that, I'd hoped to at least discover whether Brennerman was part of something I wasn't supposed to know about. I'd gotten neither. It was back to square one as far as brother Harlow was concerned. That being the case, Lockridge had no need to know anything further.

"No, just thought you might," I said in a tone that closed the topic for the time being.

"Sorry. Sit down, will you?"

I did, in a comfortable leather chair. This was my day for leather chairs. I looked around. The inner office was like the outer office, with some personal touches. The guns. Lots of old books. Framed documents on the walls. A photo of a much younger Lockridge posing with a smiling Harry Byrd, Sr., the old Virginia senator, on some long-ago hiking trip. A trophy won at some sport requiring the use of a racket.

A civilized place. A place where the unkind word remained unspoken.

"All these guns," I remarked. "I hope they're not loaded."

"Some of them are." He shrugged. "You never know."

"No, you never do. If one of your clients went berserk, it's good he'd have something to blow you away with."

He was unamused, though I had curiosity value.

"But then," he said, "they wouldn't know which one to go for, would they?" The question felt almost like a dare. I got the impression that he knew a good bit more about me than I did about him.

"I suppose not."

"Care for a drink?" The perfect host again. Too bad I disliked him so much.

"No, thank you. I can still feel the one John Majors built me a couple of hours ago."

He smiled the unctuous smile. "I can appreciate that. He likes them strong, does he not?"

"Yes, he surely doesn't not."

"But then I don't suppose you want to discuss John's prowess with the cocktail."

"No. No, I don't."

"Well, how may I help you, then?"

What I really wanted to know was whether his secretary had a steady boyfriend, but I felt instinctively that if I gave away too much, he wouldn't hesitate to ridicule me in some subtle way. So I asked him how long he'd known the Majorses.

He picked up a pipe that had been lying in his ashtray, tamped it, and started it going again. He *would* be a pipe smoker. I noted that he was left-handed.

"As a lawyer," he said, "for something over twenty years."

"And personally?"

"Since I was a boy. My father was a good friend of the Colonel's."

"Do you know Leigh well?"

"More like somewhat. I've watched her grow up, of course, but she's of a different generation. They have their own interests."

"Such as?"

"Oh, I don't know. Hang gliding. Disco music. Whatever."

"What's she like, Mr. Lockridge?"

"Beautiful," he said after a slight pause.

For a moment he'd had that look in his eye. The one that older men get when they think about desirable women much younger than themselves. The look they would have you believe denotes a certain fatherly concern. I didn't believe it. In my mind there was no doubt that Carter Lockridge had lust in his heart for Leigh Majors.

He didn't let me see it for long.

"In more than just the physical sense, Mr. Swift," he added. "That you will be aware of if you've seen her photograph. But from what I understand, she is a beautiful person, as well."

"Who do you understand that from?"

39

"John. The Colonel. And . . . her mother, of course."

He must have been choking on that one. Give him credit; it oozed out almost believably.

"And Melissa?" I tried.

"Certainly." He hesitated. Was he ready to overlook the cynicism I was deliberately showing? "Well," he went on, "actually there is a bit of sibling rivalry between the two." No, he wasn't. "I've been told that they are not the, ah, closest of sisters. But that is not uncommon when both children are equally physically beautiful." A psychologist, too. This was a well-rounded man.

"Do you think Melissa might want something to happen to Leigh?"

"Certainly not!" Just the proper degree of outrage. "And I resent your implying such a thing." I decided to go easy on him and not point out that I hadn't implied it; I'd said it straight out.

"Sorry, counselor. I was leading the witness." He didn't find that amusing, so I added, "Just a joke." I got a stony stare for that one.

"Okay. Back to business. Here's what I've done so far." I dutifully consulted my little notebook. "Interviewed a—let's see, Lisa Kaslow, Leigh Majors's roommate at the University. Do you know her?"

"I'm afraid not."

"It doesn't matter. Lisa doesn't know where Leigh is. Do you?"

"Of course not."

"Well, that's it, then," I said, closing my notebook. "Unless you can give me any help as to where to start looking."

"Try her grandmother," he said.

"Yeah, the Colonel suggested that. I got the impression he and she aren't bosom buddies anymore."

"As far as I know, Sarah Jane and the Colonel are on the best of terms."

I shrugged. "Well, I've been wrong before. Thank you for your time, Mr. Lockridge. I've left my card with your secretary if you think of anything."

"My pleasure, Mr. Swift." Good old boy to the end. Although he shook my hand with considerably less familiarity than when we'd first met.

On the way out I checked Patricia Ryan for any signs of Lockridge contamination. No way, I decided. She had too much class, and it was a whole different variety than his. Good. If he *had* slept with her, I'd surely end up having to hurt him.

"Ah, Ms. Ryan . . ."

She looked up from her typewriter. Her expression was polite, as if she were trying not to appear bored.

"Yes," she said.

Nice try, fella.

"Nothing," I said. "Could you see that Mr. Lockridge gets my card?"

"Certainly, Mr. Swift. Good day."

"You, too."

I had my hand on the doorknob when she spoke again.

"Oh, and Swift . . ."

I paused.

"Twelve-thirty. Be punctual now."

I turned, but she was back at her typewriter, all business.

"No sense of adventure, eh?" I said, and then I got the hell out of there before I somehow queered the whole deal.

Outside, I noticed a silver Datsun 280Z parked in the narrow driveway next to the office building. The license plate said, "CL II." It would.

· · ·

I drove across town and parked on a side street off University Avenue.

As usual, there were no available spaces on the street, and all the lots have meters or require a University sticker. So I settled for a no-parking zone and propped my clergy credentials in the window, the ones I'd gotten by mail from the Universal Life Church in Modesto, California. They've saved me a lot of tickets. At least I think they have. And Clementine looks great as a church vehicle if you're into the original Christian doctrine of having only the most humble of possessions.

I walked two blocks to the Corner.

The Corner is a sort of miniature Harvard Square. A three-block cluster of bars, bookstores, druggists, cafeterias, sporting goods stores, etc. A place where students and would-be students hang out. I don't go there very often, because it makes me feel old.

After a quick cafeteria meal, I crossed University Avenue to the campus proper. Two minutes later I was on the Lawn, and it was like stepping back in time. Nothing in sight had been built in this century.

The Lawn is the most prestigious area of the University in which

41

a student can live. Basically, it's a grassy rectangle the size of a football field. At its head is a Monticello look-alike building called the Rotunda. A tourist stop. Strung out behind the Rotunda, on either side of the grassy area, is a line of attached brick single rooms fronted by a covered brick walkway. The arrangement resembles an octopus with six tentacles missing and is part of the original University as designed by Thomas Jefferson, who is referred to as, simply, the Founder. This is in keeping with local custom, which likes to reduce things to a single capitalized noun whenever possible: the Corner, the Lawn, the University, etc. What this means I can't guess.

Although living on the Lawn has its drawbacks—you have to go outside if you need to take a leak, for example—rooms there are highly coveted. In order to get one, you have to be a senior who has rendered conspicuous service to the University. Delmos Venable had one. There were those who were furious about this, but you could hardly argue that he hadn't done a lot for the U.

There was one ironic little historical twist to the fact of Delmos's presence on the Lawn. The long brick structures that house the Lawn rooms are built into either side of a hill, and each room has a corresponding lower story that is invisible from the front. This lower level is where the early nineteenth-century plantation boys kept the personal slaves that they brought from home.

Delmos and I arrived at his room simultaneously.

"Good timing," I said.

"And that's everything, Mr. Swift. Come in."

Delmos grabbed some wood on the way. Each of the Lawn rooms has its own fireplace, from the days when it was the only source of heat. Now there are electric baseboard units, but students maintain the tradition of keeping stacks of wood outside their doors and fires in their hearths. Delmos worked to revive his from some faintly glowing coals.

The room was quite small, and spartan by current student housing standards. There was a bed, a dresser, some bookshelves, a desk, two straight-back chairs, and that was it. On the shelves, in among the textbooks, I spotted some things I didn't think kids read anymore. Books like *Manchild in the Promised Land* and the *Autobiography of Malcolm X* and *Wretched of the Earth*.

Nowhere in the room was there any indication that a sports su-

42

perstar lived there. No plaques on the walls, no jockstraps hanging from the bedposts. The desk was bare except for a typewriter and a small framed photo of a black man and woman.

"Mama and daddy?" I asked.

"George and Vonda, their own selves," Delmos said. "See why I'm so pretty?" He said it like Ali would, giving me a profile. It was true; the elder Venables were a strikingly handsome couple, and Delmos had gotten a lot of their good genes. Still, there was something about them, something strange or out of place; I couldn't quite put my finger on it. It would come to me eventually.

"Yeah, I see," I said. Where to begin? I still felt a little like the kid who got Mean Joe Greene's jersey. I settled for "Team's looking good."

"I believe we're gonna take it all this year," he said, stroking an imaginary beard and grinning evilly. "But you're not here to talk roundball."

"Right. But I tell you what, I'll take a raincheck on the roundball talk."

"Hey, a genuine Wahoo booster, as they say. Okay, you got it. Now set down and give me the news."

We each selected from among the two hard chairs and sat.

"This is it," I said. "John Majors called me last night. Today I went out there. Like I told you earlier, he said that Leigh's been missing for several days, and he hired me to find her. I checked first with her roommate. She put me on to you. She told me that you and Leigh had grown up together and were still good friends. True?"

"True." His answer didn't betray any further intimacy, but I hadn't really expected it to.

I shrugged. "So I was hoping you might be able to give me something to go on. Have you heard anything since you've been back?" The Virginia basketball team had just returned from its annual trip to Hawaii, during which it suns its collective body and plays a couple of patsies to fatten its early-season record.

He leaned back. "No, not much, Mr. Swift. I'm still operating on Hawaii time, and I've been sacked out a lot. Lisa called to tell me she was worried. That's about it."

"You'd expect to see her, then."

"Sure. Me and Leigh been tight since forever."

"How tight?"

He just raised his eyebrows at me. That was all, but it was enough.

"What I'd like to know," I said, trying to make my voice sound less lame than it felt, "is whether it's unusual that she wouldn't get in touch with you for a day or two after you'd been gone for a week. Are you that kind of tight?"

"I'm worried," he said. I believed him. Yes, it *was* unusual, even if he didn't say it. We looked at each other in silence for a long moment, and then he said, "Find her, Mr. Swift."

He said it quietly and without the inflection of command. Yet I was stunned at the effect it had on me. When this young man spoke about something that was important to him, his words took on an extraordinary power. It was a gift shared by all natural leaders. No wonder the white ruling elite was so afraid of him. That kind of impact crosses the color line. I suddenly had a strange premonitory thought that when they finally wrote the chapter that began, "The first black president of the U.S.," there was a dead-even chance it would continue, "travelled a long road from the basketball court to the White House." If he lived long enough.

"I will," I said. It just sort of slipped out. Stupid thing to say, really. "I'm good at this kind of thing." Even worse. I cleared my throat. "Delmos, you know the Majors family, I take it. Can you think of any reason why a private investigator from California should be hanging around them?"

"No." He seemed genuinely surprised. "Why, is there one?"

I nodded. "I met him this afternoon, and he implied that he was working on a case, although I'm not sure if it's for or against them. Do they have any connection with Sacramento that you know of?"

He thought on that one for a while.

"Now the only thing I can think of is that Leigh's grandmother lived in California for a while when she was young. That's where she had Mr. Majors. She and the Colonel had broken up when she got pregnant, and she ran away out West, but after a couple of years he talked her back. Since then, it's been all Albemarle County for the whole family, far as I know."

"The Colonel doesn't have any business dealings out there?"

"I don't think so. Course what I know about the Colonel's business wouldn't exactly fill U. Hall." He paused. "But what does this guy have to do with Leigh?"

I shook my head. "Maybe nothing. Probably nothing. It's just a strange coincidence." I told him how Brennerman and I had met on the road while I was fixing my car.

"That's strange, for sure," he said.

"Okay," I said. "Let's let that one ride for a bit. Now Leigh's mother says that she does this a lot."

"Does what?"

"Runs away like this."

Delmos's eyes narrowed. Slits in the blockhouse, with some heavy firepower behind.

"That woman" was all he ended up saying.

"It's not so?"

"Course not."

"Lisa says that Leigh's a very private person."

"Yeah, man. She likes to be by herself. But she doesn't run away, or like that. If she doesn't get in touch by now, there's a reason. Believe it."

When he said it, I did.

"Why would Elizabeth lie about it?"

"Uh, she and Leigh don't get on so good."

"She prefers Melissa?"

Delmos laughed. "That's a good one. Don't nobody get it on with Melissa, dad. Not unless they're as crazy as she is. She come on to me at times, but I wouldn't have any part of her. Once I thought she'd scratch my eyes out for it. No, Mrs. Majors doesn't prefer Melissa. Not hardly. Actually, Mrs. Majors doesn't have a kind word for Leigh *or* Melissa. Or either Bruce."

"Bruce who?"

"Bruce Majors, of course."

"Who in the hell is Bruce Majors?"

Delmos laughed again. "Oh, yeah, I bet they didn't tell you about brother Bruce. Well, welcome to the monkey farm."

"Give. Or I'll punch you in the hook shot."

"Ouch. Okay, okay." He leaned toward me. "He's the black sheep. So to speak." He chuckled. "The wayward son."

"Leigh has a brother?"

"Sure. Bruce."

"Why didn't they mention him?"

"Like I said, he's the black sheep. He turned his back on the

45

whole family, except maybe Leigh. Said their money had blood on it or something. Hey, money's money. It's all got *some*body's blood on it, right? Anyway, he joined some religious group down in Nelson." The adjacent county, heading south. "Seeks, I think they're called. I don't know if they believe in money or what, but he doesn't speak to his family anymore. They don't like to be reminded of him, neither."

I'd heard of the Sikhs, living communally down in the hills of Nelson County, and I'd occasionally seen them walking around Charlottesville in their linen robes and turbans. They didn't solicit on street corners or try to sell you incense sticks, so I hadn't paid them much attention.

"The Majors have a son who became a Sikh?"

"Sure do."

"Well, I'll be damned. Are he and Leigh close?"

"Dunno. I don't think she's seen him in a while."

"How do I get in touch with him?"

"I think they've got a phone, but he won't talk to you, my man. Anything about the family and he clams up."

"Okay, I've got my ways." We exchanged conspiratorial smiles. "Now what else can you tell me?"

He thought for a while. When he answered, I got the impression he was seeing some fondly remembered scene in his head, something buried in the distant past.

"Well," he said, "there's this place we used to go when we were kids. Me and Mama and Leigh and Bruce, and Melissa sometimes, though she'd get tore up for *days* when we didn't take her. If Leigh really wanted to be alone, she might hole up there. It's a cabin the family owns, down on the James River, pretty far from anything. They usually only use it in the summertime, but she'd probably have a key. She could be there for weeks and nobody'd notice."

"Where exactly is this place?"

"Mmmmm, that's hard to say. It's years since I've been there. Haven't been close to the family since mama left. But tell you what though, Mr. Swift—"

"How about calling me Swift for starters? The 'Mister' part makes me nervous."

"Okay, looka here, Swift. You see what you can do on your end. Day after tomorrow I don't have any morning classes. You haven't found her by then, I'll take you to the cabin."

"Fine."

"And if you do find her by then, sometime I'll take you to dinner, and we talk nothing but roundball. After the season, of course," he said, patting his stomach.

"Now there's an offer I can't refuse," I said. "I'll get her found by tomorrow."

"Good." He said good, and he meant good.

"Anything else?" I asked.

"I don't think so."

"Okay." I got up. "Thanks, Delmos. And by the way . . ."

"Yeah?"

"Just beat North Carolina, will you?"

He rolled his eyes in disbelief. "Man," he said, "we *own* Carolina." Grinning that grin.

We clasped hands with fingers upraised and thumbs locked, the way it used to be done, and I left. Being with the kid still made me feel good.

It was early evening yet.

I walked back across University Avenue to a drugstore that had some old-fashioned enclosed telephone booths. I bought a buck's worth of change and made some calls.

The first was to Sarah Jane Majors. She was in, but preparing for a dinner party. I explained who I was, and she agreed to talk to me. We made a date for breakfast the following morning.

Then I used my credit card to call my buddy Stone in San Francisco. Stone's another one who fled Massachusetts; only he went to the West Coast. Back when we were both young ops in Boston, we once drove to Illinois for the weekend just so he could buy the season's first ten cases of Meister Brau bock beer, which he claimed was the finest in the country. He's that kind of friend. Now he's a big-time San Fran P.I., like Sam Spade. But he'd do any favor I asked.

It was still working hours on the coast, so he was at his office. When I got him on the line, I asked if he could dig up what a Harlow Brennerman, of Continental Pacific Investigations, was doing in Virginia. He said no problem, but it might take a day or two. He'd get back to me.

Next I called the *Daily Press*. The *Press*—unaffectionately known to most as the *Depressor*—is what passes for Charlottesville's daily

47

newspaper. Its politics lie somewhere to the right of Alexander Haig, which makes it a little reactionary for my taste, and its staff isn't particularly professional. But it's all we've got, so I maintain a few contacts there. One of them works the night desk. I asked Jonesy to see what he could find out about the Sikhs in Nelson County. An address and phone number would do fine for starters. He thought he could have the info in an hour or so.

Finally, I called my answering service. A young female voice dripping with barely contained lust—or so I imagined—told me that I'd had one call. It was from an Elizabeth Majors. The message was that she'd be at the Jefferson Tavern in Court Square between seven and nine. If I had time, she'd like to talk to me.

I checked my watch. Not yet eight. The tavern was back across town, but in Charlottesville that's not far. I wasn't enthralled with the idea of seeing the viperous Mrs. Majors again so soon, but this case was beginning to find its way into a lot of odd little dark corners, and maybe she could do some shedding of light. I decided to meet her.

· 3 ·

The Jefferson Tavern is a rarity for Charlottesville. In a town that caters primarily to the desires of fifteen thousand college-age juveniles, it's an adult bar. They have nice authentic butcher-block tables. Stained-glass windows. Subdued lighting. A music system that doesn't intrude but which, if you want to listen, is playing something you'd want to hear. Plus the area's largest selection of imported beers.

I go there for the imported beer and the atmosphere, though the clientele leaves a good bit to be desired. Being on Court Square, the tavern attracts a high percentage of lawyers. Personally, I've got nothing against lawyers; just think of all the laughs we got out of Nixon, Mitchell, Liddy, that bunch. But in my experience they're usually either loudmouth egomaniacs or quiet and abysmally boring. In other words, not your better class of bar companion.

It didn't seem like Elizabeth Majors's sort of place, and I wondered how she'd happened to choose it as a spot to wait in until I maybe contacted her. Logic suggested that she'd had some other business in the area. Legal business, perhaps. It occurred to me that she might have been consulting her lawyer, the smarmy Lockridge. That was an interesting possibility, considering the presence of the California P.I. on the scene.

I pushed through the old-timey, heavy glass-and-brass double doors that admitted you to the Jefferson Tavern. Elizabeth Majors was sitting at a corner table, as far from the next nearest customer as she could get. She was drinking something brown with ice in it and smoking a cigarette. With her high-fashion clothes and stunning hair she drew attention, even at the Jefferson. If she was aiming to be unobtrusive, she wasn't succeeding.

"Mrs. Majors," I said, and extended my hand. She took it and dropped it immediately, giving me the Big Lie smile. No one here but us old buddy-buddies.

"I appreciate your coming, Swift," she said.

"You're paying for the time."

The waitress, my friend Anne, bellied up to the table and asked if I wanted the usual. I said sure. Watneys Red Barrel, like always.

When she'd gone, Elizabeth said, "Not exactly. John's paying for your time."

"Correct me if I'm wrong, but he is your husband, is he not?"

"Of course he is."

"Then—"

"Don't play dumb," she said, mashing out her cigarette. "*John's* hired you to find that little ninny over my objections."

"You don't want your daughter found?"

"That isn't the point. My daughter's not lost."

Anne arrived with the Watneys, and I took a long pull at it, from the bottle. Delicious. Imagine living in a country where you could get one of them for the price of a Schlitz.

Elizabeth excused herself to go the rest room. When she got back, I picked up the thread.

"There are those who disagree with you," I said. "About Leigh being lost."

"Swift, it has been my misfortune in life to be surrounded by idiots. The fact is that Leigh loves to make grandstand plays for John's benefit. If it wasn't this, it would be something else. It's like she has to keep reminding him that she's the favorite daughter. God only knows why; it couldn't be more obvious already. She's done it before, and she'll do it again. It's part of her neurosis now. You'll eventually find her shacked up with some friend of hers."

"Lisa says she doesn't have any close friends."

"Lisa's a nitwit."

"Other people concur with Lisa."

"What other people?"

"Other."

"Well, don't believe everything you hear."

"I don't."

"This isn't getting us anywhere, Swift."

"I know. It's beginning to sound like the Watergate tapes."

"Very funny."

"I suppose. But I'm serious, Mrs. Majors. Everybody I meet's got an angle. They're all talking at cross-purposes, and I'm stuck in the middle, trying to make some sense out of it."

She lit another cigarette. A Virginia Slim. She'd come a long way, baby; her grandparents were probably Tidewater swamp rats. Her mouth left a garish red phantom lip on the cigarette filter.

"Look," she said after thinking on it, "how about leaving off the world-weary cynical act for a few minutes? I don't suppose it ever occurred to you that I might actually be trying to help you . . . No, obviously not. I imagine you think I'm some sort of vampire, that I hate my own daughter. Well, let me tell you something. Just because the child is a simpleton doesn't mean I don't care about her. Besides which, you're in no position to judge me or anyone else in my family. There's a great deal about us that you'll never know. At this point, I may have to play the ogre to you, and so be it. I don't have to impress you, and I don't care whether you like me. But I do have problems of my own in this life, believe it or not, and I have to do what I think is best to resolve them. Now do you think you could give me the benefit of the doubt long enough for us to have a half-civilized conversation?"

She had a point. Maybe I was prejudging her because of her interactions with John. Maybe Leigh really was a little ninny and Elizabeth was the only one who allowed herself to see it. Maybe anything.

At moments like this, there was definitely something compelling about Elizabeth, a devastating combination of blue eyes, honey hair, and that flower-of-womanhood thing that only southerners seem to know about. It was difficult to doubt her sincerity. She forced you to start warming up to her, whether you wanted to or not.

I didn't trust it. But then I've been wrong before.

"Okay," I said neutrally. "Will you help me?"

"What would you like to know?"

"We could start with something simple, like why you wanted to talk to me tonight."

She smoked on that for a bit, giving me the old southern belle look. I didn't mind. The night was young, and the Jefferson had plenty of Red Barrel, and Brennerman probably wasn't going anywhere. I passed the time thinking how I'd hit Delmos up for a couple of tickets to a Virginia basketball game—they were scarce as an honest face on Capitol Hill—and invite Patricia Ryan to go with me. She'd turn out to be a fan, of course, and would accept immediately. And that would be the best of all possible worlds.

Elizabeth seemed to make up her mind about something.

"Swift," she said, "as you may have gathered by now, I'm not real enthused about our—about John's having employed you."

"And here I've been believing that you thought I was swell people."

She ignored me. "Number one, I think it's silly, given Leigh's history, but there's more to it than that."

"What a surprise. Do go on."

She leaned toward me. "Listen, let's cut the crap, all right? The point is, I'd rather not have someone poking around the family's affairs just now."

"Because of Harlow Brennerman?"

"Who's he?" She said it sharply, as if surprised and suddenly concerned at the same time. If it had been anyone else, I would have sworn that she'd never heard of him. Yet Brennerman had been on his way to her house to meet *someone*. It would be odd if she didn't know about it. Still, what could Brennerman possibly have to do with Leigh Majors? I decided not to press the point. I filed it away under Peculiarities and Inconsistencies.

"Just some guy I met. If you don't know him, you don't know him. Okay, so why would you rather I not be hanging around?"

"Personal reasons."

"Such as?"

"Come on, Swift. I said personal; I meant personal. It just happens to be a difficult time for the family. There are some delicate business matters involved. Wouldn't you know she'd pick now to run away." It wasn't a question.

"I'm sorry, Mrs. Majors, but I've been hired to—"

"Screw that! *I'll* hire you to take it slow. Not quit, just ease up. In a couple of days the little waif will show up on our doorstep, and you'll have both John's money and mine."

"I'm sorry, Mrs. Majors, but—"

"Damn you, Swift! I'm offering you good money and all you have to do is not do anything. You're so rich you can turn up your nose at that?"

"I only do one job at a time, Mrs. Majors, and I like to finish what I start."

"Your stupid morality makes me sick."

"It's not morality; it's only the way I am." Morality's something you choose, but the way you are comes with the deal. I don't know why people find that so difficult to understand, but they do.

"You're a smug bastard."

She glared at me. Then, abruptly, the contempt was gone, wiped away completely. It was as if she could turn her moods on and off as readily as a good actor can tears. Now she was all southern sweetness and light.

"Swift," she said huskily, "what do I have to do to get you to listen to me?" She was about as seductive as daughter Melissa. They must watch the same TV programs.

"I am listening."

"No, I mean *really* listen, like you do to your lover at three in the morning."

Jesus. What the hell *was* this? I don't know a soul who has anything worthwhile to say at three in the morning.

"I'm sorry," I said. "I don't think I can give you what you want."

In an instant she had flipped the switch again. It unnerved me. I felt like I was trapped in a cage with some alien being whose behavior patterns were totally unpredictable.

"You people piss me off," she snapped. "You think you can come down here with your Yankee ways and tell us how to do our business. Well, I'll tell *you* something. We run you off once, and we can do it again. And all of your little brown lackeys won't be able to help you out then."

I didn't know what in Christ's world she was talking about. I opened my mouth to make some inane comment. No words came out.

I shrugged. I had nothing further to say to this woman.

She didn't let it go, though. Despite the crazy mood swings, there was more than a trace of the pit bull in her. Get something between her teeth and she'd worry it until it was a disintegrating pulp of gristle and hair.

"Leave it be, Swift," she said. She was trying to sound matter-of-fact, but there was a strong undertone of warning. "Just for a few days. It'll be a lot better for you if you do."

I got up.

"Mrs. Majors," I said, "I don't like being run around and around the goddam barn. I don't like being talked down to. I don't like crude attempts to buy me off. And I especially don't like being threatened. Now, your husband has hired me to do a job, and I'm going to do my damndest to get it done, and then I hope I never have to deal with the Majors family again. So if you'll excuse me, I've got work to do." And I left her to pay the check.

On my way out, I walked down to the rest room in the basement to take a quick leak. I passed a public telephone and thought about giving Brennerman a call and canceling our meeting. After all, he was just some California shamus. He wouldn't know where Leigh was, and I really didn't want to get involved in whatever other weird deals were going down within the family. But of course my curiosity got the best of me. It always does. Generally to my regret. So I saved a couple of dimes.

Back outside, the air was cold but tasted good. I decided I needed a drink before keeping my appointment. I also needed to put some gas in Clementine. Mac's would fit the bill nicely. It's a combination roadhouse and two-pump gas station over on Route 29, just south of the Interstate. And it was on my way. From there, it would be a straight eight-mile shot down 29 to the Mountain Vista Motel.

I drove out of downtown Charlottesville, cut across the Interstate, and exited at Route 29 South. Then came the tricky part: 29 is a divided highway, and Mac's is over on the northbound side, so you have to cut across the two southbound lanes as soon as you come off the feeder ramp in order to make the necessary immediate left turn. But at that hour traffic was light, and I made it without mishap. I watched the cars pass by while the attendant pumped nine and one half gallons of regular into the VW.

Had I still been heading toward the Mountain Vista, I never would have noticed him across the median strip. The strip is wide, and the night was cloudy dark. But now we were both on the same side of the highway, and he slowed just as he passed me. I could hear the Datsun gear down as it slipped into the exit lane that would take it up onto the Interstate. The license plate read: CL II.

Brother Lockridge, I thought. Out cruising, eh? Well, I hope you find whatever it is you're looking for. Unless it's your beautiful secretary, of course.

After I paid for the gas, I went into the bar and settled myself down to a nice steaming cup of Irish coffee. If the Irish didn't really invent the drink, as I've been told, then they should have. It's the perfect antidote to damp chilly nights. I understand they have a lot of those in Ireland.

There was a TV on, up above the stacks of bottled liquors. It was tuned to the local station, and they were broadcasting a show on University of Virginia basketball.

Jeez, I thought, in prime time no less. They were going to milk the sucker for all it was worth this year. And why not? After Delmos left, the team would be a good one among many others. But while he was here, the national championship was only inches away.

I watched for a half hour or so. Always the pushover for a little good roundball.

They were replaying the highlights of the previous year, capped by the final minutes of the second Wake Forest game. It was exciting. Wake, the conference's third-place team, had led by eight with just over three minutes to go. Virginia had then staged a furious comeback as Wake tried to run out the clock. Now, for what it's worth, if I was a coach, I'd never stall. It takes you right out of your rhythm, and I think it loses many more games than it wins. In any case, with ten seconds to play, Virginia got the ball under its own basket, still trailing by two. Delmos took the inbounds pass, dribbled it over, under, around, and through the defense, going the length of the court in the process, and capping the trip with a soft lay-up. The last Wake defender tried in vain to block the shot and picked up a foul instead. With no time left on the clock, Delmos calmly sank the free throw. Virginia by one.

After a commercial break, they showed an interview with Virginia's head coach, Storm Taylor. When they asked him about the Cavaliers' chances this season, he said, "Well, I think we've got a great nucleus here, with all of our starters coming back. But there are a lot of fine teams in the country, as you know. Right now our primary objective is to win the conference title, which won't be easy. After that, we'll take it from there."

Then they interviewed Delmos.

When asked the same question, he just grinned and said, "We're gonna win it all."

I finished my drink and called the *Daily Press* back.

My man Jonesy on the night desk had done a good job. He'd

come up with an unlisted phone number for the Nelson County Sikhs, plus the approximate location of what he called their "ashram."

"What the hell is that?" I asked. I thought he'd said "ashcan."

"An ashram is a spiritual community, you illiterate," he said. "Where followers of a great teacher live."

Now me, I haven't had a great teacher since Miss Heavener in the third grade, who scandalized the school by showing up without underwear and then failing to cross her legs. We learned a lot from Miss Heavener, but I don't think anyone ever suggested building an ashram for her. So I let it slide.

Jonesy even had a capsule history of the local branch of Sikhdom for me. It was some very interesting information indeed. I filed it away for future reference.

"Thanks Jonesy," I said. "Slow night, eh?"

"Aren't they all in this half-ass town?" Jonesy had *Washington Post* aspirations.

"I suppose. Still, I owe you one. That was a lot of digging."

"You set up the drinks at Mac's on Super Sunday if the Redskins get in?"

"You got it."

I hung up and headed down Route 29 South.

• • •

U.S. 29 is one of those few remaining federal highways that hasn't been made obsolete by the Interstate system. It's still the primary route through central Virginia, connecting Washington, D.C., with Charlottesville, Lynchburg (home of the inimitable Jerry Falwell), Danville, and the tri-city cluster of upper North Carolina. A heavily traveled road in excellent condition, favored by salesmen and truckers and those on the tourist trail south who choose to pass up the glories of Interstates 81 and 95.

As I slid along it, Clementine's heater tried in vain to keep up with the cold that seeped in at a couple of dozen key points. And Volkswagens are supposed to be airtight? Maybe when she was new she had been.

To distract myself, I considered the events of the day.

Here I was, on the same road and headed in the same direction as this morning, and I didn't like the way things were going. It

56

should have been simple. Girl disappears. Investigator locates her. Everyone is happy. The end.

Now basically I agreed with Elizabeth Majors; I didn't think Leigh was going to be that hard to find. Ninety-nine times out of a hundred that's the way it works out. It's difficult enough for anyone to vanish without a trace in this society, Jimmy Hoffa notwithstanding. Doubly so for someone her age who's still financially dependent on her parents. The only exception of any significance is kidnaping, and there was no evidence of that here.

Of more immediate concern was the question of Leigh Majors's character. Most people appeared to consider her a candidate for sainthood, at the very least, and were surprised at her disappearance. On the other hand, a vocal minority called her a tramp and insisted that this sort of behavior was not uncommon. Naturally, I wanted to be on the side of the good guys. But I learned long ago that it can be a very bad mistake to assume someone is lying simply because you don't like them. Best to stay neutral until the facts were in, and that would hopefully be soon.

I resolved that my trip to see Brennerman would be the last detour I'd take in this case. If he really wanted to talk to me, I wouldn't be able to avoid him, anyway. But after this I was going to stay clear of anything that didn't relate directly to Leigh Majors and her whereabouts.

The night road pulled me south like a magnet, and I almost cruised on past my destination. At the last minute the glowing neon advertising the Mountain Vista caught my eye. I managed to brake in time to skitter in at the far entrance. The "Vacancy" part of the sign was lighted, but the "No" wasn't. Just in case I needed a quick room.

The Mountain Vista is a small brick job. Sixteen units with the office in the middle. It attracts those who don't like the bright lights, fast-food joints, and inflated prices of Charlottesville's motel strip and catches the overflow from town on big football weekends.

I drove slowly past the units, looking for number 14. It was seventh out of eight in the even-numbered wing. Brennerman's car was parked out front, and there was a light on inside the room. I pulled up and looked at my watch. Ten past ten. The Irish whiskey and coffee I'd recently had were debating inside me like the 1980 presidential candidates. The alcohol said I was as old and slow-witted as Reagan, while the caffeine tried to persuade me that I was as jacked up as Anderson. The winner got to go head-to-head with Harlow Brennerman.

Anderson lost. I hauled myself to the door thinking that I'd much rather be home in bed with a Robert Parker novel and a glass of Jameson on the rocks.

Nobody answered the knock.

"Mr. Brennerman," I said, not too loud, and knocked again. Nothing. My stomach suddenly felt like a bottomless pit.

I tried the door. It was open.

Now I'm no more brave or cowardly than the next guy. Confronted with the unknown, especially when my stomach is in a state of open rebellion, my natural impulse is to run like hell in the other direction. As I imagine most people's would be. But again, like I suspect most people would have, I went on into the room, anyway. Call it curiosity or a latent self-destructive urge or simply the desire to complete an action once begun. Whatever you wish.

The room was hot, much hotter than it needed to be. It was a motel room like any other, with one double bed; a desk and writing chair; two easy chairs; and a color TV. The TV rested on a shelf suspended from the wall by two lengths of chain. Harlow Brennerman's suitcase was on the floor, its contents scattered about. An open attaché case was on the desk, empty.

Brennerman himself was lying on the bed, looking much as I'd last seen him except for the small hole above his right eyebrow. An entry wound producing very little blood. That meant a small-caliber pistol, probably a .22. A generally ineffective handgun. Unless you could put the bullet right where you wanted it. Then there was nothing any better, nothing at all. Dead was dead.

I closed the door behind me.

Cautiously, with my heart trip-hammering, I checked the rest of number 14. Closet and bathroom, that's all there was, and no one was lurking in either. The late Mr. Brennerman and I were alone.

I went through his things. Whoever had preceded me had done a thorough job. They'd left only his clothes. No papers, no billfold, nothing. I didn't doubt that the car would be clean, too.

Gingerly, I felt the side of Brennerman's face. He hadn't been dead long. Indirectly, Elizabeth Majors may have saved my life. If I hadn't met her and then stopped for an Irish coffee, I might have walked right into the middle of things. That gave me the creeps.

I sat on the edge of the bed and tried to decide what to do. On the one hand, I didn't want to get mixed up in whatever had gotten Harlow killed. On the other, I didn't want to be spotted leaving the scene of a homicide. Clementine was too identifiable a car to take the chance. Besides, I reasoned, I don't have the slightest idea who killed Brennerman or why, so I have nothing to fear from the cops.

There was no choice, really. I trudged to the motel office.

The pimply-faced young clerk was catching some heavy Z's behind the desk. He came awake with a start when I entered the office, as if I'd been playing a nasty role in his dreams and it was frightening to see me now in the flesh. But he recovered quickly. His prominent Adam's apple bobbed violently when he spoke.

"Room, sir?" he asked. Bob, bob.

I flashed my special deputy's badge. The kid didn't study it too closely. They never do. Just flash a badge, any badge, and your average citizen snaps immediately to attention. It makes you realize that we're a military society at heart. It also helps a lot in my line of work.

The kid looked at me with eyes that said he didn't do it, whatever it was. "Wh— what is it?" he said.

"There's a stiff in fourteen," I said.

"Huh?" Bob.

"I said, you've got a stiff on your hands. A corpse. A cadaver. A dead man. There is a late person in room fourteen."

"Wh— what do you mean?"

"Okay." I sighed. "Here's what you do. You call the sheriff's office, and you tell them you want to report a homicide, and then you tell them where you are, and then they'll send somebody over. Think you can handle that?"

He started to say something, then nodded. His Adam's apple bobbed even when he was just thinking about speaking.

"Good," I said. "When they get here, send them to number fourteen. I'll be waiting there. All right?"

He nodded again and was reaching for the phone as I left the office.

It took Ridley Campbell about fifteen minutes to get there. Sheriff Campbell and I are old buddies.

59

"Hi, Rid," I said. "What kept you? Catch a peeping tom in the act and stick around to see what he was peeping at?"

"Swift," he said, "you sit in that chair over there and see how long you can go without your lips get separated from each other."

I sat down and shut up. Rid Campbell is six-one and about 225. He looks a little like Jack Lambert, maybe the toughest linebacker ever to play in the NFL. I once saw Rid single-handedly end a bar brawl. One of the brawlers, a guy about the size of a quarter horse, had the bad judgment to take a swing at the sheriff. Rid broke his arm like maybe it was a number 2 pencil, and suddenly everyone in the place was into the pleasures of quiet drinking. That sort of thing might understandably cause you not to notice that he's a primarily nonviolent man, with a first-rate mind. Nevertheless, he is. But when he tells you to sit, you sit.

The cop crew went over the room thoroughly, not once asking for the assistance of the special deputy. They found exactly as much as I had. Finally, Campbell turned the fingerprint guy loose and rediscovered me. He came over and sat next to me, real neighborly, and lit a cigarette.

I cleared my throat and put on my cooperation face.

"Okay, Swift," he said. "My working assumption is that you didn't grease the man. You got an alibi we can check, right?"

"If it comes to that. I was with a client."

"Great. So who's the dead one?"

"Well, I'm glad you value my assistance, Rid. Now before I—"

"Swift." He paused. "Don't jerk me off." His look said don't jerk him off.

"His name's Harlow Brennerman. Was."

"Good. Who's that?"

"Some guy from California. He was a P.I. Worked for something called Continental Pacific Investigations, out of Sacramento."

"No kidding. Now ain't that a wonderment? And what was your brother P.I. doing in Virginia?"

I shrugged. Campbell gave me the don't-jerk-me-off look again.

"I'm serious, Rid. I don't know."

"All right, let me put it this way. How'd you happen to know the fella?"

I told him how I'd met Brennerman when my car broke down.

"I get it," he said. "He just happened by when you was broke

60

down, and then, you both being P.I.s and all, he invited you back
to his place for a drink. That how it went?"

"Something like that."

"And how'd you two discover you was in the same line?"

"It came up in the course of conversation."

"It come up in the course of conversation. That's very convenient.
And did this course of conversation by any chance give you a hint
as to why Mr. Brennerman now has a nonfunctional orifice?" Ridley
loved to do that, use a phrase like "nonfunctional orifice" to keep
you on your toes.

"No, it didn't."

"Well, what *did* he say, then?"

"He said he had some kind of deal going that he wanted to talk
to me about. I don't have the vaguest idea what. He thought I could
help him with whatever it was since I knew the local scene. I agreed
to meet him and hear what he had to say. That's all there was, I
swear it."

"Who you working for, Swift?"

"That's confidential, Rid; you know that."

"Who you working for, Swift?"

"Sorry."

"You want me to lean a trifle?"

"Look, Rid, here's what it is. The people I'm working for could
buy and sell the likes of me a hundred times out of their monthly
bar bill and never miss a drink. If I blow them, I'm finished around
here. Even you they could probably make uncomfortable, but let
that be. I'll make you an offer. You don't lean, and I don't give up
my client. In return, I promise you that what happened here couldn't
possibly have anything to do with what I'm working on. If you find
later that I was bullshitting you, I'll give you my license in seventeen
pieces. Plus, if I should stumble by chance across anything that even
remotely connects to Brennerman, you've got it the same hour.
How about that?"

He gave me that soulful brown-eyed look that makes you think
the good guy inside him is plugging away, constantly working to
keep the bad guy in check.

"All right," he said finally. "But you better be leveling with me,
Swift. If you're not, I will do two things. I will have the license you
so gracefully offered me. And I will carve you a nonfunctional orifice

of your very own. Make a formal statement before you go."

Then he smiled.

I didn't care what it meant. All I wanted was out of that goddam motel room and away from Harlow Brennerman and his three eyes. I was so anxious that I tripped getting out of my chair and pitched forward into Sheriff Campbell's lap. He levered me back up with one hand.

"He ain't yer type, Rid," one of the boys called.

"You're a mess, Swift." Campbell chuckled. "Get some sleep, will you?" Pause. "And don't forget my phone number, y'hear?"

"I won't."

"Good." The word the way he said it still had only one syllable, but it took him as long as if it had had two or three.

I made my statement as quickly as I could.

"Oh, Swift," Campbell called after me as I was headed out the door.

"What?"

"Don't let your inspection sticker expire."

They thought that was a laugh riot, all the good old boys.

• • •

I was tired. Not that it had been such a long day, but it had put a heavy drain on the spirit. It had produced more questions than answers. And it had ended with my putting myself in a very hairy position with respect to Ridley Campbell. That was particularly dangerous, like owing a favor to Michael Corleone.

I was glad to see my home neighborhood. I live in the Belmont section of Charlottesville, east and south of the city center. It's a hilly area of mostly pre-World War II frame houses. Primarily white. Blue-collar workers. The mountain kids who move to town end up in Belmont, with their jacked-up Chevvies parked out front. There's a flock of Baptist churches within walking distance, should my soul need saving.

Belmont is not one of your more fashionable addresses, but traditionally it's cheap. That's why I chose to live there. Me and a few thousand others on the wrong end of the economic stick. Lately, though, with the increase in popularity of funky old neighborhoods, Belmont's been rediscovered. People have I ♡ Belmont stickers on their cars. Stuff like that, suggesting that the old slums aren't so bad, after all. And the rise in property values has started to keep pace with the surrounding countryside. Someday I'll probably be driven out by the speculators, but for the moment the area still suits both my taste and my budget.

Home is one of those two-story frame houses built into the side of a hill so that the first floor sits level with the road. The lower story is my half, and you have to go around back to get into it. I like the arrangement. It's very private. The earth in back of my north wall isolates me from street noise and acts to keep me cool in summer and warm in winter. Of course, the place is also damp, but you can't have everything.

My landlady, Mrs. Detweiler, is eighty something and a little hard of hearing. Back in the twenties and thirties she was one of those socialist activists who fought the good fight against the capitalist bosses and lost. She claims to have known Red Emma Goldman and the rest of them and maintains to this day that America blew its big chance to help promote world peace by failing to join the Revolution when it had the opportunity. Mrs. Detweiler's hearing impairment hasn't stilled her tongue or fogged her brain any. When I'm in the mood, I can listen for hours as she draws on a bottomless well filled with colorful stories about the early labor movement in this country. Part of the deal each time is having to examine the scar on her scalp that was left by an overzealous Chicago cop long ago.

Despite her unusual history my landlady never intrudes where she hasn't been invited, which is another reason I like where I live.

I parked on the street and walked to my house. Later, I figured I must have passed the car, but in my fuzzy-headed state it hadn't registered.

When I reached the door, I froze with the key in my hand. I could see light leaking from under my bedroom door. There shouldn't have been any.

Very quietly, I let myself in. I went immediately to the couch in the front room and reached behind it. I keep a loaded .38 Police Positive there. Though I've felt it'll probably never do me any good, at least it's something I have that an intruder won't know about, and that might be worth a little. Like tonight. I pulled it loose from the tape that holds it in place and checked it out. It was ready.

I went into the bedroom fast, slightly crouched, with the safety off.

She hardly batted an eye, probably more from the drugs than any natural courage.

"Hi, Swift," she said.

She was propped up in my bed with the covers tucked under her chin. Drinking my Irish whiskey and reading my Robert Parker novel. Exactly what I wanted to be doing. It annoyed me more than somewhat. I lowered the gun.

"Melissa," I said wearily, "what are you doing here?"

"Seeing what you like to read. This is a good one," flashing *The Judas Goat* at me.

"Well, you can check it out of the library when I'm done with it. So put it away and let's say good night."

For an answer she leaned forward, and the blankets dropped away from her shoulders. Just like they do it in the movies. Her breasts looked even better than they had behind the filmy blouse this afternoon, and she knew it. She'd done this sort of thing before. I'd have given a hundred to one she hadn't gotten a rejection yet.

I forced myself to look instead at her face. That made things easier, which I needed them to be since I hadn't had a woman in some time. Her face was also beautiful, true, but with the not uncommon hint of cruelty you sometimes find in otherwise-beautiful faces.

She was doing the pouty child-woman thing again. It was damned effective but not quite enough. I could focus on the cruelty.

"How'd you get in?" I asked.

She gave me a secretive smile that suggested she could get into anyplace she wanted. I didn't care for it.

"Get up, Melissa," I said.

"You're not going to send me away, are you?" She pouted.

I walked over to the bed and stripped the covers away from her. Lord God. They didn't make them like that in my day. I looked at her nose. I was angry at her effrontery and excited by her body at the same time. And I was angry with myself for being excited and further excited by my anger. The situation was almost out of hand.

"Melissa," I said, striving for an icy tone before my resolve began to give way, "a few minutes ago I might easily have taken a shot at you. That is not the way I like to go about these things. Plus I'm tired, and I need some sleep. Now will you please get dressed and get the hell out of here?"

She was still looking up at me with that kittenish expression she'd learned from the TV. I think she might have won the war of nerves if it hadn't been for the cold. She didn't have a stitch on, and the chill was starting to get to her.

"Please," she said.

"No!"

The rage came over her again then, the same blind childish rage I'd already seen a couple of times. When it did, you wondered how she'd ever seemed beautiful. I thought, How many other men have wondered the same thing as the knife was sliding in?

She threw herself out of the bed, snatched up her blue jeans and sweater, and jammed herself into them.

"You wish I was my sister," she muttered.

"That has nothing to do with it—"

"Don't *lie* to me, you fucker! That's all you've ever wanted was to stick it in *her*. You and all the *rest* of them!"

"Melissa," I said.

But she was into it now. Her intensity was frightening. Tonight she was no sloppy downer freak, despite the whiskey she'd been drinking. This was someone riding the manic energy of an upper trip. Coke or speed or something equally tricky. The other side of the drug coin. Though at times she'd be a zombie, at others she'd be capable of clearheaded decisive action. Whenever she was cooking on the unshakable self-confidence of the white powder. Eventually, of course, she'd schiz herself out, and I didn't want to be around when that happened. I didn't want to be around when she was at one of the ends of the spectrum, either. Actually, I didn't want to be around her, period.

"I know *you*!" she screamed, poking a forefinger at me. "You're nothing! You're old, and you're nothing! Just like my parents! Well, someday I'll have *all* their money. Someday they'll kick off, and I'll have it all! And when I do"— she leaned toward me, eyes blazing —"when I do, I'll make you *crawl*."

The way she drew out that last word made my skin do just that. God, she needed help, and I wasn't sure I could give her any. Still, I was the one in the room with her.

"Melissa," I started. And then I quit. You couldn't talk to someone in a state like this. Just let her get the hell out of here. I sat on the edge of the bed.

She glared at me as she pulled on the rest of her clothes. Boots.

Gloves. The green car coat. She shoved her hands into her pockets. When she did, she hesitated, just for an instant. As if something had suddenly occurred to her.

Whatever it was passed quickly. She turned and left the room without another word. I didn't bother to follow her.

Her grand exit was punctuated with a nasty, high-pitched shriek: "I *hate* you, you faggot!"

She slammed the door, of course.

And even that was apparently not enough. A moment later there was a crash of splintering glass. I rushed into the living room. One of its windows was letting the outside in where it wasn't welcome. A small rock lay on the carpet. I ran outside, not a little enraged myself, but she was gone, in which direction I couldn't tell. Shortly, I heard the telltale rumble of the Mustang pulling away. I didn't go after her. Giving chase in Clementine would have been silly.

I swore at the night. That didn't help any. Then I realized that I was standing around with a loaded .38 Police Positive in my hand. It made me feel like an idiot.

I went back inside, dropped the pistol into one of the drawers, and set about repairing the damage. Already it felt ten degrees colder in there. I taped some cardboard over the broken pane, mentally submitting a bill to John Majors that included a heavy surcharge for the aggravation. Poor predictable Melissa, I thought. A true child of the TV generation. If you don't get your way, resort immediately to violence. It doesn't matter because violence isn't real; no one ever truly gets hurt on the tube, and when you switch it off, it ceases to exist. I shook my head. After the TV generation, what next?

And then I thought, Look at me. At thirty-three I'm nostalgic for the good old days before we became a global village. As if it were better in the laissez-faire times when open sewers ran next to every street. Yeah, give me a year or two and I'd be a neo-fascist to rival any of the bright young men of the Nixon administration.

That depressed me almost as much as having spent two hours in the same room as a guy with a nonfunctional orifice. I drank a stiff shot of Jameson before falling into bed with more than my usual amount of clothes on. As I was drifting off, I found myself wondering who Melissa meant by "all the rest of them."

66

·4·

I arrived at Sarah Jane Majors's at nine on the nose, still trying to
shake off the effects of the previous day. It's tough enough to make
a living in this business, what with being hired by people out of
some demented R. Crumb comic or stumbling on fellows with too
many holes in their heads. But after the day's work is over with,
you want to be able to spend a few comfortable hours in the rack.
You don't want the coldest December on record to come whistling
in through broken windows. The whiskey had helped some, but I'd
still awakened around seven with no chance of going back to sleep.
So I'd gotten up and had a couple of Irish coffees, without the
whipped cream, while waiting for it to be late enough for me to
show up at Sarah Jane's.

She lived in a modest house two blocks from Court Square, an
area I seemed destined to spend a lot of time in. The place was two
stories, of—what else?—weathered brick, and had a couple of small
white columns supporting a roof over the front stoop. Eight rooms,
maybe. Pretty big, relative to where I live, but not much by the
standards of this part of town. Genteel. A quiet statement concerning
the net worth of the owner rather than a gaudy proclamation. I had
the feeling that the neighbors approved of the elder Mrs. Majors,
in that sterling-silver-tea-service-at-three-in-the-afternoon kind of
way. No one on this street would have a can of Pabst Blue Ribbon
in the refrigerator. Then again, neither would I, but that's another
matter.

I always feel a little nervous in such neighborhoods, as if the
inhabitants are scrutinizing me through the crack between the lace

67

curtains and debating whether to call the law down on me. You'd think I would have adjusted by now, since most of my clients have to be fairly well off simply to be able to afford me. But I haven't. I'm more at home among people who kick and scream and throw plates of spaghetti at one another than I am with those who retreat behind their evening papers at the dinner table. That comes with a half-Italian blood line.

Sarah Jane answered the door herself. She wasn't as old as the Colonel. Sixty, or maybe a little over. She was short and had hundreds of little crinkles around her eyes. I suppose she laughed a lot, which made her a minority of one in this family. Her helmet-cut hair was white and still soft and fine enough to flop around when she moved. There was more than a little of the elf about her, but behind the lively gray eyes you could see a wicked, keen intelligence at work. She had a reputation as an extremely capable businesswoman, and I could see why. She could be charming you with that innocent elfin face while her mind was three steps ahead of you. I liked her immediately and wanted her on my side.

We took breakfast at a small table in the kitchen. She had a formal dining room but explained that she found the kitchen more relaxed for casual conversation. I agreed. There was no sign of any servants. I assumed she ran the house by herself; she seemed the type. The Colonel had made a major mistake when he let this one get away.

Breakfast came out of the warming oven. Cheese and mushroom omelets, bacon, English muffins, all in covered serving dishes. Delicious. I felt the night's cold begin to dissipate.

I soon discovered that she was an enthusiastic Virginia basketball fan, and we chatted about the team during the meal. It was an unexpected delight to find someone of her age who could talk intelligently about the trap press, collapsing zones, and the double set pick. In addition, of course, she knew Delmos Venable well. She admired his athletic gifts and agreed with me that his strength of character would carry him far beyond the sports world. That had been evident ever since he was a kid whom all the other kids followed.

Over coffee we got down to it.

"Now, you want to talk about Leigh, Mr. Swift."

"Just Swift is fine, Mrs. Majors."

"All right. Sarah Jane here." She grinned. The little crinkles crinkled. "How can I help you?"

68

"You could tell me where Leigh is, if you knew."

She shrugged. "I don't."

"Oh, well. They can't all come easily. Tell me what she's like, then."

She sat back, then steepled her fingers and touched them to her lower lip.

"That's not a simple question, Swift," she said. "Let me give it some thought." She thought. After a while she went on. "You see, Leigh is a complex person. Not many people will tell you that about her. But then not many people know her as well as I. She comes to me when she has nowhere else to go. I'm the least, ah, up-*tight* member of the family."

"Yeah, I noticed that the Majorses like to keep their sphincters locked." She laughed. "Except for Melissa, that is."

"Oh, yes, that one. Did she make a play for you?"

"Sort of."

"For her, 'sort of' begins when the clothes start coming off." My turn to laugh. "But to get back to your question, Leigh needs someone she can talk to candidly. She never got that at home. John worships her, but from afar. He's more comfortable with lawyers and bankers than he is with people. The Colonel adores her, too, but he's a flinty old bastard, too set in his ways to respond to the problems of a teenager. As for Elizabeth, well, I don't have much good to say for my daughter-in-law."

"She seems to be what used to be called the proverbial bad apple," I put in.

Sarah Jane nodded. "Sometimes the old expressions are best."

"How did she and John happen to get hooked up? They seem an odd couple."

"The oldest story in the book. Elizabeth's maiden name was Fauquier, which you probably recognize as a name of some importance in central Virginia." I did. The Fauquiers were old-time money. They even had a county named after them. "Well, Elizabeth's branch of the family, FFV or whatever notwithstanding, had fallen on hard times. In order for her to live in the style to which she aspired, she basically had to find a rich husband. Even as a teenager she realized that. Anyway, she found John. The Colonel went for the idea, and who can blame him? Elizabeth was offering admission to a society from which he, as a nouveau riche, had been excluded. John I don't think cared one way or the other; he's always been an . . . asexual

69

sort of man. He saw it as an advantageous match from the business point of view, of course, and she *was* an attractive-enough girl. So they got married. But"—she threw up her hands in a gesture of helplessness—"how they managed to produce three children I'll never know."

We chuckled and drank some coffee. While I had her talking, I asked how long she and the Colonel had been living apart.

"About forty years," she said.

"Huh?" I said. One of my all-purpose comeback lines.

"Sounds strange, doesn't it?" She laughed. "But it isn't really. I married the Colonel when I was seventeen. I was quite a looker in those days—"

"I'll bet."

"—thank you, and the Colonel liked to show me off. Two years later I got pregnant with John, and that didn't go down at all well. It seems the Colonel loved his child bride when she was all trim and sexy but not when she began to swell up. So I told him to stuff it and took off on my own. I ended up in California, along with a few million other wanderers. I had John. Things were tough for a while, but World War II was coming on, and there were always jobs. Plus people helped one another more in those days. We got by. I don't know why the Colonel never came after me at that point. Probably half because he was really into preparing to go to war and half because he was embarrassed by the whole thing. In any case, after the war he asked me to come back and said that he wanted to help raise our son. I agreed on condition that he not try to get me to live with him again, that time with John be equally shared between us, that we remain friendly, and that he help me get started in business here. To his credit, he's done it all."

"And you have apparently prospered."

"I've had my . . . successes, yes."

"You never remarried?"

"What for?" Mischievously.

"I don't know. Love, companionship, whatever."

"I've had plenty of that, young Swift. My feeling is that not only does marriage not nourish such things; it quite often kills them altogether. I've been spared the misery of watching the process."

"You must have been a real curiosity forty years ago."

"Outcast is more like it. The protohippie, that's me," she said with a grin that had more than humor behind it.

"Tell me, do you still have connections in California?"

I'd meant the question to sound casual, but she immediately picked up that it wasn't. It didn't seem to bother her any.

"No. Why?"

"Just wondering."

That didn't work. She said, "I'll be happy to be straight with you if you return the favor."

I thought it over. One man somehow connected to the Majors family was dead. One younger daughter was missing. It might well turn out that I needed a reliable ally in this case, and the woman across from me was the only potentially trustworthy member of the family that I'd met so far. I decided to trust her.

"Have you ever heard of a man named Harlow Brennerman?"

"No. Who's he?" She was sincere.

"He's a private investigator from California. Was. Someone murdered him last night in a motel on 29 South."

"How awful."

"Yeah. I found the body. It was."

"But why should I know this man?"

"He was here on some business involving the Majors family."

"What kind of business?"

"I don't know. He died before he could tell me."

"That's very strange."

"Yes, it is. And the only connection to California is you. Can you think of any reason why an investigator from Sacramento would be here?"

She hesitated. It was brief, as though she started to say one thing and switched to another track before her vocal cords got moving. There *was* something; I was sure of it. Yet she hadn't hesitated at all when I'd asked her if she still had any connections out there. The obvious inference was that there wasn't anything in the present that a P.I. would be interested in but that the past might be another matter.

"No," she said, "I can't."

I decided to let it lie. Her slight hesitation was filed away. It didn't seem relevant at the moment, and I knew I could come back to her if the Brennerman thing began to tie in. Or send Ridley Campbell. I hoped I wouldn't have to do that.

"I didn't expect you would," I said. "But you never know; I had to ask. The timing is odd, is all."

"Yes, I can see that. I'm sorry I can't help you. Will the police be coming round?"

"I don't know. Maybe later. As far as I'm concerned, Brennerman's murder doesn't look at all connected to Leigh Majors, so I invoked my privileged client relationship with the cops and didn't tell them who I was working for. But sooner or later they're going to find out what he was doing in Virginia, and then they might want to talk to people in the family."

"Who's investigating the murder?" she asked.

"Sheriff Campbell. It was in his jurisdiction."

"Ah," she said, her eyes lighting. "Ridley. That's good. He and I will have lots of . . . old times to talk about."

Sarah Jane and Ridley Campbell? Well, you never knew. She had a good fifteen years on him, but she was a live wire, this woman.

"We seem to have gotten a bit far afield," I said. "Could we get back to the subject of Leigh Majors? I think you were saying something about her being a complex person."

"Yes, she is that. On the one hand, she's very introverted. Shy, you might think at first glance. But it's not shyness exactly. Because on the other hand she has a lot to say, and she's very eager to communicate. What it is, is that it takes her a while to formulate her thoughts and then to articulate them. Which is why a lot of people think she's not too bright. That couldn't be further from the truth. But her inability to say things quickly doubles back on her, do you see? If you're not patient with her, she becomes less and less able to deal with the interchange, because what she wants to express just can't keep pace with her feelings. So she gets frustrated with herself, and the end result is that she turns inward some more. Eventually, she gets a reputation for being a loner who, though beautiful, is socially inept and doesn't have much of a mind. That's a tough rep to carry on a college campus, especially this one. It makes her prey to every horny jerk who thinks he sees the opportunity to rip off a quick fuck." She said the words "quick fuck" not as an antisexual person but as one who realized there was something better. "Sometimes," she went on, "I think the only thing that keeps her going is having a couple of friends who'll let her be herself."

"And who would they be?"

She ticked them off on her fingers. "Me, of course. Delmos Venable. They were inseparable as kids. Maybe her brother at one time, though I don't know when she last saw him. He and the family are estranged, you know."

"I'd heard. Do she and Delmos have a, ah, relationship?" I was thinking of what Melissa had said in her delicate fashion: that Leigh "runs around with the niggers."

"I'm not sure," she said without batting an eye. I'd chosen the right person to ask the question directly. "But I will say that Leigh is the most genuinely colorblind person I've ever known."

"He *is* an attractive fellow."

"Yes, he is. If you're thinking that he might have something to do with her disappearance, you may be right. But it won't be because of anything he did to her. That boy is as gentle as they come."

"With lovers you never know, Sarah Jane."

"With some you do," she shot right back, defying me to question her judgment.

"I admire your trust," I said, "if I may say that without seeming patronizing. In my business, you see, we make a personal philosophy out of suspicion."

"That's your loss."

"Yes, it is." I meant it. Sometimes I wished for the days before I hit the long slide with a grim intensity that didn't accompany any of my other longings.

But this wasn't the place for soul-searching.

"Melissa and Delmos," I tried. "How about them? Do they get along?"

"Not as well as I think she'd like them to."

"Hmmmm. How would she feel about Delmos and her sister, then?"

"Not that good, I would imagine."

Well, there that was, though I didn't want to make too much out of it at this point. I'd just started this job, and I didn't even know if Leigh was truly lost yet. It was much too early to start hatching a heavy sibling rivalry theory.

"So . . . what can you tell me about Bruce?" I asked.

"Ah, Bruce. He's an odd one, that boy, though a lot like his father, in a way. They both keep things so bottled up, you know?"

"I know John, at least."

"Yes. You know Melissa, too, of course, and you know how she is. Very much the flamboyant little rebel, telling the world 'kiss off'

73

to its face and all that sort of thing. While under the surface she's a scared, very conventional teenager."

"You don't think her capable of violence?" I cut in, thinking of my former window.

"I don't know," she said. "She certainly has some strong feelings. She's always been unreasonably jealous of her sister, and not just where Delmos is concerned. The people she hates, she hates with a passion. I suppose, under the right circumstances, we're all of us capable of just about anything. Still, I'm more inclined to think that Melissa will turn into somebody's bored housewife with a social-drinking problem."

"I'm not sure I agree with you," I said. "But let's get back to Bruce."

"Right. On the surface, *he's* been the conventional one, very straitlaced, always in control. Melissa's alter ego, in a way. But inside all the time there was this incredible mass of hostility building up. I don't think many people even suspected its existence until it blew. One day he just confronted the Colonel and his parents. For over an hour he ranted and raved, screaming at them about what pigs and hypocrites they were and about all the blood on their hands. Then he left the house, swearing that he didn't want any further contact with them, ever. He joined a Sikh group down in Nelson County. They're some kind of militant Hindus or something. I guess that suits his temperament, because he hasn't been back yet."

"And he's still friends with Leigh?"

"Possibly. She doesn't like to talk about him, and as I said, it's useless to press her about things she doesn't want to discuss."

"All right. What else about Leigh?" I asked.

"I don't know." She sighed. "Just make sure she's okay. It's not like her to be out of touch like this." I think she'd been worrying more than she let on.

"I'll do my best, Sarah Jane."

I got up. We'd spent quite a while at that kitchen table, but I hadn't even begun to squirm in my chair. Someday, after the case, we'd have to do it again. I wanted to know what it was like being twenty years old in California in the 1940s with an infant and no husband.

We exchanged pleasantries, and I left her one of my cards. I told her I had the feeling that we hadn't seen the last of each other. She just smiled that mischievous smile.

· · ·

I walked over to Court Square and located a pay phone. I dialed my answering service. Jonesy had called. He'd found out exactly where the Sikhs lived and had left detailed directions. That was it. Nothing from any of my groupies out at the Majors place.

Since it looked like Sikhtown might be my next stop, I carefully copied the directions into my little notebook.

Then I thought, What the hell, and made a credit-card call to the number Jonesy had given me. A man with a deep voice answered.

"Yes?" was all he said. No reference to the group. Nothing about Allah, or whoever it is that they worship. Not even a hello. It appeared that I was expected to state my business before we could continue.

"Hi," I said, trying to be my most winsome, "my name is Swift, and I'm calling from Charlottesville." I paused to let the importance of that sink in, but nothing came from the other end, so I continued, using the info Jonesy had fed me. "Well, I'm kind of interested in the Sikhs. You see, I read about Yogi Bhajan, and I can dig what he's trying to do. I was wondering if I could maybe meet you'all and get to know you, ah, personally."

"Do you live in Charlottesville?" the deep voice asked.

"Yes."

"If you'll leave a phone number, we'll have someone get in touch with you when they come to town next."

"Well, gee, I don't have a phone, you see. And I was kind of hoping I'd be able to see the ashram and all. Would it be all right if I came down to visit?"

"That wouldn't be possible."

"Well, what can I *do*, then?" I pitched it so that a pitiable feeling of disappointment went sliding down the wire. No person of compassion could have been unmoved.

"I'd suggest that you watch the paper for one of our lectures. Thank you for your interest."

With that, he hung up.

"Yeah, and thank you for your courtesy and wit," I said to the dead receiver. It looked like I was going to have to visit the turban freaks uninvited.

I arrived at Lockridge & Lee at noon.

"You're early," Patricia Ryan said.

"I know. But I've got to see the man again," I said, jerking my thumb toward the inner sanctum.

"I'm sorry, he's with someone. Could I help you perhaps?"

"You could have lunch with me."

"Let me check my calendar . . . no, I'm afraid I already have a date."

"I'll wait for Mr. Lockridge, then."

I sat down, and we played secretary and client for a while. She looked great again today. A simple tartan plaid skirt and white cable-knit sweater that looked authentically Irish. Tiny gold earrings. Masterful understatement for our first date. As if she'd thought about it.

After twenty minutes or so a man came out of Lockridge's office. He looked as untrustworthy as the lawyer he'd been consulting. I'd heard that these sorts ran in packs.

Patricia did her phone thing again, then cupped the receiver.

"He wants to know how much time you need," she said.

"Five minutes, maybe."

She relayed the information to Lockridge and got the go-ahead. I let myself into his office.

"Mr. Swift," he said, giving with the unctuous handshake.

"Brennerman's dead," I said.

God, he was cool. Nary a feather ruffled. Still, I had the gut feeling that he knew exactly who I was talking about.

"I'm afraid I don't—"

"He's the guy I asked you about yesterday. You sure you never heard the name?"

"I do not know the man any more today than I did yesterday. You say he's dead?"

"Yeah. Somebody iced him at the Mountain Vista Motel on 29 South last night."

"How terrible. But should this concern me? Who was he?"

"A private investigator from California. When I met him, he said that he was here on some job involving the Majors family. That ring any bells?"

76

He shook his head calmly. "I'm afraid it doesn't. I do handle their legal business, but of course I'm not privy to every decision that they make. I think you'd best talk to John or the Colonel."

"I will. But let me tell you something. Ridley Campbell is handling the case. You know the man?"

"Certainly."

"Then you know he doesn't like to be jerked around. Now, I didn't feel I had to tell him that Brennerman had mentioned the Majors family to me, since there's no apparent connection to what I'm working on. And he'll find out soon enough what the guy was up to. But my tit is nevertheless in the wringer here, and Ridley is the wrong person to be in that kind of spot with. You see what I mean?"

"I understand your position. And I certainly appreciate your keeping the Majors name—"

"Yeah, yeah. But here's what I'm saying to you. Don't hold out on me, pal. It could be your tit in the wringer, too."

"Mr. Swift, are you threatening me?" He looked very amused. The intimidator, that's me; grown men tremble when they see me coming.

"I'm just trying to get you to play it straight with me," I said rather lamely.

"But I am, Mr. Swift." You could almost smell the oil as his gears meshed smoothly.

"All right. Anyone in that family breathes Brennerman's name to you, I don't care if they're only reading a story in the paper, I want to hear about it. Deal?"

"Certainly, Mr. Swift. Now if there's nothing else . . ."

I gave him a hefty dose of the old hairy eyeball as I thought about it. The son of a bitch knew something, I could feel it. But he wasn't in the least worried by what he knew. That bothered me.

Then I thought of Patricia Ryan, waiting in the next room, and I reminded myself that I wasn't going to get involved in whatever it was that Brennerman and the Majorses and their sleazy lawyer were up to.

Lockridge's phone buzzed once. He picked it up.

"Yes," he said. "Of course, put him through." He palmed the phone's mouthpiece. "Mr. Swift, if you wouldn't mind . . ."

I shrugged and got up to leave.

Behind me, I heard, "Yes, Ed, what is it? . . . *What!?* . . . Jesus *Christ*, of *course* I'll be right down!"

The phone slammed back into its cradle. I turned. Lockridge looked like he was in shock. He beat on the beautiful oak desk.

"What—" I said.

"God *damn* them!" he was yelling. "God *damn* the bastards to hell!"

He was looking at but not seeing me. He yanked open one of his drawers and pulled out an expensive leather attaché case. Then he jumped to his feet and rushed from the room. I'd been forgotten, an unwanted piece of furniture.

"Mr. Lockridge," I heard Patricia say, "what's going on?"

"I'll be at the Joint Security Complex," he said. "Cancel all my afternoon appointments."

"Is it Williams?"

I arrived at the door in time to see him nod, tight-lipped.

"What—" Patricia said.

"Trouble," he said. "Bad trouble." And he was gone.

Patricia looked my way. I raised an eyebrow.

"Beats me," she said. "It was Ed Goolsby on the phone. He's Carter's man over at the Charlottesville-Albemarle Joint Security Complex. That's where they're holding Williams."

"Ward Williams?"

"Ward Williams. Carter's helping handle the case. Something . . . something appears to have gone wrong."

Patricia was visibly disturbed, as well she should be. The Williams case was a biggie.

"Well," I said, "no use it spoiling lunch. You'll know soon enough."

"You're right," she said. "There's no point in worrying. I don't know why I get so involved."

"So where to, young lady?"

"Would Le Soir suit the gentleman?"

You could walk to Le Soir. "Good," I said.

• • •

Le Soir is on the downtown mall, five minutes by foot from Court Square. The mall is part of Charlottesville's urban revitalization program. It's several blocks of Main Street in the old commercial district that they resurfaced and closed to vehicular traffic. They

78

planted trees and put in fountains and park benches and metal sculpture. They have outdoor concerts when the weather's nice. By and large, they did a good job. On a summer day, it's a favorite spot of mine to sit and watch the ladies go by. Here they're not all as young as they are over near the University, and that suits me just fine.

The general idea behind the mall project was to encourage businesses to stay in the downtown area, which had been slowly dying like downtown areas all over the country. Nearly the whole community was behind it, and several million dollars later it was enough of a showpiece to help Charlottesville win an All-America City Award. People were proud of what they'd accomplished. The stores that were already there were now only too happy to stay on, and a lot of new little shops opened up in the formerly vacant buildings.

A modern urban success story, you might say. Ah, yes. But then somebody got the bright idea that what Charlottesville really needed was a shopping mall, one of the other kind that has fifty-seven stores under one roof and year-round climate control and unceasing Muzak and twenty-foot-high plastic trees. Such structures do, after all, represent the pinnacle of American merchandising expertise. You might expect there to have been a lot of opposition from those who realized what effect this mall would have on the outdoor one, on which so much time and energy had already been spent. And they did oppose. But need I say who won in the end?

So now the downtown shopping district is dying once again. There are those diehards like myself who still go there, out of stubbornness and a distaste for unchanging sixty-eight-degree temperatures. But its days are numbered. The big chains were the first to close their doors; the smaller shops can't help but follow. No one doubts that before long we'll see the first plans to raze the old frame and brick buildings in favor of concrete and glass offices and apartment complexes. To "revitalize" downtown, of course.

In spite of all this, Le Soir seems to be thriving. It's a small restaurant that does a brisk luncheon business serving soups and salads, quiches and crepes, yogurt and sprouts, whatever's trendy with the health-conscious beautiful people who work downtown. On nice days, you can eat at wrought-iron tables out on the mall itself and pretend you're in Paris or some other outdoorsy Old World city. Today, everyone was inside.

Patricia appeared to know most of the people in the place. When we finally sat down, she ordered a vodka and Perrier with lime to my Stroh's. There's no accounting for taste.

"Well," she said when we'd settled in, "looks like we're alone at last."

"Patricia," I said, "what are you doing working for a scurve like Lockridge?"

She regarded me noncommittally. "That what you think of him?"

"Yeah, somewhere I just get the feeling the man is up to no good."

"Well, then," she said, "I suppose the same question could be asked of you, couldn't it?"

"Good point. But I'm not working directly for him, and not every day."

She shrugged. "Like the good German said, 'I wasn't involved.' "

"Oooh, you're a sharp one, Patricia Ryan. Consider the question withdrawn."

She laughed. "It's all right; you just shouldn't start a conversation with an accusation like that. It might turn some people off. Actually, I basically agree with you. Carter does have a distinctly shady side to him. But I wasn't about to let you get away with something like that at the beginning."

I felt like a teenager when she said "at the beginning." It implied there would be something to follow.

"And," she continued, "I wanted to find out how much of this 'date' is social and how much . . . business." The green eyes would have made me squirm if I was the guilty type. Instead, I decided to be honest about things. This was the kind of woman for whom nothing less would do.

"Mostly social," I said.

"The truth?"

"The truth."

"Okay, then, Mr. Swift, you want to get the business out of the way before it has a chance to sour our lunch?" She was tough.

"Could you call me Swift?"

She shook her head. "Don't like it. Your first name was?"

"Loren."

"Nice name. What can we do for you, Loren?"

I wet my lips. "All right. First, have you ever seen or heard of a

Harlow Brennerman?" I gave her his description. "Second, have any of the Majors family been to the office recently, or has Lockridge gone to their place that you know of? That's all I got for business."

"Two easy ones. No to the first. Neither seen nor heard. And yes to the second. The Colonel was in a couple of days ago. He's the only one. Of course, what Carter does after working hours only he could tell you. He often stays late."

"Thanks."

"You sure that's all?" She teased me with her eyes.

"Positive." Except, what are you doing the rest of your life?

"Painless it was. Let's order."

She ordered soup. And quiche and salad and bread on the side. If she always ate that heartily, it didn't show on her trim frame. Maybe she worked out. Maybe she could beat me up. I ordered a BLT on wheat and some fries to go with the beer.

"Now," I said, "what *are* you doing working for Lockridge?"

She laughed. "Good one. As I said, the man's not my type, either." She pronounced it eye-ther; it's the little things will make you lose your heart. "Al*though* . . . he's not all bad, by any means. You knew that he was defending Ward Williams?"

"So you said."

"What I didn't say was that he's defending him for free."

"It'll put money in his pocket in the long run."

"Still, he's doing it," she said. Then she added, "And there *is* some risk involved."

I nodded. Okay, a small grudging point in Carter Lockridge's favor. I was right that Locky would eventually benefit, if only from the publicity generated by the case. But she had a point about the danger. Ward Williams's life had already been threatened numerous times. It was not illogical to assume that some ill will might be felt for the man who defended him.

Essentially, the Williams case was a variation on the old black-man-rapes-white-woman scenario that's been used to frame innocent people for hundreds of years. Such incidents always generate a lot of heat in the South and rarely much light. Not that legitimate interracial rapes don't happen, of course. They do. But so do the phony ones. This one had yet to be considered by a jury.

What made it so much out of the ordinary was the defendant himself. Ward Williams was a man who'd fought his way up from a poverty-stricken childhood to a spot on the Charlottesville City Council. He'd done it through a backbreaking political organization effort among the local black population, a community that now almost worshiped him. He was their voice in local government, their only voice, the first member of his race to climb so high.

As such, he was bound to stir up some controversy. How much, no one could have suspected.

The other council members had probably hoped they were getting a nice Uncle Tom. Instead, they got a Jesse Jackson. Williams plunged into his job with the energy of half a dozen lesser mortals, and he conducted his business out front, preferably on page 1 of the daily paper. He fought for affirmative hiring policies, across the board, but especially in the city police department. He fought for money to help the town's destitute, a disproportionate number of whom are black, like everywhere. He openly criticized the University for keeping the vast majority of its black employees in menial minimum-wage jobs where there is no hope of advancement, ever. He worked with Delmos Venable to encourage more aggressive minority faculty recruitment efforts at the U. And so on. It wasn't long before the hate letters began arriving.

Then, two days before my lunch date with Patricia, Ward Williams had been arrested. For rape. A seventeen-year-old white girl, still in high school.

The results were predictable. The bigots began screaming for his scalp. And the black community screamed frame-up just as loudly. The facts seemed to support the latter group. There was what appeared to be significant evidence that rapist and victim were nowhere near each other when the alleged crime took place.

But the strangest thing was that Ward Williams was still in the slammer. After two days you'd expect that a public official would have long since been out on bail. Had the races of the two principals been exchanged, there's no question that he would have been. Even the newspaper, the voice of the local white establishment, was beginning to wonder what was going on. Charlottesville was on high simmer.

"And by the way," Patricia Ryan said, "are you only a professional cynic? Or is that the real you?"

Ward Williams receded from my consciousness.

"I don't know," I said. "I'd like to trust people, but in my line of

82

work it's more often a mistake than not. A lot of times when I have, I've paid for it."

"That sounds like an honest answer. So I'll be honest with you. If you noticed the sign on our office door, it said Lockridge and *Lee*. Bob Lee's a prince. He did a very large favor for my family once. He's the one I'm really there for. If it was only Carter, I think I would have left by now."

I suddenly realized that she no longer made me think of Marilyn. She'd become a real person all her own. It was better that way. Now I could do away with the notion that I was in some hall of mirrors where Marilyn and I were going to fall in love all over again and somehow make it come out right this time. I wanted to kiss Patricia on the tip of her nose.

"What *are* you thinking?" she asked.

"I was thinking I'd like to kiss the tip of your nose." Worth a try.

That really got her off. My best lines are apparently the unrehearsed ones.

Well, what the hell, I thought, and leaned over and kissed her nose. She only smiled. It could mean anything.

We sat in silence while they served our lunch. She dug right into it. I liked that. People who play with their food make me nervous.

"What do you do when you're not thinking about noses?" she asked.

"This and that," I said. "I read a lot. I've always been something of a bookworm."

"Odd line of work for a bookworm."

"Not really. This job, you spend a lot of time waiting for something to happen that you can write up in the little spiral notebook. There isn't much action, contrary to popular belief."

"What sort of things do you read?"

"Well, I like a good mystery, of course. Ha, ha. I read a lot of novels, all kinds. Then I'll get sick of them and just read nonfiction for a while. Unstructured self-education, you might say."

"Interesting," she said as if she meant it. "And how'd you happen to choose this particular field?"

I wanted to tell her all of it. About the war and the long slide and the abandoned dreams, and the strange thing is that I absolutely believed she'd understand, on very little evidence. But I didn't try to tell her, of course. It was too soon, way too soon.

"I don't know exactly" is what I said instead. "I flunked out of college, right here at Mr. Jefferson's University. I guess I found the parties more interesting than the courses. Then there was the war. I was in that for a while. When I got out of the army, I didn't know *what* to do. So I got married. That wasn't the answer, either. I got my start in investigative work with an insurance company while my wife went to school. When she finished, she took a regular job, and I decided I'd rather be my own boss. So I got my P.I.'s license. And here I am as you see me today."

"That's a sad story. I take it you lost the wife along the way."

"Yeah."

"I've got a missing husband myself. I guess that just makes us two typical children of our times."

"Do you think it used to be easier?"

"I don't know. My grandparents were together for fifty years."

"That's nice."

"It is, except they hated every minute of it."

I laughed. It had been a while since I enjoyed someone else's company.

"That would be the Irish branch of the family?" I said.

"Sure and it would, me boy."

"You wouldn't happen to be related to Mrs. Nixon, would you?"

"I think not."

"Whew . . . come to think of it, I guess I should have asked if Ryan was your name or your late husband's. Some women do get attached to their married names."

"It's mine."

We ordered dessert. She had a slice of Irish whiskey pie. A woman after my own heart. I settled for plain coffee.

We chatted, whereas five years ago I would have been smoking my afterdinner cigarette. I gave up the weeds when I abandoned my marriage. It seemed an appropriate time. Now being in a smoke-filled room for too long can make me nauseous.

"And you," I said. "What's your story?"

"It's a trite one," she answered. "Married young. Failed at it, as we've noted, so I had to get a job. Bob Lee helped me out. I've been there, let's see, four years now. I haven't had a very exciting life."

"Any kids?"

"None by Martin."

"Martin?"

"Oh. My ex. I meant, no kids of my own."

"You adopted a Vietnamese war orphan?"

"No." She laughed. "I'm making this unnecessarily complicated. I live with my kid brother. He was hurt in a car accident."

"Wheelchair?"

She nodded.

"I'm sorry," I said.

"No, no need to be. Patrick gets around quite well, and he's studying computer programming, which is a great field if you're confined to a chair. It's just that he needed a place to live that was accessible, so we modified my house a bit—you'd be surprised how little awareness of this kind of problem there is in the world. And how small an effort is required to make sufficient changes so that basic needs are met. It's incredible, the apathy you run up against. People just don't give a damn until it happens to them or someone close to them. Excuse the soap box."

Yeah, I thought, excuse you for being a caring human being.

"Anyway, Patrick was always very athletic before the accident, and he likes to have someone around to help him through the . . . rough spots."

"He's a lucky kid."

She smiled. "Me, too," she said, and she meant it.

That seemed like a nice note to wind up lunch on. I tried to pay the bill, but she insisted on splitting it, seeing as how the date was "mostly social." She left twenty-five percent for the waitress, saying that if I'd ever had to do it for a living, I'd do the same. I said I tipped as well as lawyers. That got a laugh. I hastened to assure her that I was kidding. They're the worst.

I walked her back to Lockridge & Lee, and we agreed to do it again sometime soon. I tried hard not to sound like a refugee from the Clearasil years.

The last thing she said was "You never did show me your collection of Italian hand gestures."

Next time, I promised.

Out on the street, the afternoon air was cold, and it still looked like it might start snowing at any moment. I didn't feel much like driving to Nelson County. But then what were my options? That and nothing. Leigh's brother Bruce was the only lead I currently had. It wasn't much of a choice; I decided against nothing.

First things first, though. On my way out of town I stopped at an imported auto parts store, picked up a new gas filter for Clementine, and stuck it in the fuel line. If there was something I truly didn't need, it was to break down in Nelson County in the middle of a snowstorm. The population of the county is only about twelve thousand, total, and they have little in the way of facilities for stranded motorists there.

·5·

Rolling down U.S. 29 again. Past the Mountain Vista Motel. Past the S.R. 666 turnoff that led to the Majors place. Down into real rural Virginia. The foothills of the Blue Ridge. Back country, where you can still run across an occasional blood feud that's been raging between families for five or six generations.

I reviewed what Jonesy had told me the night before about the Sikhs.

The Sikhs had moved into central Virginia some five years earlier. They were followers of Yogi Bhajan, a former customs inspector at the New Delhi airport who decided one day that his future didn't lie in India and made his way to the United States. Once here, he soon discovered that the religious/ethnic grouping known as Sikhs didn't have a supreme authority figure in this country, so he proclaimed himself to be that man. The orthodox Sikh leaders back home quickly denounced him as a pretender, but that hasn't prevented him from attracting the sort of following that seems to inevitably gather around any brown-skinned fellow from the East who adopts the style of a prophet. In America they come and they go, the yogis and the swamis, the babas and the gurus, krishna this and rama that. The only thing you can be certain of is that each one's devotees will swear by the eye of Vishnu that their man is *the* One, the holiest of holies, the true incarnation of God for our times. And that all others are somewhat lesser beings.

Now I'm not one to put down someone's spiritual beliefs, whatever they might be. If it does the job for you, that's all that matters. Still, it seems to me that all these jolly little brown fellows are

87

running down the oldest con of them all: that God in his or her wisdom has created us all equal but that some are more equal than others. And what can't be denied is that no matter how much they preach against wealth and material possessions, these guys have really set the old American cash registers jangling.

Yogi Bhajan, for example, has a particularly profitable scam going. He opened up some restaurants and put his disciples to work in them. That nets him a lot of nice free labor, since the faithful are expected to routinely put in fourteen-hour days. On top of that, the workers live communally and are supposed to plow their earnings back into the brotherhood. So the Master makes out twice, the way I see it. That ain't bad, if you can get someone to dance to the tune.

Early on, the good Yogi decided that his organization ought to be geographically diverse. He put the restaurants and communal houses in the big cities. Then he bought large tracts of land in remote areas for his rural retreat centers. Ashrams, Jonesy had called them. The biggest one was out in the Southwest someplace. Another was in the mountains of Nelson County, Virginia, maybe thirty miles from my house in Belmont.

After giving me all this, Jonesy had paused dramatically. Now for the good part, he had said. The difference between this group and all the others is that these people are armed. Armed? Yeah, armed. Back in India and Pakistan the Sikhs are renowned for two things: the fact that they never cut their hair and their prowess as warriors. In the States, they've decided to maintain both traditions.

I'd asked Jonesy if he was sure about this. He was. Sikh retreats consisted of yoga, meditation, and training in the use of small arms and automatic weapons. Come the Revolution, these dudes were going to be able to defend themselves, Jim.

Jonesy asked me if I remembered a few years back when some rednecks had raided a Hindu community in West Virginia and shot up the place. I did, vaguely. Well, he told me, the same thing almost happened in Nelson County. No kidding? Yeah, a bunch of drunk good old boys planned to put a scare into the Sikhs. The newcomers didn't belong in Nelson County, they felt, what with their robes and turbans and all, plus who knows what kind of weird drugs and sex. Well, the county sheriff got wind of the plan and called a couple of the leaders into his office for a little chat. He told them he didn't like the idea of shoot-outs in his county but that he wasn't about to spend a lot of time watching the boys to see that they behaved themselves. So if they were bound and determined to do such a stupid thing, there wasn't much he could do to prevent it. Only thing was, he wanted the boys to know that they were going up against people who were well trained and heavily armed. Just thought they'd like to know. He smiled and showed the good old boys out of his office. The attack never came off.

I told Jonesy I hadn't heard that one, and he said yeah, it was kept quiet. The paper had decided not to publicize it.

So these were the people Bruce Majors had hooked up with. The "ragheads," as Jonesy referred to them. I'd deliberately left all of my handguns at home.

• • •

The Sikhs lived up the Jack Creek hollow, in the mountains west of Route 29. It's an area where the log cabin is still the predominant form of architecture. Hitherto, Jack Creek had been in the news only once. During Hurricane Camille it had jumped its banks and swept seven people to their deaths. Driving along it today, you'd hardly believe the creek capable of much in the way of destruction; give me three or four beers to build up pressure, and I could nearly pee from one side to the other. But it was. It had been filled to overflowing by thirty-some inches of rain in less than ten hours, possibly a world record. Reminders of that wild night were everywhere. Massive logs that had to be bulldozed out of the road. Mounds of boulders that had come tumbling out of the mountains to pile up against some natural obstruction. The tailings of an elemental violence beyond belief.

Halfway up the hollow the tar road changed to what is laughingly referred to on maps as "maintained gravel surface." Two miles farther on, the Sikhs had bought five hundred acres, which ranged from fairly level hay fields to sheer mountainside. They probably got it for a good price, too. After the flood, land prices plummeted as ruined hill folk were forced to sell out.

The drive into their property was defended by a heavy chain stretched between two iron posts and padlocked at one end. I parked Clementine and hiked in.

The main building was a quarter of a mile from the gravel road. It was a massive thing of rough-hewn logs, with modern touches like a large solar greenhouse attached to the south-facing wall. It put me more in mind of a fortress than a religious structure. There were also numerous outbuildings. Sheds and barns. Things with no function that was evident from the outside. I wondered which was the armory.

Someone must have spotted me coming up the drive because a large turbaned fellow came out on the front porch. He wasn't smiling and whistling a happy tune.

"Yes?" he said. His look told me I could leave anytime I wanted.

"Hi, there," I said. "I'm a newspaperman, and I'm doing a story on the Hollywood stars of yesteryear. Where are they now, that sort of thing, you know? I was told that Sabu lived out here, and I thought I might interview him." I put on my finest investigative-reporter face, but he wasn't buying any. How soon they forget. If he was old enough to remember in the first place.

"All right," he said, "you've had your fun. What do you want?"

I was hurt that he'd seen through me so easily, but he was right. It wasn't fun anymore. In fact, fun was increasingly hard to come by these days.

"I'd like to talk to Bruce Majors," I said.

"There's no one here by that name."

"Now that's a shame, because if there was, your whole family would have just won a free trip to the Cayman Islands."

At this point, my host was joined by another raghead. The second man was short and wiry and looked to be in excellent shape. He also had the air of authority. I guessed that I was looking at the head honcho around here, or close to it.

He asked the first guy what was up. The first guy told him, and the second guy nodded and dismissed him. The big one went back into the house, and the second guy came down the steps to greet me. He took his time and seemed not unfriendly. Next to me, the top of his head came to my eyes, and that was counting the turban. Nevertheless, in a fight I'd want to have a good-sized club on my side.

"I'm Dorjé Khan," he said. "How may I serve you?" I recognized his first name only because I used to read Talbot Mundy adventure novels. He pronounced it "door-zhay," with the accent on the first syllable, and it means something like "the savage thunderbolt that strikes from the sky without warning." Oddly enough, and for no

90

reason I could put my finger on, I found myself sort of liking the little guy, and I decided to play it straight with him.

"My name is Swift," I said, "and I need to speak to Bruce Majors. It won't take long."

"Concerning what?"

"I'm a private investigator working for the Majors family. The matter is confidential."

"I see. You are aware that when one joins our group, he or she gives up the parental name?" I nodded as if I had been. "Good. Then it is Ali Gupta Hassan with whom you wish to speak."

"Okay, fine."

"You will also undoubtedly be aware that Gupta Hassan does not desire to receive members of his former family or their representatives."

"So I've heard. But I think he will want to discuss this particular matter with me."

"I can't guarantee that, but I will speak to him. You may wait inside."

"Thank you."

The front door let onto a small entrance hall with three closed doors leading off in different directions. It was weirdly reminiscent of the foyer at the Majors mansion. Dorjé headed east.

"Mr. Khan," I said, and he turned politely. "Please tell Bruce—please tell Gupta Hassan that if he talks to me, he probably won't have to talk to the cops."

"This is a police matter?" He asked the question without betraying the slightest concern for the answer.

"Not yet," I said. "And I think I can prevent it from becoming one."

"Very well."

I settled myself on a padded bench with a hard wooden back while Khan went to roust Gupta Bruce. The bench was surprisingly comfortable. I entertained myself with carnal thoughts about Patricia Ryan. We were into some heavy foreplay when Khan returned.

"Mr. Swift," he said. "Gupta Hassan wishes to know if this concerns his sister."

"It does."

"In that case, please come with me."

I followed him to Gupta's room, which he let me into and then

91

left. The room was like a cell. There was a sleeping mat on the floor and a framed photo of someone I took to be Yogi Bhajan on the wall. Other than that, nothing. The room was apparently also unheated, perhaps as a test of faith. I kept my coat on, being unready to take the vows.

The former Bruce Majors was very slender, almost emaciated, and about my height with his turban on. He had his mother's blue eyes and a thick brownish blond beard that rested on his chest. He was as cold and remote as his father, maybe more so. Norman Rockwell would have shot heroin before he would have painted this family.

"I'm Loren Swift," I said. Start them off with something they can handle.

He didn't offer to shake hands.

"They're freaked out because they don't know where Leigh is," he said, "and they want you to make sure their baby girl is okay."

"Aw, you peeked," I said.

"You can go home now." He was pretending I wasn't there.

"Are you pretending I'm not here?" I asked.

"No, you're here," he said, looking me in the eye for the first time. "But you can leave now."

"I need to ask you some questions first."

He brushed my questions away with his hand.

"Leigh's all right."

"How do you know that?"

"Because . . ." He held it for a long moment, then said flatly, "Because she's here. Now will you kindly leave?"

"She's what?" Hit 'em with the tough ones.

"I said she was here. She's safe. Are you hard of hearing?"

"No, but I'm hard of understanding sometimes. What's she doing here?"

"That's none of your business."

"I know that, but it is her family's business—"

"It's none of theirs, either!"

"Okay, let's just say that I was hired to verify that she's in one piece, and I'm going to have to do that. I'm afraid I can't take your word for it."

"That's impossible."

"Why?"

He was having difficulty controlling himself. I had no problem picturing the young man who slung words of hate at his parents before leaving their house forever. For a moment I saw his father looking out through his eyes, the hopelessly imprisoned being inside, crying for help. Somehow I knew that both father and son were beyond help. Or beyond my help, at least.

"I have nothing more to say," he said.

"Bruce—"

"That's not my name!" He shouted like nothing so much as a cranky little kid.

"I'm sorry. Listen Gupta Hassan, there's more involved here than just your sister's health."

"What do you mean?"

"Exactly that. Didn't Khan tell you?"

"He said that you'd offered to keep the cops out of it. But you were lying," he sneered. "My parents would never go to the cops. The good family name is too important for that." He said the last sentence as if the family name weren't worth a bag of chicken droppings to a poultry farmer.

"Yes," I said, "you're right. They wouldn't go to the cops, not about Leigh. But there's murder involved now."

"Huh?"

"A guy from California got himself croaked last night. He had something to do with your family, but the cops don't know that yet."

"So what does that have to do with you? Or me? Or Leigh?" I'd had him off balance for a moment, but he'd recovered nicely. The ice man cometh.

"What it means is that if I can wrap up the job I was hired to do, then I can leave the cops to find their own way. They might well solve the murder without ever involving the family. The longer I stay on the case, the more likely I am to run into them, and sooner or later I'll have to tell what I know. Then there'll be cops here, there, and everywhere." I hoped it sounded less flimsy to him than it did to me.

Gupta Bruce didn't reply right away. Instead, he turned and walked to the window. The view was of a dormant hayfield fringed by a mixed oak and poplar forest. He looked like he might be waiting for the grass to start growing again. I hung on as long as I could, but eventually the cold began to get to me. I cleared my throat. The master of subtlety. When I did, he faced me across the room.

"Leigh's been having a tough time of it lately," he said. "That's why she's here. I won't let you take her back to those bloodsuckers."

"I'm only paid to find her, not to force her to go somewhere against her will."

"Good. Otherwise, you wouldn't be permitted to leave."

I felt a chill that had nothing to do with the air temperature, remembering the Sikh arsenal that was concealed somewhere on the property. This fellow was one in whose hands I wouldn't want to see an M-16. I reminded myself that the job was nearly over now.

"A few minutes with her will be fine," I said.

"Well, that's her decision. I make you no promises," he said. "Wait here."

He left. I sat down on the sleeping mat, pretending it was one of those leather chairs that I'd become accustomed to on this case. It was an unconvincing lie.

Fortunately, Bruce returned in a couple of minutes.

"She'll see you," he said.

• • •

I followed him upstairs and to the rear of the house. It was warmer up there. We paused in front of a closed door.

"Keep it short," he said, "and I warn you, don't upset her."

I felt like yanking his turban off and stomping on it, but I only nodded agreement. He let me into the room.

It was a garret with a six-and-a-half-foot ceiling, but it was considerably more homey than Bruce's. For one thing, it was warm. There was a regular platform bed and a couple of chairs. A desk that looked like an antique. A nice dormer window with cushions for setting and looking out. On the floor, a braided rug of many colors. On the wall, the obligatory photo of Yogi Bazoom.

The girl was looking at me as if the Black Death had come to pay a social call.

"It's okay, Leigh," I said. "I'm not here to make you do anything you don't want to do."

I took a step forward. She took a step back.

"Wait," she said.

94

I stood still while she vibed me out. She was less pretty than her photograph but more beautiful. The true extent of her vulnerability hadn't come through in two dimensions, and it grabbed me more than I would have thought possible. You could look at her, standing there in her blue jeans and U. Va. sweatshirt, and it was as though she were stark naked. She made you want to swear to protect her from the evils of the world. Forever and ever. Amen.

No wonder the vultures of collegiate society hovered around her. When your heart's that far out on your sleeve, they'll line up to bleed it for you.

I suddenly felt way out of my depth.

"Who are you?" she asked finally.

"My name's Swift. I'm a private investigator from Charlottesville. Hopefully, I'm also your friend."

"I don't know you."

"That's true, but— Look, why don't we sit down, okay?"

She nodded and sat on the edge of the bed. The very edge. I pulled a chair over.

"That's better," I said. "Now, Leigh, the reason I'm here is that your parents were worried about you and they hired me to find you and see that you were all right. That's the extent of my commitment to them. I didn't promise to drag you home or anything like that."

"Well, I'm all right, as you can see."

"Your grandmother was also concerned, and your friends Lisa and Delmos, as well."

"How do you know Delmos?" She said it sharply.

"I had to talk with your friends. It's the way you find people."

"Well, you shouldn't have."

"Why not?"

She looked at me, then down at her lap. She shook her head slowly.

"Leigh," I said as gently as possible, "I know you're alive and kicking now, and I can leave if you want me to. But you've obviously got a lot on your mind these days. I'm willing to be your friend if you like. Sometimes it can help to talk to someone you don't know."

"Why would you want to help me?" She didn't say it bitterly; she was just surprised.

"Mmmmm. Well, let me put it this way. The investigation business is ugly and dirty a lot of the time; I can't deny it. But every now and then I do bumble my way into an opportunity to help someone. I try not to blow too many of those chances. They tend to make the work more tolerable.

"Besides"—I grinned—"I'll get to tell all my friends how I came to the aid of the Six Million Dollar Man."

She smiled maybe a teeny bit.

"That's so old," she said.

"You think that's bad; the newest thing I got is a Rochester imitation." She looked puzzled; obviously didn't know who he was. "Just a guy who used to be on the radio. You remember; it's like TV except you didn't have to look like your voice."

She smiled for real. "I hate my voice," she said. "It's so . . . squeaky like."

I did my Rochester imitation for her. "Now there was a voice," I said. That got her laughing.

"Sounds like Louis Armstrong," she said.

"Ah, you remember the Satchmo."

"Not really, but I've seen some old films."

"Well, David Bowie he wasn't, but the Satch was one of a kind in his own way."

We sat quietly for a bit. Gupta Bruce stuck his head in momentarily to make sure his sister wasn't being abducted or we weren't doing it right there on the floor. She told him she was fine and that he could leave us alone without concern.

When he'd gone, I said, "Would you like to talk, Leigh?"

"I don't know, Mr. Swift. Things are just—"

"You can call me Swift. I'm not that much older than you."

She smiled shyly. "Okay. Things are just so screwed up now, I don't know if I can talk sense."

"That's okay. The last time I heard anybody talk sense was the day Nixon announced his resignation."

"I was just a kid then, but I remember feeling sorry for him."

I laughed at that one. "No need," I said, "no need at all."

"I did, though. I even cried. It seemed like such an awful thing to have to do."

"He'll get over it. But tell me. How did you happen to come here?"

"I had no place else to go."

"Sarah Jane would have taken you in. I think she cares for you a lot."

96

"Yeah, Grandma's good people. But— I'm not really sure— Maybe she isn't— Damn!" She was grappling with her feelings, and her verbalization was obviously failing to keep pace. "It's all so complicated, Mr.— uh, Swift."

"Let me see if I can help. There's a fellow. You've known him all your life. You grew up together, and as kids you were inseparable. You get older, though, and you have different interests. Maybe you drift apart for a while. Then you end up at college together, away from your families for the first time. The friendship blooms again. Time passes, and to the surprise of both of you, you find yourselves falling in love. But it's very tough; the two of you come from such different worlds. None of your parents are going to approve. Many of your friends will desert you if they find out, as will many of his. The odds are really stacked against you. You begin to wonder if you have the strength to be true to your feelings." I smiled my Ed Koch smile. "How'm I doing?"

"You're a good guesser. Do you disapprove?"

"Not at all. I think he's a fine man. Besides, anyone who can do a reverse helicopter slam dunk and make it look easy is a friend of mine."

"What did he say about me?"

"He said if you didn't show up soon, he was going to come looking with me. He thought you might be at the cabin down on the James."

"I thought about going there. If it doesn't—if it didn't work out here." She stared at her lap again. "I shouldn't have let him worry."

I reached out and patted her hand. When I did, she jumped like she'd been hit by a copperhead.

"Hey," I said, "I don't bite. That was part of the ground rules, remember? No biting without at least twenty-four hours' notice."

"I'm sorry. I just feel very— There's been a lot of—" She gave it up. This time I kept quiet and gave her time to find the right words. Watching her was like watching a couple of street dogs fight for the scraps coming out the back door of a Chinese restaurant. There was something terrible about her struggles but something fascinating, too. I was more than a little spooked by her, yet irresistibly drawn into her life. I would have given anything to be able to put a permanent smile on her face.

"It's not," she began, "it's not like we're . . . lovers or anything. Yet . . . I'm saying this all wrong. We didn't realize we were in

97

love until this fall. We still don't know what to do. When Delmos went away, I thought I would, too. Just for a little while. And then— And then there's—"

She faltered. As she did, the feeling of being out of my element came over me again. There was a heavy load sitting inside of her, and she'd been more than a little neurotic to start with, in my unprofessional opinion. I was the blind man trying to mark the contours of the cliff edge in my head without falling over.

"What is it, Leigh?" I asked.

"You don't understand how awful—"

"No, I can't be you. But other people have faced your kind of problem before. I've been in love myself once or twice, too. And it's never easy." I laughed. "In fact, I think I even fell in love today."

"You did?"

"Well, it was only a first date, you understand, but you never can tell. Say, you might even know the lady in question."

"Oh, I doubt that."

"No, really. Her name's Patricia Ryan. She's the secretary of your father's lawyer. Lockridge."

Whatever I'd said, it was the wrong thing. Her eyes went blank, like someone had snapped off the light behind them. She gripped her knees and began moaning, rocking steadily forward and back, forward and back. I hopped over onto the edge of the bed and put my arm around her shoulders. I stroked her and mumbled harmless inanities, not knowing for certain what I ought to be doing. Eventually, she stopped moaning and said something.

"What?" I couldn't make it out.

"Evil." The word came through loud and clear, then again. "Evil." It wasn't what she said; it was the way she said it. She drew out the first syllable in a long, ominous monotone. It was eerie. I reminded myself that this was not a scene from some mindless novel about demonic possession. The girl in front of me was a jittery teenager who'd grown up with some really crappy role models and needed help.

"What is it, Leigh? Tell me what it is."

"An evil man," she said, stressing the "e"again.

Well, at least she wasn't freaked out about Patricia. For some reason that made me feel a little better.

"Who's evil, Leigh? Is it Lockridge?"

She nodded. "Evil."

I put a hand on her shoulder and slowly turned her to face me.

"Leigh," I said, "I'm your friend. I want you to tell me why you're saying that Carter Lockridge is an evil man."

Her eyes moved to the left and then to the right, as if she had to take me in in segments, before looking into mine.

"He hurts people," she said.

"What do you mean?" She sounded rational again.

"He fucked my grandmother." She said it almost without expression, but it snapped my head back. The word still has the power to shock, depending on who says it and when.

"Sarah *Jane?*"

She nodded. "He fucked her, and then he hurt her. She told me."

"When was *this?*"

"A long time ago." She seemed calm now, although she was reciting all this woodenly, as if there were a reporter inside her who wasn't her. "He fucks my mother, and he hurts her, too."

"Your *mother?*" Elizabeth and Lockridge. Now there was a match made in heaven. And I did notice that in this instance she'd used the present tense. "Is this still going on, Leigh?"

She nodded. "He tried to fuck me, but I wouldn't let him."

Jesus.

"I wouldn't let him, so he hurt me."

No wonder this kid was badly bent. If I didn't get off this case soon, it looked like I might end up getting into something with the oily little weasel, after all. Then again maybe we'd get into it even if I didn't get off the case.

"When I wouldn't let him, he got angry with me. He called me terrible names. So I told him I know he fucks my mother and that I thought he was a disgusting man. Then he got more angry, and he said more terrible things. He told me that he could fuck my mother any time he wanted to, and she didn't have anything to say about it. And he said that he didn't really want to fuck me, after all, because, because . . . people don't fuck their own daughters. It isn't true, is it, Swift? It isn't true, is it?" She had ahold of my shirt front, and she was crying. I took her in my arms. Christ, how did I know what was true? In this lunatic family, anything was possible.

I let her cry herself out.

It took some time. Huddled together as we were, with some intense emotions charging the air, I began to get uncomfortably aware of her as a woman. She was truly the flip side of Melissa. One would break your heart for the fun of it; the other could break it without even trying. I didn't want my heart broken just now. And besides, I'd already fallen in love once today. I concentrated on thoughts of Elizabeth and Lockridge. That did the trick. It caused my awareness to shrivel until all that was left was a clot of cold, calculated anger. I wondered if Lockridge had ever tried anything with Patricia and whether he'd hurt her when she turned him down. I imagined myself walking into his office and pistol-whipping him with one of his own Colt Woodsmans. The fantasy was highly satisfying.

Eventually, Leigh came around. "I'm sorry," she said, her voice still catching a little in her throat. "I haven't been able to tell anyone the whole thing yet and— It just—it just all came out. I'm sorry."

"No need to be. You would have had to get it out sooner or later. It'll be better now."

"Yes, I'll be better."

Yeah, I thought. You'll heal in a year or three. But you're stuck with the scar. Somehow it's always the nicest ones who take the biggest beatings. Maybe that's why there are people like me around. The ones who eat the big shit sandwiches are usually too nice to even the score. Me, I've got my principles, sure, but I'm not nice. And I like to balance things when I can.

In the meantime, what to do next?

"Look, Leigh," I said, "I'd better get going."

"Yes, your job's over now, isn't it?"

"Yes and no. I found you, and I can tell John that you're okay. That's what he is paying me to do, and it's done. But I'm not so insensitive that I don't care what happens to you now. Let me think for a minute." I thought. "All right. Are you comfortable staying here?"

She shrugged. "It's better than nothing."

"Then why don't you hang on for another night. I'll clear things up with your parents. After that I can talk to Delmos. I'll pass along whatever you tell me to. If tomorrow you still feel like you need to be alone or if you two need to be alone together, I'll find someplace you can stay for a while. How's that?"

"Why are you doing this for me?"

"I'm doing it for both of you."

"But why?"

"I don't know. You're nice kids, and you deserve a better shot than you're getting. Something like that. Besides"—I grinned—"we've got a great team this year, and if Delmos is bummed out, he won't play as well, and then the only person who'll be happy is my bookie."

She smiled weakly. I would have done anything she'd asked, and she wanted to know why. Oh, well.

"Please don't tell him what I've told you, Mr. Swift. Or my parents, either. I don't know what people will do anymore."

"I won't."

"Just tell him that it doesn't really have anything to do with him but that I've got to be by myself for a while. Say that it won't be for long. And tell him that—that I miss him."

"I will."

"Thank you for helping me."

"All in a day's work, lady, all in a day's work." Complete with a passable Bogart imitation. Me Bogie, you Betty. I don't think she got it, but she smiled as if she had.

"How can I repay you?"

I played at giving it deep thought, then snapped my fingers. "Two tickets to the Carolina game would do nicely." I winked.

"I'll see what I can do," she said.

"Good. Meanwhile, just stick around here. If I come across anything you need to know, I'll phone. Otherwise, give me a call tomorrow and tell me how you're doing. I don't care if you feel on top of the world; call me, anyway. If you can't get me, leave a message with my answering service." I gave her a card. She thought it was cute. If only she were ten years older . . . I mentally slapped my face. I was already in love with someone my own age. "I'll move as fast as I can to get something set up for you in town," I went on. "Until then, if you want my impartial opinion, I think you're better off here than most anywhere else."

"You're probably right."

I got up and held out my hand.

101

"Now how about helping me find my way out of this place?"

She took my hand and smiled that shy smile again. So chaste she could have been a bride of Christ and me her favorite monk.

Bruce was lounging at the end of the hall. When he'd determined that his sister was still unmolested, he volunteered to show me out, and Leigh and I said good-bye.

Along the way, I said, "How long has she been here?"

"A couple of days."

"Where was she before that?"

"I don't know. Why? What did she tell you?"

I ignored him. "Has she talked with anyone since she got here?"

"She's hardly left that room."

"Ali Gupta, I think right now she could use some companionship. Are there other women here?" He nodded. "I think another woman would be best, but not someone who's going to ask a lot of questions. Someone who'll let Leigh talk and be supportive. Anybody come to mind?"

"All the women here are supportive of each other." He said it as if any other state of affairs was unthinkable.

"Good. Pick the most. That kid's under a lot of pressure. She needs to know that she has friends. And look, don't let her run off anywhere if you can help it, okay?"

"Why should I do what *you* tell me?"

I sighed. "I'm not trying to tell you what to do. I'm an objective observer who thinks that your sister is better off with the folks here than on her own someplace, in her current state of mind. If you need to know exactly what that state is, you can ask her, of course. But I'd advise that you stay in the background until she comes to you. Which she will. And I guarantee she'll think more highly of you if you do."

"I can't think of any reason why I should trust you. You work for my father."

"Worked. The job's over, Ali. What happens to Leigh is the important thing now." I looked him in the eye. "As for the trust, I ask you to give it to me, but if you can't, at least allow me the benefit of the doubt for the time being."

I left Gupta Bruce in the front hall, trying to figure out what the cool parting word might be.

The big guy who'd first greeted me was on the porch, leaning against one of the posts that supported the roof.

"Holding the place up, big guy?" I said. Couldn't resist.

He just looked at me out of that arms-folded-across-the-chest stance. I don't think he liked me. Maybe he'd like my Peter Lorre imitation. Nah, everyone does Peter Lorre. I decided to leave him to entertain himself.

"Have a nice day." I waved.

·6·

It was dark by the time I got to the turnoff for Route 666. I stopped at a small family grocery store on 29 and called my answering service. Sure enough, Ridley Campbell was after me. He wanted me to get in touch with him, like yesterday. And Delmos Venable had called, leaving a number to call back.

There was also a message from Stone in San Francisco. He'd pried some information out of Continental Pacific. Brennerman had been working on an insurance case. A John Grimsley was the beneficiary of a modest life insurance policy in the names of his grandparents, George and Alice Grimsley of Sacramento, who had been killed in an automobile accident. Double indemnity. Whereabouts of the beneficiary was unknown, and Brennerman had been employed by the insurance company, through Continental Pacific, to find him. Somehow, presumably, the trail led to Virginia.

I no longer cared what it all meant. Brennerman had mentioned money, so he probably had some scheme to rip off the insurance company, thought I could help, and planned to cut me in if I could. Something like that. And the payoff must have been substantial, because it got him as dead as the Grimsleys of Sacramento in their ill-fated auto. But that didn't concern me now. The thing might have something to do with the Majors family, and it might not, but it certainly didn't have anything to do with Leigh Majors and her problems.

So long, Harlow. Sorry it didn't work out.

Ridley Campbell was another matter. When he said drop trou,

that's what you did. I figured he might be working late because of the murder, so I called him at his office. He was in.

"Swift," he said, "you been jerking me off."

"Hey, not me, Rid."

"Yeah, you have. I heard you knew that Brennerman had been nosing around the Majors family. Any reason you overlooked that little item when we was talking?"

"Ah, I believe I have a right to protect a client."

"Uh huh. And I got the right to haul your sorry ass in here and whop it a little. Any reason I shouldn't do that?"

"Well, it's the only one I got," I said hopefully. "I use it a lot for sitting and such."

"But you sure don't need it for talking out of, do you?."

"No, sir. No, I sure don't."

"You intend to play it straight with me from here on out?"

"Yes, I do."

"Tell you what. I'm a little busy right at the moment, as you might expect with all the shit that's flying hereabouts. But let's you and me have a more informed chat sometime soon. Don't leave town in the next couple of days, hear? And one other thing. How about that alibi you said you had?"

"I was with Elizabeth Majors at the time," I said. No client to protect anymore.

"Now that's very interesting, Swift. I think you and me, we got a whole lot to talk about. You don't mind if we check with the lady in question, do you?"

"I'd appreciate about an hour. I'm wrapping up the case."

"And I'd appreciate you call me in the morning."

"You got it."

"Good, good. One other little thing while we find ourselves on the subject. If you're in this any deeper than you say you are, you're in a flock of trouble, my boy."

"I'm not, I promise you."

" 'Bye, Swift."

" 'Bye, sheriff. Tomorrow."

It wasn't until after we'd hung up that I began to wonder what he'd meant by all the shit that was flying thereabouts. Surely not the Brennerman thing. That was small potatoes, even if it was a homicide. What, then?

105

I gave up. Whatever it was, Ridley would be sure to fill me in when next we met. Besides, I had more important things to think about. Like the new wrinkle in my current case. Someone had tipped Campbell that I knew Brennerman was tied to the Majorses. Now that was a surprise. Who had I told? Patricia. Assume it wasn't her. Sarah Jane? Not unless my judgment was slipping badly. Delmos? Unthinkable. Elizabeth? Maybe, but it would mean bringing herself directly to the cops' attention. And she had given every indication of not wanting that right now. Which left Lockridge, the bastard. It fit. He'd have the sheriff's ear without having to involve himself, being the Majorses' lawyer and all. But why would he want to call Ridley down on me? It was a puzzle, and I didn't like some of the solutions that were occurring to me.

No. The case is over, I said to myself, the case is over, the case is over. Carter and I could have a nice brotherly chat once all the loose ends were tied up. Like maybe in the parking lot behind that fancy office of his.

Anyway, that was for later.

I called the number Delmos had left. A woman answered.

"I'd like to speak to Delmos Venable, please," I said. "I understand that I can reach him at this number."

"Who's calling, please?"

"Loren Swift. Who's this?"

"Oh, yes, Mr. Swift. He said you might be calling. I'm Joanna Taylor, Storm's wife." Storm Taylor, the University's basketball coach. "We all felt it would be better if Delmos stayed here for a while, considering."

"Considering what?" I had an evil feeling in my gut.

"The, uh, unpleasantness, you know."

"Mrs. Taylor, I don't know. Could you please tell me what you're talking about."

"Oh, I thought everyone knew. Forgive me. Last night—well, early this morning actually, someone, uh, shot Delmos and—"

"*Shot* him!? What—"

"Please, Mr. Swift. He's okay. He's—"

"Put him on, will you? Can I *talk* to him?"

"Could you calm down, Mr. Swift? I'm sorry, he's not here right now. He and Storm went out to try and help with the disturbance. He's okay, I assure you. Someone took a shot at him early this morning while he was sleeping. They shot through the window, but

106

they missed. Well, not missed actually. The bullet grazed his skull, just barely. People heard the shot, and they got him to the hospital right away. He only had to stay a couple of hours."

"Who did it?"

"I'm sure I don't know. They got away without being seen. The police are working on it, of course. Delmos said to tell you he'll come by your apartment about ten tonight. Is that okay? He said you could leave word with me if it wasn't okay."

I looked at my watch.

"That'll be fine. Tell him I'll be there when you hear from him."

"I will. Good-bye, Mr. Swift."

I'd been so upset about Delmos that it wasn't until after I'd hung up that Mrs. Taylor's words completely sank in. Delmos was out "helping with the disturbance," she'd said. What in hell did that mean? I recalled Ridley's remark about the shit flying. Something was going on in Charlottesville. What was it? Did it have to do with the attempt on Delmos's life? If Clementine's radio worked, I'd know. But it didn't. I almost called Joanna Taylor back, and then I thought, What for? I'd see Delmos in a couple of hours, and I was sure he'd have the whole story, including perhaps an idea as to who might be taking potshots through his window in the night. Meanwhile, I had some other things to wrap up.

I leaned against the side of the phone booth, trying to let the anger drain out of my system. Swift, I said to myself, you are too involved in all this. Do not become personally involved in your cases. I repeated the motto until I began to half believe it. That'd be the day.

I made my last call, to the Majors place. This time I wouldn't be arriving with darling Melissa, and I didn't feel like climbing the fence. John agreed to meet with me despite the shortness of notice and the awkwardness of the hour. I guess I was supposed to be grateful that they could find a slot for me in their busy evening. But it felt more like being a faithful precinct worker who is rewarded with the privilege of paying a hundred bucks to attend the senator's campaign dinner.

One thing I *was* grateful for, though. To be paying my last visit to the house that Majors built.

· · ·

A little light snow had fallen while I was down in Nelson County, and it made the Majors manse look smaller, but not much. If you wanted to play off the NCAA Final Four inside, you still could.

Since the courtyard was brightly illuminated, the white stuff also presented me with a record of recent vehicular traffic in the area, and there was plenty of it. Upon such evidence are tricky cases often broken. So, without peeking, I decided to see if I could deduce who was at home. I studied the crisscross pattern of tire tracks. Conclusion: John and Elizabeth had both gone out earlier. So had Melissa. But all vehicles had returned. Everyone should be home now. I checked the garage. Gold star for the fearless investigator. The cars were all there.

I turned and faced the house again. Why, I wondered, did the good Lord allow brutal insensitive people like these to have such mind-boggling play toys? I took a deep breath and trudged up the marble steps.

Deya showed me into the east-wing ballroom again.

John and Elizabeth were in the exact positions they'd been in when I first met them. It resembled some twisted restaging of *American Gothic*. Elizabeth sitting there looking her most jolly rotten. John standing dutifully next to her.

We went through the hand-shaking, drink-mixing ritual; then I settled myself in the couch and said, "Your daughter's safe, Mr. and Mrs. Majors."

John was visibly relieved; Elizabeth couldn't have cared less.

"You've found her, then?" John asked.

"No, he's only teasing," Elizabeth said.

"I've found her," I said.

"Well, where is she?"

"Let me ask you something, Mr. Majors. Why didn't you tell me you had a son?"

"I have no son anymore. No one in the family has anything to do with my former son."

"Leigh does."

He was genuinely astonished. "She went to *him?*"

"She did."

"But—but what for?"

"I don't know all the details. All I know is that she needed to get away from things for a while. Apparently, she thought of Bruce."

"I told you," Elizabeth said.

"Shut up!" John said. Then he added, "Mr. Swift, you said she was 'safe' rather than 'well.' Was that meaningful?"

I nodded. "She's safe, like I said. Otherwise, she's an unhappy, confused young girl who's carrying a lot of weight through no fault of her own."

"What are you implying?" asked Elizabeth.

I turned to her. "I'm not implying anything; I'm saying it flat out. She's a nice kid who happens to be highly emotional, and she hasn't gotten a whole hell of a lot of support from her family."

"How dare you!?" John demanded.

Elizabeth laughed. "The perfect father speaks. How touching. Well, Swift, I see you've been taken in by one of Leigh's sob stories. But fortunately you don't have to listen to any more of them. Did you bring her home?"

"No, I didn't."

"Why not?" John asked.

"Because she didn't want to come, and I have no legal authority to force someone to do something against their will. And . . . because I think she's better off where she is."

"So don't we all," Elizabeth muttered. John sideswiped her with a glance, but it wasn't intended to be effective.

He reserved the hard stare for me. "Mr. Swift," he said finally, "I don't care for your insinuations. What Leigh's home life may or may not be is no concern of yours. You've been hired to find her—"

"Which I've done," I pointed out.

"—which you've done. Would you care to inform us as to what she is planning to do next?"

"I think she needs to be by herself a while longer."

"And then what? Is she returning to school?"

"As far as I know."

"Do you think she requires the services of a, uh, doctor?"

"I don't think she requires anything more than a few sympathetic people in her life," I said.

"May I ask if there is a, uh, young man involved?"

"I'm afraid that Leigh's social life is outside the scope of my investigation."

"Very well," John said. "Then I don't suppose we have anything further to discuss. We thank you for your services. Good evening, Mr. Swift."

"Before I go," I said, "I'd like to speak to Mrs. Majors privately."

"We have no secrets—"

"Oh, beat it, John," Elizabeth said.

He left, looking grim. Maybe later tonight he'd finally blow up at her. Yeah, and maybe the Red Sox would finally take the pennant next summer.

Elizabeth was regarding me with that aloof, patronizing expression of patient tolerance that I loved so well. The wealthy really have it down, that look. Let them try to carry it through the eye of the needle.

"Swift," she said, "you know, as much as I dislike you, there's something about you that I admire."

"Well, that's swell, Elizabeth, because I neither like nor admire you. I think you're rotten to the tips of your phony eyelashes. Leigh is a hell of a lot more than you deserve."

"What do you know about it?" she said acidly. "I don't see any little Swifts trailing after you."

It stung more than I would have imagined, even coming from someone I disliked. Probably because, despite the source, there was more than a grain of truth in it. The childless always have a surplus of opinion about raising the little devils.

On the defensive, I lashed out more strongly than I'd intended to.

"A good thing," I said, "if they had to grow up with the kind of parental confusion you offer."

"What the hell is *that* supposed to mean!?"

She was good, but she couldn't cut it. Righteous indignation was as remote a possibility with her as leading a Girl Scout troop. But it was time to backpedal a bit. I hoped she hadn't picked up that I might have reason to suspect John's paternity. Who Leigh's father was, was truly none of my business.

"It means that I've learned a little about your extracurricular activities the past two days."

"Oh, for God's sake. Stay out of my life, will you, Swift? It's no concern of yours."

"Actually, you're right, Elizabeth. I don't care a dime's worth who you get it on with. But I don't think your daughter should have to suffer for the company *you* keep."

"I don't involve my daughter in my personal affairs." Just as cool as you please.

"Maybe not. But you'd better check your personal affairs to see who *they* involve themselves with."

"That's a vile accusation, Swift."

It suddenly dawned on me that I was a hell of a lot deeper into this than I wanted to be. Just what was I trying to accomplish, anyway? I was through with John and Elizabeth. I'd never be able to make her into a better mother. All I was doing was venting my own stupid self-righteousness.

I shrugged. "Some people can't help boasting about what they do," I said. It was a lie, and I felt ugly saying it. But I needed to get Leigh off the hook now that Elizabeth knew that I knew. Hinting that Lockridge had told me was one way I was sure she would go for. Besides, she and Carter richly deserved whatever wounds they would eventually inflict on each other.

"You bastard," she said venomously, "get out of here."

"With pleasure," I said. "Don't bother to see me out. I'll find my way."

This time I made it all the way to the foyer before Deya caught up with me.

"Don't tell me," I said. "It's the Colonel."

"The very one," she said with a sly smile.

"Tell him that I don't have the slightest interest in working for him. In fact, tell him if it wasn't for you, I'd set his house on fire." I winked and patted her shoulder. She laughed.

I slid on out the door.

• • •

I drove back to Charlottesville on U.S. 29, wanting only to get to my apartment and wash the taste of Elizabeth Majors out of my mouth with some good whiskey from the land of the banshees. Then I'd meet with Delmos. Tomorrow I'd see what I could do for Leigh.

I was pretty close to the city before I realized what was wrong. There was a reddish glow behind the hills that enclose the southwestern edge of town. It didn't belong there. A fire, I thought, and from the look of things a good-sized one.

I turned east on Interstate 64, from which I had a better view of the University area. I couldn't tell exactly which building was on fire, but it was definitely on the campus. That didn't surprise me.

The University maintains a number of old frame buildings that would go up quickly under the right circumstances. I returned my attention to the road; it would be soon enough to read about it in the paper tomorrow.

I got off the Interstate at Route 20 and drove into Belmont. There seemed to be an awful lot of activity in the streets for a cold winter's night. I'd been right earlier; something was going on. I began to get that old spooky feeling, the same one I'd had every day of the world when I was in Southeast Asia. The feeling that I'd been dropped into the middle of an ongoing game where I didn't know the rules or who was playing at any given moment. Nor even quite what the game itself was supposed to be.

I pulled up in front of my apartment. I'd only been parked for a few seconds when the rock hit Clementine's side window, turning it into a jumble of cracks radiating out from the point of impact. It just wasn't my week for windows.

The second rock bounced off the hood.

I rolled out of the car on the passenger's side, silently apologizing to Clementine for putting her between me and whoever was doing the throwing.

"Hey!" I yelled. "Don't shoot. I didn't do it."

A bunch of voices yelled back, saying who knows what.

Tentatively, I stuck my head above the car's roof line. Half a dozen black teenagers were coming across the street toward me. Now, I suppose I could have made a run for my apartment and grabbed my .38 Police Positive and scared the hell out of them. But then again there was at best only an even chance that I'd be able to beat them to the door. Besides, I couldn't think of anything I'd done to make an unknown black teenager angry at me. I moved out from behind the car to meet them halfway; surely reason would prevail here.

Sometimes I'm not too bright.

"Hey, my man, what's the trouble?" I said to no one of them in particular. Old Swift, as blood as they come.

"You the trouble, white boy," said the tallest, leanest, and meanest looking. This was not good. I went into defensive posture, keeping Clementine at my back. "You and yo' murderin' white brothers."

"Ah, hold on here a minute," I said, raising my right hand palm out. Miraculously, they stopped, about two feet from me. "I think you got the wrong fella. Sounds like you're looking for the Ku Klux

112

Klan or something, and I don't belong to no Klan. Hell"—I chuck-led—"I'm a registered Democrat." That amused precisely no one.

"Fuck it, Lewis," one of them said. "Let's git his ass."

There was a chorus of "yeahs."

"Yeah," Lewis said, "you *all* Klan tonight, white stuff."

"Look, guys," I said, trying to keep the shakes out of my voice, "you scare up a Klansman, and I'll go stomp him with you. But I don't know *what* you're talking about."

"You lyin' mothafuckah" came from my left, followed by an amateurish hook. I caught it on my forearm, then pivoted on the ball of my right foot, driving a jab full into Lewis's nose with all my weight behind it. The nose broke like an eggshell and blood flowed onto his face as he went down. Get the leader and the followers will become disorganized and scatter, right?

Wrong.

Decking Lewis only stirred up the hornet's nest. Using the car as an immovable ally, I gave a pretty good account of myself. I stiffed one with a forearm shot to the windpipe and stopped another with a side kick to the kneecap. But there were too many of them and not enough of me, and they kept coming. Somebody clipped me decently on the side of the head, and I was on the ground with no recollection of falling. Instinctively, I assumed the tuck position. After that, they just beat the living Jesus out of me.

I drifted into a state where I felt no pain, only the force of the blows hitting me. Strangely, I never lost consciousness, but I doubt I would have survived the beating if help hadn't arrived.

I heard the car coming down the street in some tiny corner of my mind that was still usable. Then there were some slamming doors and some shouting and some running and stuff. Then voices.

I got my eyes open to a squint.

To one side of me was the group that had lately been playing Johnny-jump-up on my body. To the other was a semicircle of four young men. Big young men. One of them was Delmos Venable. There was a white bandage around his head.

"What you want to help the white boy for, Venable?" one of the bad guys was saying.

"He's okay," Delmos said. "He ain't the one you want."

"It none of your business, roundball man. We got to make the mothafuckahs *pay* for what they done."

"This ain't the way to do it, man. I know what you're feeling right

113

now. Brother Ward was my personal friend, y'dig? He was family to me. But this jive ain't gonna do a thing to bring him back. He's gone. All you're gonna get outta this is bad shit down on your own head and more trouble for all of us. Let it alone. Go on home, and I'll see if I can persuade the white man to forget about it."

Thanks a lot, I thought. Guys beat me senseless, and my buddy's going to have me telling people I fell off my bicycle. But then I suppose it beats dying.

There was general grumbling among my tormentors. One of them spit on me. I just soaked it up. It didn't hurt nearly as much as his foot had.

"We see you again, boy," another said to me.

In the end, though, they shoved off. Delmos and his colleagues—two of whom I recognized from the varsity football team—were an imposing sight. No one in their right mind would have wanted to get into it with such a collection of beef.

Then friendly arms were scraping me off the pavement.

"Careful," someone said. "I think this guy might be hurt bad."

"No'm not," a stranger said through my mouth. "M'okay."

Delmos got my arm around his shoulder. The road was tilted at a peculiar angle, making it difficult to figure out which way to lean. Other than that, I felt like I could probably walk.

"Thankth," I said. "I dunno wh'they wannid. They dutht dumped me." The "J" and "S" sounds were having a tough time making a comeback.

"Man," one of the others said, "you gotta be crazy to be out on the street tonight. You're lucky Delmos was headed this way. Those kids mighta killed ya."

No kidding.

"Yeah," another said, "we been on patrol three hours now, and we busted up four fights already."

"Patrow?" "L's." They were tough, too.

"Yeah, you know. Groups of athletes are helping patrol the streets, trying to cool things out a little."

I must have looked as confused as I felt.

"I don't think he knows what's going on, guys," Delmos said. "Help me get him inside, and I'll stay with him for a while. Y'all can pick me up in an hour." The three nodded and walked back to their car. "Which building's yours, Swift?"

114

"Over there." I made a painful gesture with my head.

Delmos half supported and half carried me down the embankment to my apartment.

"Coolin' what out?" I said along the way. My "L's" were back.

"Hush up," Delmos said. "Wait'll we get a glass of whiskey in you."

We staggered into the apartment, and Delmos poured me onto the living-room sofa.

"Where's the whiskey?"

"Should be a bottle next to my bed. In there."

He went into the bedroom, got the Jameson, and splashed me half a tumblerful.

"Thanks," I said. The "S" sound had returned. Or something close to it.

"Do you need a doctor?" he asked. "Do you want to go to the hospital?"

"No, to both." I shook my head, gently. Hospitals tend to have a negative effect on me. Too many people go into them and never come out alive.

I drank the whiskey in three well-measured swallows. It made me realize why the Irish keep it around for when they finish brawling. I decided that however difficult it might be, I would try to go on living. I breathed deeply. It hurt.

Delmos sat down next to me. "You look terrible." He grinned.

"And you on the outside at that. But you don't look so great yourself."

"Oh, that's right. I tend to forget about this." He touched his head bandage.

"What happened?"

"I don't know. I was sleeping. Someone fired a shot through the window of my room on the Lawn. Small caliber. It just nicked my head. By the time I knew what was happening, my neighbors had me on my way to see the team doc. He said there might be a slight concussion. Coach took me in after that, and I spent most of the day in bed. I feel okay now."

"Yeah," I said, "I talked to Joanna. You have any idea who might have done it?" I managed to get the "J" about right. My pronunciation apparatus had suffered no permanent damage.

"Hell, it could've been anybody," he said. "Most of the folks in this town tolerate me, but there's always those that don't like to see a black man get too raised up. Speaking of which, I allow that you don't know why you got beat up tonight. You don't, do you?"

"I don't. I've been concentrating on finding Leigh—"

"Damn! Should've been my first question. Did you find her?" The way he said it, I realized that whatever else was going on, this was more important to him.

"Yeah, I found her. She's all right."

He let out the breath he'd been holding in.

"Well?"

"Well what?"

"C'mon, Swift, where is she? When can I see her?"

"It's not quite as simple as that."

"Look," he said. "You seem straight. You know about Leigh and me?"

"I'd guessed. She more or less confirmed it."

"How you— how do you feel about that?"

I shrugged. "It's your business . . . No, it's more than that. I like you both. I'll help you if I can."

"Is that the private eye speaking, or is it you?"

I had to think on that one a while.

"Mostly me," I said. "Officially speaking, I'm off the case. John dismissed me this evening. Though he did pay me for three days and the clock's still running, if you want to look at it that way. But I don't feel finished. For one thing, I promised to help Leigh. And then there's all the shooting. Somebody knocked off Brennerman. Later that same night somebody took a shot at you. Now that might be a coincidence, and then again it might not. Either way, though, someone's trying to kill you. I'll feel better when he's off the streets."

"And who's Brennerman?"

"Oh, yeah. He's the guy I asked you about yesterday, the private investigator from California who was somehow involved with the Majorses."

"And he's *dead*?"

"Yup. Someone shot him last night in his motel room. I found the body."

"Whew. That's strange, all right. But hell, Swift, I don't know this Brennerman from Uncle Joe. I just want to know where my girl is."

116

"She's at her brother's."

"She's okay?"

"Physically, she's fine."

"But what?"

"But— Delmos, I think you ought to hold off on seeing her until she comes to you. She will. She told me it'd only be a couple of days. It's just that right now she needs breathing room. To think things over."

"Like me and her?"

"Partly. Jesus, I don't know what to say that won't cause you worry. Look, my take on her is that she cares about you very much. I don't think that's going to change, ever. But she's a very emotional girl, and right now she's got to sort things out for herself. Now you could go charging down there to see her if you want to. No one can stop you. But I'd really advise against it. Trust me. Give her a little time. It'll be best for both of you in the long run. How about it?"

"Okay," he said, but he wasn't happy about it. I wouldn't have been, either.

"Good. Now I been talking here more than I should have considering my mouth feels like a flannel factory. It's your turn, kid. How about pouring me a little more Jameson and telling me what in hell is going on in this town."

He poured the drink, and I settled back to listen.

"You know Ward Williams?" he asked.

I nodded.

"Well, he's dead."

I nearly choked on the whiskey. I coughed and sputtered until it went down the right way.

"What?" I said hoarsely.

"It's true. It happened this afternoon, over to the Security Complex."

"Who?"

"Some racist. You know how in every jail they've got gangs divided along the color line, right? The guy who hit Ward was a member of something called the White Brothers. Stabbed him to death with a homemade knife."

"Jesus."

"Yeah. The black community is a little upset about this, as you might expect. We've felt all along that there was something funny

117

about how long he was being held without bail. A lot of people are blaming the authorities for his death."

"They've got a point."

"They do. But it's not going to do us any good. Ward's gone. Someone will take his place. The struggle will continue. It's a struggle that has to take place in the schools, in the courts, in local government. Not in the streets. All that can happen there is that more of us will get killed. The Man has all the best guns on his side."

"I take it there's a lot of action in the streets like I ran into."

"Unfortunately," he said wearily. "The word about Ward was all over the city by late afternoon. The people are mad. They torched the Poe Annex over on Grounds, and when the firemen came, they threw rocks at them. The cops are out in force, but the whole thing's pretty decentralized. Small groups attacking whites here and there—that sort of thing. A couple of people may have died. The governor's considering calling out the guard. I hope that won't happen."

"Me, neither." I remembered Kent State all too well. We ex-army types don't think that well of the guard. "Let's hope the snow gets here before he does it. That ought to quiet things."

"Right. Anyway," he went on, "some of the black athletes—and whites, too—at the University got together and decided to form unarmed patrols to drive around and try to head off some of the violence before it gets started. That's who I was with when we found you earlier. You're pretty lucky I was on my way over here when I was. Otherwise, we might have been in a whole 'nother part of town."

"Whew," I said. "What a story. You know, I really ought to get a working radio in my Volkswagen."

He laughed.

"You should at that."

Then his buddies arrived.

"Delmos," I said, "I'll keep in touch through the Taylors. And with my answering service, if you need anything. Tomorrow I'll nose around and see what I can turn up in the areas we talked about. And thanks for breaking up the fight. I owe you one."

"No, you don't," he said. I knew what he meant without him having to say it in front of the guys.

They left.

I got to my feet, which wasn't that easy. It was less a question of

118

what hurt than of what didn't hurt. Now I knew how Ali felt the morning after the Thrilla in Manila. Do people actually do this for a living? God.

I looked around the apartment. No sign that anyone had tried to torch it. Nobody'd fixed the window, either. The pipes were laboring mightily to heat the place, with moderate success at best. I realized I was getting cold. The whiskey only warms you for so long.

Jameson in hand, I dragged myself to the bathroom as if I were working one of the heavyweight Nautilus machines set at maximum resistance. I clicked on the little electric heater, closed the door against the draft from the living room, and stripped down. Tentatively, I checked myself in the mirror for damage. It wasn't as bad as I might have thought, if I'd listened only to the pain. My right eye was swollen half shut, and there was a nice bruise forming over the cheekbone. There were a couple of small blood-clotted places in my hair. Other than that, it was all abuse to the body. They hadn't gotten between my legs, but most other spots were sore. Here and there were the beginnings of yellow and purple discolorations. Before long, I'd look like the Illustrated Man. I took a few deep breaths. My ribs hurt, but I didn't think any were broken.

I'd live.

I filled the tub with steaming water, gingerly lowered myself in, and put my battered brain to use.

Working assumption: everything that had crossed my path in the previous two days—the Majorses, Brennerman, Delmos, everything—was connected. In my business, you tend not to believe much in coincidence. Then along comes a coincidence like Ward Williams's murder and the subsequent riot. That wouldn't be connected. Of course, Lockridge *was* Williams's lawyer. And Delmos had worked closely with the dead man on some pretty touchy racial issues. Maybe there was something . . . No. That kind of speculation would take me way too far afield. Put Ward Williams aside and stick with the working assumption: that the attempt on Delmos's life was the last link in an interrelated chain of events that, on the surface, might appear to be random. If that was the case, then somewhere there was a key that would make sense out of things.

I took a healthy swallow of whiskey and submerged myself up to my chin. Damn if it didn't feel good. There is a certain pleasure in being in pain, because then you can do things to alleviate it.

So what did I know for sure? First, a P.I. from California was real interested in the Majors family concerning some uncollected insurance money. But there must be more to it than a straight death benefit case, or he never would have bothered to try and involve me. With people as wealthy as the Majorses, the idea of blackmail always suggests itself, but who and how? Elizabeth's determined efforts to get me off the case might tend to support the blackmail theory. Then again, they might mean something entirely other.

It occurred to me that I'd never asked Melissa what she knew about Brennerman. Maybe I should. Then again, maybe not. Our conversations hadn't exactly tended toward the congenial. The likelihood of her knowing anything of value didn't seem to justify going out of my way to find out. If I saw her again and she was straight, I'd ask. If not, I wouldn't.

Of more immediate interest was Lockridge. He appeared to be Elizabeth's lover, and formerly, perhaps, Sarah Jane's. He might also be Leigh's father. There could be a blackmail angle in there somewhere, but how would Brennerman have found out about it? Leigh didn't have any idea who he was. Whatever the case, Lockridge had tried to get me in trouble with the sheriff. That had to mean something more than that he thought I was a crummy dresser. He was waist deep in the whole business.

There was also the relationship between Leigh and Delmos. Interracial love affairs are still not terrifically popular in Virginia, and the potential for violence is always there. Sibling jealousy was a possibility, too, as was parental anger. But how would one of those connect up with the California end of the deal?

Motive. Motive was everything. Over the years I'd had to deduce or flat out guess people's motives for all sorts of weird and sometimes violent behavior. Nine times out of ten it was as simple as greed. Basic, down-home, sticky-fingered greed, as all-American as the whore with a cashbox mind and a heart of gold.

Scenario: Brennerman comes East looking for the missing beneficiary of George and Alice Grimsley. While poking around, he comes across something that looks like it will make him a lot bigger bucks than locating the lost heir. It's big enough to risk bringing someone else in on it, namely me. At about the same time, I get hired to find Leigh, whose disappearance has nothing to do with all this. Elizabeth and Lockridge get antsy about my being on the scene and try to buy me off. That doesn't work. Then persons unknown send Brennerman to the daisy farm, and Lockridge tries to implicate me. The simplest conclusion is that Elizabeth and Lockridge are into some scam together, that Brennerman finds out about it, and that they're worried I might, too. Though Elizabeth couldn't very easily have killed Brennerman, Lockridge could have. I'd seen his car coming from the direction of the motel, at just the right time. Now he might not have gone there with the *intention* of killing Brennerman. An argument might have gotten out of hand; Brennerman might have pulled his gun first; anything was possible. On the other hand, the stakes could be big enough that he *did* intend to plant the California shamus. And if Elizabeth knew it was going to happen and set me up to be her alibi, then that makes her accessory to murder one, which is almost as big a crime as pulling the trigger.

Sheer speculation, of course. But it did nicely fit the facts. Except for the part where Lockridge tries to divert Campbell's attention my way. In order to do that, he had to mention the Majors name, which is precisely the sort of publicity that Elizabeth seemed hell-bent on avoiding. Possibility: Lockridge and Elizabeth were into something together, and he was beginning to feel that the time had come to cut her loose. Pointing the cops in the right direction could be the first step. I liked the idea. If true, it meant that sooner or later the two of them would be at each other's throats.

Then there was one other thing I'd learned that might be relevant. Colonel Majors had made a trip to Lockridge's office a couple of days earlier. I got the impression that the Colonel didn't go out much, so I could assume a matter of some importance was involved. It could mean that the Colonel was mixed up with Lockridge. Considering the Colonel's feelings about his daughter-in-law, I thought that unlikely. The other possibility was that the Colonel said something to Lockridge that threatened the little weasel in some way. More likely.

All of this left me with a loose connection. Delmos Venable. I couldn't see him on either side of a blackmail scheme. Yet I couldn't write him out of the scenario. Someone wanted him dead, and my gut feeling was that it was one of the principals in the case. A nagging voice at the fringe of my awareness kept telling me that I *knew* what the connection was, that I'd already seen something that should have tipped me off. Try as I might, I couldn't remember what it was. It would come.

I knocked down the rest of the Irish whiskey and drew some fresh hot water. The warmth seeped into my muscles like a gift from God.

I thought some more. Supposing Lockridge and the younger Mrs. Majors *had* been running a scam together. That would make the Colonel the most likely target, since he controlled the bulk of the family money. That could explain the visit to Lockridge's office. The Colonel might have been making a payoff, or something like that. Yet the old man didn't seem the type to sit still for blackmail, especially from his own lawyer and daughter-in-law. Perhaps the scheme was just getting underway and the Colonel was receiving the initial bite. That didn't seem right, either. He'd tried to hire me to find out who Elizabeth was sleeping with, as if he wanted to give John some evidence for divorcing her. At no time did he act like a man who was under the gun himself, nor did he give me any indication that I might wind up investigating criminal activity against the family. None of the pieces was fitting together correctly here.

Try it another way. I knew that Brennerman had gone to the Majors place after I'd been there. Presumably he'd made his pitch to whoever was going to get squeezed. If it wasn't the Colonel, then it was either Elizabeth or John. Chances are it wasn't John. He wanted his daughter back, and he wanted me working on the case, and it didn't feel like there was anything more to it than that. If he was involved, it was likely that *he* would have ended up playing Elizabeth's part at the Jefferson Tavern last night, and he hadn't. Assume she was the projected loser in Brennerman's game. If so, she moved fast, especially considering the suddenness with which the tables had been turned on her. She would have tipped her partner, Lockridge, that something bad was up. He hadn't met Brennerman at that point, at least as far as Patricia Ryan knew, so whatever she said must have hit him hard. Hard enough to send him to the Mountain Vista Motel for a rendezvous with Brennerman that ended in death. Then she left the message for me to meet her at the Jefferson. For reasons still unclear she wanted my nose out of things for a while. In addition, I could serve as her alibi while Brennerman was getting knocked over. If I didn't show, that would've been okay. She could have rescheduled the chat about my laying off the case. Plus enough people would likely remember her to provide the alibi. She could easily come up with a plausible reason as to why she'd been waiting for me.

I wondered fleetingly whether Brennerman might have told Elizabeth about his encounter with me. No, that didn't make any sense at all. She was working hard at covering her butt, for whatever reasons and in however many ways. None of the potential reasons suggested that it would benefit her to bring me, Brennerman, and Lockridge together. I'd just been lucky. Had I decided against going to the Jefferson, as I almost did, I might have walked in on dear Carter right at the moment of truth. Unarmed. But I hadn't, and now Elizabeth's position was looking very good. Unless she and Lockridge could be turned against one another, she stood a good chance of walking away from it all clean as a born-again Christian. Not a pleasant thought.

At that point, I went back to the beginning. I replayed the scenario in my mind, step-by-step, carefully checking fact against theory. What I had made sense so long as I admitted that there were some major holes in the plot. One important thing I still didn't have was an overall motive. And I still couldn't fit Delmos in.

Thinking about Delmos, my mind began to wander. I saw in my head what I feel was his finest moment. It was in the second Carolina game last year. Carolina leading by one, and they had the ball with ten seconds left. The point guard was bringing it up the floor, and Delmos was going one-on-one with him. At midcourt, Carolina's guard looked up for the tiniest fraction of a second to see how much time was on the clock. In that instant, Delmos reached in and picked him clean. No foul, just great defense. Before the Carolina guard knew what had happened, Delmos had raced down the court and slam dunked the game winner. Considering the situation and the teams involved, it was the greatest single play I've ever seen in a basketball game.

But for a slightly shaky aim, it would now be just a highlight to show when they made the commemorative film of his life. If the would-be killer had succeeded, I'd have had him with my own hands. I'm one of those old-fashioned people who believes that vengeance is sometimes the only appropriate response.

That train of thought ended when I realized that someone was knocking on my front door. Jesus. When would it be over?

"Come in!" I yelled. I felt like getting out of the tub about as much as I felt like going a few rounds with Sugar Ray Leonard.

Nothing happened. Eventually, they knocked again.

Cursing, I got up, wrapped the big towel around my body, and went to the door.

Surprise. It wasn't a pretty girl popping out of a layer cake to wish me a speedy recovery from the indignities of the night. In fact, it was a very big male person who looked at that moment exceedingly ugly. And a couple of his equally ugly friends. Sheriff Ridley Campbell and the boys.

"You're about an hour late, Rid," I said. "But that's the way it is with the law these days. The more you pay 'em, the less they're there when you need 'em most."

He took in my collection of pornographic purple and yellow spots. They made him smile in a detached sort of way. He started into my apartment.

I caught his arm. "You got a warrant, Rid?"

He looked at my arm as if it were an enigma. "Save me the trouble, will you?" he said.

"All right." I let him go. The boys followed him in, checking me over.

"Hey, Swift," one of them called, "what happened? You come on to a lady truck driver?" They guffawed. That was funny, the boys thought.

"Naw," I said, "your wife's just a little heavier into S & M than I expected."

The deputy tensed and balled his fists. Strain lines formed at the corners of his mouth. I guess he didn't like the joke. For a moment I was sure I was going to get my second beating of the night. But the deputy looked first to Campbell, and Ridley stopped him with a tiny shake of the head. He retreated to the corner of the room and glared at me.

"Mind if I put some clothes on, sheriff?" I asked.

"Not at all. You mind if we take a look around?"

"And what would you be looking for? If it's the missing half of your buddy's brain, I didn't take it."

The deputy took a step toward me, but Ridley held up his hand, and the guy stopped again.

"Routine search, Swift," Campbell said. "You know, controlled substances, whatnot. We'll be real gentle, seeing as how we're here at your invite and all. That sound okay to you?"

He was looking for controlled substances about like I was looking for the Magic Kingdom, but I nodded.

"Whatever you need."

"Good. And Swift, stop needling Thurman, okay? You don't look

124

in such hot shape as it is." He smiled that smile that said: I've been as patient with you as I'm going to be.

I went into the bedroom and toweled off whatever hadn't drip-dried. Then I put on a pair of jeans and an old U. Va. sweatshirt that I'd picked up long after my student days. I took my time about it. Beyond the door they were going through my stuff. It was an audible search, but you could tell they weren't throwing things around.

When I emerged, they'd finished the living room, and the deputies were working on the kitchen. The sheriff was lounging on my couch. He patted the spot next to him, and I sat down. My guns were on the coffee table. The .38 Police Positive revolver and the 7.65mm Walther automatic. An instrument of death for every season. Campbell pointed at them.

"That it?" he asked.

"Yes."

"Swift," Campbell said, "you're in a pile of trouble here." Smile that smile.

"C'mon, Sheriff," I said. "What's going on?"

"In time, in good time. Meanwhile, who did the pop-art job on your torso?" Cute.

I filled him in on the night's events. He listened reasonably sympathetically.

"It's a jungle out there, ain't it?" he said. "Can't say as I blame them, though. That guy was something else. I'd want to kick somebody's butt if he was one of mine."

"He *was* one of yours, Sheriff."

"Yeah . . . yeah, I guess he was at that. I 'spose I *would* like to handle the stiff who did it."

"Well, it's done. Now how about telling me what you and the hired help are looking for?" The deputies had come back into the living room and were standing around with arms folded across their chests, looking like they'd watched too many reruns of *Cool Hand Luke*.

"Nothing," the one named Thurman said, obviously disappointed.

Campbell nodded, then turned slowly to me.

"Okay, Swift. Tell me about last night. And let's get it right this time."

"I've already told it right."

"Tell me again. My memory's beginning to go in my old age."
Yeah, like I'm going senile.

"Jesus." I sighed and repeated it all again the very same way.

"Well, that's fine," Ridley said when I'd finished, "but there appear to be certain, ah, discrepancies in your story. There's the matter of your foreknowledge of the decedent's interest in the Majors family, for example."

"Yeah, there's that," I agreed. "Who'd you get that little ditty from, if I may ask."

He shook his head. "Police privilege."

"Figures. But I've got a decent idea. Let's say I have the candidates narrowed to a field of one. Wouldn't be your man at the county courthouse, would it?"

"Swift," he said with exaggerated patience, "it doesn't matter a damn who it is, and you know that. What matters is that you withheld information in a murder case."

"I have a right to protect my clients."

"Up to a point. We're past that point now. Give."

When the man said "give" like that, you gave generously.

"I met Brennerman on the road for the first time in my life. The only thing I didn't tell you was that he indicated that he was on to something with the family that might be worth some bucks and he figured I could help him out. But he never told me what that something was. That's the truth. He intended to spell it out when I met him last night, but he was dead when I got there. I figured you'd find the Majors connection for yourself soon enough if it was important, and in the meantime I had a job to do for my clients that had nothing to do with Harlow Brennerman."

"I've only got your word for that."

"Look, Rid, the job's over, and I don't care anymore. They hired me to find their daughter. I found her. She's safe and sound and hasn't fallen in with a bunch of dope fiends. That's all they were afraid of. It was a simple case, and it doesn't tie in with Brennerman any kind of way. Finis."

"Where's the daughter now?"

"Sorry."

"All right. I don't think it ties in, either. Did you know that Brennerman was working on an inheritance case?"

I nodded.

"Well, you do work fast. Maybe next year you should run for my job."

"I don't think your boys would like that much."

He laughed. "No, I don't reckon they would at that. You got any idea what Brennerman might of had in mind?"

"Not in the slightest, but I have been thinking on it. Blackmail occurred to me."

"Who and how?"

"You got me again."

"Ain't exactly the bubbling fountain of wisdom here, are ya?" The man could turn a phrase.

"It's been kind of a rough night."

"Too bad. I wouldn't want to see it get any worse."

Spoken with an unnerving kind of understatement that Campbell could flick on and off at will. Very intimidating. He was toying with me again. I didn't like it, but there was nothing I could do. It meant that he was here for more reason than to rehash last night. I liked that idea even less.

"You weren't there, Rid," I said. "It doesn't get any worse than that. I heard a couple of people have died already. You ain't planning to take my life, I trust."

"Not just yet, anyways. But how about you tell me when you left the Jefferson Tavern."

"I don't know. Around nine."

"Mrs. Majors says maybe quarter till."

"It could have been. What's the point?"

"She also says you had an argument."

"Of sorts. Get to the point, Rid."

"Mrs. Majors says that you threatened her. Says that you told her you were on your way to meet somebody who could make it very hot for her."

"That's a damn lie—"

"What'd you two argue about, Swift?"

"Nothing important. I don't like the way she relates to her kids."

"That your business?"

"When I'm trying to find one of them, it is. What are you getting at?"

"This," he said. He reached into his jacket pocket and pulled out a plastic baggie. Inside was a small automatic pistol, one of those

127

cheap nickel-plated jobs designed to fit comfortably inside a woman's handbag. "Twenty-two caliber, wouldn't you say?"

"Yeah. So what?"

"So this, buddy. I thought those two there were your only guns," he said, pointing at the coffee table.

"They are."

"Then what's this?"

"How should I know?"

"You should *know* because we found it in *your* apartment."

I just gawked at him. He pointed.

"Under this very sofa."

"Under my *sofa?* Oh, for Christ's sake, that's the dumbest thing I've ever heard. You've got to be kidding."

"No, Swift," he said. "I'm serious. Here's what I think happened. Brennerman came to you with a scheme to bilk the Majorses based on whatever he had on them. For some reason, he thought he needed your help to pull it off. But you got greedy and decided you wanted the whole pie yourself. That meant Brennerman had to go. I think after you left Mrs. Majors, you drove to the motel and shot him, and I believe we got the murder weapon right here. Then you took off, stashed the gun someplace, and went back to 'discover' the body. How's that? That about the way it went?"

I just laughed. I leaned back in the couch and laughed and laughed.

"You're pretty loose for a man in your situation," Ridley said.

"Of course I am, Sheriff. I've never seen that gun in my life. I wouldn't own such a piece of crap, would you? Besides, I'm not a killer, Rid. You've known me long enough to know that."

"I don't *know* anything. Brennerman was killed around nine, nine-thirty. You called us at ten twenty-five. That gives you plenty of time to have done it. Plus we got a twenty-two pistol, and I'll bet it fired the shot."

"I'll bet it did, too. Somebody's setting me up, Rid. Find out who, and you've got your killer."

"I think I'm looking at him."

"Sorry, not this time. Whoever planted that gun had what seemed like a great idea, once they found out that it was me who discovered the body. I'm the perfect patsy. You've been tipped that I knew what Brennerman was up to. There's motive. I left the Jefferson in time to do the deed. There's opportunity. And now you've got the gun from my desk drawer. There's your method. Method, motive, and opportunity. The old police procedural Big Three. You've got it all except for one minor flaw, which the person who set me up obviously couldn't have known about. I didn't go directly from the Jefferson to the motel."

"You talking alibi?"

I nodded. He looked crestfallen.

"Annie at the Jefferson will tell you I was there till nine, or nearly so. After I left, I stopped at Mac's for an Irish coffee to get rid of a bad taste in my mouth. There was a show on the Virginia basketball team on the TV. I didn't leave until close to ten."

"Witnesses?"

"Call the bartender."

Campbell snapped his fingers, and one of the deputies did just that. He had a brief conversation, then came back and announced, "He was there," disgustedly.

"Sorry, fellas," I said.

Give the sheriff credit; he didn't miss a beat. Immediately, he was into alternatives.

"All right," he said, "who do you think planted the gun?"

I shrugged. "Your killer."

"Very clever," he said. "And who would that be?"

"I hesitate to say, but Elizabeth Majors comes to mind. Oops, excuse me, that just slipped out. Don't want to commit slander here."

"She couldn't have. She was with you."

"You're right, and I'll bet she stayed on at the Jefferson for another hour or so, in sight of many people. So she had to have help. She could have planted the gun, though. In fact, I strongly suspect it. This place isn't too tough to get into with that window out."

"Maybe. Who's the helper?"

"Why don't you try her lover?"

"Swift, you seem to know a lot about these people's private lives."

"You forgot it's what I do for a living?"

Campbell sighed. "All right. And the lover is?"

I spread my arms. "Far be it from me to indulge in malicious gossip. But you might try the fellow who stirred you up against me in the first place. Like I said, the people who want me implicated have got to be involved themselves."

129

Campbell's eyes got hard. "You'd better be careful how you sling your accusations around."

"I'm not accusing anybody," I said. "I'm merely responding to your request for suggestions. Cooperation with the law and all that. You know. And here's something else for you. You check that gun out, not only will you find no fingerprints, much less mine, but you're also gonna find that it's dead cold. What you want to bet? So who would you expect to catch holding a cold handgun? A professional hit man, for one. That's a little unlikely in this case. How about somebody who deals with criminals all the time in his line of work? I'm not making any wild accusations, you understand. But like my mama used to tell me, if a man is hip deep in the Big Muddy, you're bound to find a fishing line nearby."

"Your mama never said that in her life."

I grinned. "Right you are." I think he smiled, too, just a mite, but it could have been a trick of the light.

"You got any other bright ideas?" he asked.

I ran some of my favorite scenarios at him. Off the record, of course. Ridley Campbell could be trusted in matters like that, and what the hell, it wouldn't hurt to have him working on the case, too. I told him everything except the part about Leigh and Delmos. That was still privileged information. They had no connection with the Brennerman killing, and Ridley had no need to know about their relationship. I played it as if I'd stumbled accidentally into a complex web of intrigue that ended in murder. Which was exactly what I had done.

When I was finished, he grunted like a man who'd just had a three-course meal in a very bad Italian restaurant.

"Do you think the Colonel's in danger?" he asked.

"Mmmmm. Assuming he *is* the target, I doubt it. Another murder so soon would be a bit much. But you never know. What with every cop in the world out tending to the riot, they might think this is the perfect opportunity."

"Okay. I'll question Elizabeth Majors. She's in the middle of this thing. If she gives me anything at all, I'll pull Lockridge in, too. That's a big if. I don't have anything hard here, Swift, and I can't go treating people like suspects on the basis of your speculations. I'll also stop out there to visit with the Colonel. That way I can put him on guard and also let her know that we're watching. If she runs to your buddy, I'll make it my business to know about it."

130

"Now what else you got?"

"That's the lot," I said.

Without further ado, the guys prepared to leave. As usual, the sheriff had some parting words for me.

"Swift," he said, "I want you to know that you're not out of the woods on this one yet. I could bust you for half a dozen things already. I won't, because I think right now you're leveling with me and you're more use to me out on the street. But keep your nose out of this case, you understand me? If they come after you, that's one thing. Call me. Just don't go looking for them, or you got yourself beaucoups of troubles."

"All this and multilingual, too." He'd pronounced the word *boocooz*. "Where do his talents end?"

"And watch your mouth. I wouldn't want you should meet Thurman someday when I'm not around." Thurman, on the other hand, was quite obviously looking forward to the occasion.

"No problem," I said. "Just make sure he got his Burger-Bits that morning."

They left without having been amused. There's just no accounting for people's taste in humor.

I collapsed into my favorite chair. About the last thing I wanted this interminable night was more talk, but I needed some. I called Jonesy. Late as it was, I figured the *Press* would be cranking at top speed. The next day's issue was going to be one of the meatiest in their history. They'd want it to be a good one.

I was right. The background sounds of frantic activity were clearly audible over the phone. It took a while for them to locate Jonesy and get him on the line.

"Swift," he said, "of all the goddam times to call. Make it quick, will you?"

"What have the cops got in the Venable shooting?" I asked.

There was one of those pauses that hangs there like a layer of smog. When Jonesy spoke again, the hurry-up had gone out of his voice.

"What's your interest in that?" he said.

"I'm concerned."

"Don't jive me, Swift! You didn't call in the middle of the busiest night of the year because you're a concerned citizen. Give."

"Look, his name came up during a case I'm working on. I'd like to know if the cops have made any progress, that's all."

"What case?"

"Don't jive *me*, Jonesy. You know I can't give you that. Now there's obviously something up. How about filling me in?"

There was another long pause.

"Swift," he said finally, "I've got something that you'll probably never hear if I don't tell you. Suppose I do? And suppose it ties in with whatever you're working on? What do I get in return? A couple of six-packs isn't going to be enough."

I thought it over. Jonesy had something hot concerning Delmos. If it helped me in what I was doing, he deserved a payback. Jonesy was my friend, but he was also an ambitious journalist. It wasn't hard to figure what he wanted.

"If it's big," I said, "I'll tell you the story. Exclusive."

"How big?"

"I don't know what you have. I'm looking at one murder and a near miss. Maybe some heavy doings behind the scenes in this town. It may tie in, or it may not. That's all I can say right now."

"Okay"—he sighed—"this is it. Earlier tonight somebody dropped an anonymous note at the front desk. No one here saw who it was or when it happened. With all the craziness, it didn't even get opened until around eleven. The note claimed responsibility for the attempt on Delmos Venable's life. It instructed us to print a message to the black community warning that what happened to Williams and Venable is going to happen to any blacks who quote forget their proper place unquote. The note was signed 'The White Brothers'."

"Jesus," I said. "You're not going to print it, are you?"

"Of course we're not going to print it. Do you think we're totally irresponsible down here?"

The thought had occurred to me, but I didn't say so.

"You sure the note actually came from the White Brothers?"

"Pretty sure. We called the cops immediately, and they rousted the guy who knifed Williams. He said sure, they did it, Venable had it coming, etcetera. Now they're trying to get the names of some of his buddies on the outside. Last I heard, he hadn't cracked."

"What're the cops doing for Delmos?"

"He'll have an around-the-clock bodyguard until the case is broken."

"Good. Thanks, Jonesy."

"This ain't charity, Swift. See you scratch my back when the time comes."

I hung up.

My head felt like the proverbial five-pound can crammed with ten pounds of goodies. I gulped down a shot of Jameson, straight, and fell into bed without having another thought.

· 7 ·

When I woke up, it was five-thirty in the morning, and I felt like
the Six Million Dollar Man before they rebuilt his body. There was
too much pain involved to consider going back to sleep, so I swal-
lowed four aspirin and chased them with a tumblerful of Jameson.
That helped some. I took another long hot bath. That helped
some, too.

Then I settled myself on the sofa with my down sleeping bag
wrapped around me to wait for an appropriate hour to begin the
day. I drank lots of coffee and thought things over.

Although my head still didn't look too hot, the abbreviated night's
sleep had helped clear it a little on the inside. Looked at from the
perspective of my original involvement with the case, I now had a
pattern. It was a vague one, with lots of fuzzy areas, but it existed.
And the starting point was obvious. Something had happened in
California that precipitated the entire sequence of events. Nothing
else made any sense. And the person who would know what that
something was, was Sarah Jane Majors. John's mother. Carter Lockridge's former lover.

Okay, but what about Delmos Venable? Did he somehow connect
with Lockridge and Elizabeth and Brennerman and the rest of it,
or didn't he? In my gut I still felt that he did, but I was going to
have to allow that my gut feeling might be wrong. There was now
evidence that the attempt on his life had been made by members
of a racist hate group. The same group that had unquestionably been
responsible for the murder of Ward Williams. If the White Brothers
had shot Delmos, then that aspect of the case was no longer any of

my business. The cops were much better equipped to deal with gangs of armed lunatics than I. But if they *weren't* responsible, then who was? Probably someone I'd already met.

Another chat with Carter Lockridge suggested itself. He'd been Williams's lawyer and might have some further information on the White Brothers. Besides, there was the whole question of Leigh Majors's paternity and who had been sleeping with whom over the years. A lot of stuff, all told. It would require considerable ingenuity to get anything of value out of someone as crafty as Lockridge. I decided to defer my visit to the lawyer's office until I formulated an effective plan for working him over. Otherwise, I'd end up merely chasing my own fantasies.

For the moment it was best to concentrate on Sarah Jane.

At eight-thirty, I knocked on her door. I figured she'd be an early riser, and I was right.

She appeared at the door like someone who always accomplished at least three things of major importance before nine in the morning.

"I need to talk to you," I said.

She hesitated, giving me the hard appraising stare that you somehow knew wasn't out of place on the pixieish face.

"All right," she said, "come in."

We took up our accustomed places at the kitchen table. No fancy breakfasts this time, though. Just straight coffee.

"What happened to you?" she asked. "You look like you got beat up."

"I got beat up."

"Is Leigh . . ." She couldn't finish the sentence.

"Leigh's all right. She's with Bruce. Or Ali Gupta Hassan, as he now wishes to be known. I found her late yesterday. By the time I got home, there was a war going on in my neighborhood, and I got drafted against my wishes."

"I'm sorry."

"Hardly your fault. It's no problem as long as they don't suddenly uninvent aspirin and Irish whiskey." Yeah, no problem except when I walked, talked, moved, or breathed.

"Would you like a drink now?"

"Thanks, but I'd better not. We should be clearheaded for this."

"For what?" She was wary but didn't seem paranoid.

"Sarah Jane," I said slowly, "there's something going on here that

135

I don't understand, and it all started when a private investigator from California showed up in town. Now he's dead, and there's been an attempt on Delmos Venable's life, as well. You heard?"

"I heard. You think that what happened to Delmos is connected?"

I thought briefly of telling her about the White Brothers note and decided against it. It was privileged information, and I didn't want to start spreading it around. If it got out, a bad situation could get a lot worse. I'd stick with my original theories for the time being.

"Some way. It's been a lot of years since I was able to believe in coincidence, especially when interrelated people start dying on me. I think you've got the key, though you may not even realize it."

"Why me?"

"You're the only one with a California history. And for one other reason, which I'll go into later."

"I don't think—"

"Brennerman was working for an insurance company, through Continental Pacific Investigations. The insurance company had an accidental death policy to pay off, and they couldn't find the beneficiary. The name of the insured was Grimsley. Does that help any?"

She was silent for a long time. Her eyes were on me, but they weren't seeing anything in front of her. They were scanning scenes from long ago. She had the answer, I knew that now for sure. I was equally sure that she'd open up to me.

She did.

"Swift," she said, "you have to understand how difficult things were in those days for a woman on her own. I was a cantankerous young girl. I don't know how I ever got into that miserable marriage. Just because it was what you did, I guess. There weren't supposed to be any other options. My parents wanted me off their hands, so the first eligible bachelor who came along and showed interest got me. We hadn't been married two weeks before I realized what a terrible mistake it had been."

"But you stuck with it for two years and got pregnant to boot."

"Yes, I did. Even today it takes a lot of courage to walk away from a failing marriage. Back then it took that much more. I was years building up to it. As for being pregnant, well, all I can say is that despite our personal problems the Colonel and I maintained an active sex life right up to the end. The pregnancy was an accident, but in hindsight it wasn't too surprising, considering my general ignorance of proper precautionary measures. At first I thought that nothing worse could possibly have happened to me. But as time passed, I found myself really wanting to have the baby."

"Not that you had much in the way of alternatives."

She chuckled. "No, not that I did. The primary instrument of abortion at the time was the coat hanger. But I wanted the kid, so it didn't matter. It seems strange now that I would have had such feelings as a teenager . . ."

She'd lost the thread. "So you ran to California," I prompted.

"Yes. I ran as far from everything I'd grown up with as I could get. I didn't want anyone to know where I was, and I didn't want to ever come back. You know how it is when you're young; things seem so final. Well . . . it was awful. I was scared, and alone for the first time in my life. I . . . lost the baby."

"Huh?"

"I lost the child. Miscarried. I spent a week in a hospital in Sacramento. When I got out, I was almost broke."

"But—"

She smiled ruefully. "I know what you're thinking. No, John isn't the Colonel's."

And there it was. The hook on which you could hang the rest of the mess. Brennerman and Lockridge and Sarah Jane, the lot. No wonder the Colonel had said that John was always scrawny as a kid. It wasn't because he was naturally frail; it was only that he was younger than any of his classmates. Surprising that I hadn't guessed something along that line, considering the clues. Well, I've heard it said that deductive reasoning is one of the first faculties to go when they start going.

"What happened?" I asked gently.

"The usual." She shrugged. "I got out of the hospital and took a factory job. I was lonely. Bob Grimsley was there. We became lovers right away. I'd developed an appetite for sex when I was with the Colonel, and I didn't believe in delayed gratification." She laughed. "I never bothered to get a divorce from the Colonel. It seemed superfluous, and besides, I didn't have the money. In fact, the Colonel and I didn't get legally divorced until John started having children. Anyway, Bob and I just moved in together. It was a funny time. People could sense that we were going to get involved in a horrible war, so almost anything you did was okay. There wasn't that dreadful conservatism that you got in the late forties and fifties."

"Ah, yes," I said, "those lovely years to which we seem to be returning under full steam."

"Don't we now?" She laughed. "It seems such a shame that we should have come so far only to start running so hard in the opposite direction. But I guess everything comes full circle in the end. In a way I think it might be tougher to do what I did now than it was then. At least in 1940 people still remembered the Depression and understood how dependent they were on each other. Nowadays it's fuck you, Jack, there's no more room in *my* lifeboat."

I smiled but not out of any real amusement. She was right. If I wanted examples, I had to look no further than the people I'd met on this case.

"Maybe we need another good Depression to shake us all up again," I said.

"Lord, I hope not."

"What happened to Bob?" I asked.

"We had some really fine days together," she said. Her wistful expression made her look as if the youth fairy had just singled her out for the full treatment. Minus the white hair she could have passed for forty. "Weekends we never even got out of bed. Made love and then made more love. A couple of months after my miscarriage I was pregnant again. I didn't care; I loved the feeling. Bob was happy, too. John was born a little less than a year after my first child would have been, and we both loved him like crazy. That was right before Pearl Harbor."

"Bob enlisted?"

"Yes. And then he was gone. At least he got to enjoy the baby for a little while."

"You ever see him again?"

She shook her head. "He was killed on one of those little islands out there. I don't even remember which."

"It must have been hard."

"It was. But there was plenty of work for women because of the war. We got by. George and Alice helped some. I regret that I eventually had to take John out of their lives, but I felt I had to do what I thought was best for him."

"So he was about five when the Colonel came looking for you?"

"Right. I don't know how I got started with the lie about whose son he was. I guess it simply seemed easier to let the Colonel believe what he wanted to believe. I'd about had it with my life, anyway. John needed more stability, and so did I. The Colonel made us a very good offer, and I decided to take it."

"That meant not letting George and Alice know where you were taking him."

"My only regret, as I said. I'm surprised they still had a policy in his name after all these years."

"Grandparents are like that. Wouldn't you do the same for Leigh, no matter what?"

She smiled. "How is my girl?"

"Not good, Sarah Jane. She took off because she and Delmos had fallen in love and she didn't know how to cope with the situation. She was right on the edge when I talked with her yesterday. I don't think it's going to get any better now that someone's gunning for her boyfriend."

"Bring her to me, will you, Swift?"

"The idea had occurred to me, but she's going to need a lot of taking care of. You up to it?"

"I hope so. She doesn't have anyone else."

"All right, I'll bring her here."

We paused for a while. I wanted to give her time to collect her thoughts before I slogged on into even more unsavory matters about her past. We drank coffee and looked past each other.

She broke the silence.

"When can you get her?" she asked.

"I don't know," I said. "Maybe this evening."

"No sooner?"

"Well, I'll call and see what's up. It'll be easy enough to tell if she's already heard about the shooting. If she has, she may not want to go anywhere just now, or she may want to come home immediately. If she hasn't, I think it would be best to leave it that way for the time being."

"I think you're right."

"Meanwhile, I've got a murderer or two to locate. And that brings me to the key question of the day."

"Which is?" You could see the tension in her now. The crinkles around her eyes weren't playing the role of laugh lines anymore.

139

This dredging of the past was painful for her. She wasn't at all sure she wanted to hear what came next. Which made me feel bad, since I still considered her an ally. But the words had to be said. I had to know for sure.

"Which is: who else knew about John?"

"Well, *he* knows, of course."

"Of course. Anyone else?"

"No one."

"Not even your lover, Carter Lockridge?"

The air went out of her in a rush, like the back draft from a railroad tunnel. She looked her age again.

"How'd you find out about that?" she said softly.

"Leigh told me."

"She shouldn't have."

"Yes, she should've, as you'll see. Would you mind telling me about it?"

"I guess not"—she sighed—"since you already know. It was . . . a long time ago, twenty years, who remembers? It was just a fling, nothing serious. Carter had been the family lawyer since he got out of U. Va. law school. His father and the Colonel were great buddies in the old days, so it was only natural. He was young, quite handsome, sort of a dashing figure. I was already over forty. It was very flattering to have someone like that interested in me. We had an affair, not especially torrid but fun. When it was over, it was over; there were no regrets on either side. Until now. I suppose you're going to tell me he was just using me."

"It looks that way."

"He couldn't have known ahead of time that I had anything worth finding out."

"No. But ruthless people use others as a matter of course; it's a part of their m.o. You were attractive and available. You were tied into a very wealthy family. You were a good connection. It was just a lucky chance that he picked up something of value."

"I never suspected," she groaned.

"Of course you didn't, Sarah Jane. If you had, you'd be a very different person. It's not your fault."

"All for a few moments of satisfied lust." She shook her head slowly.

"It's done," I said. "How'd he find out?"

140

"The usual. I got loaded one night. It just slipped out when I was talking about California. I never dreamed it might not be in safe hands. Since he knew most of the family secrets, anyway."

We fell silent. I busied myself slotting the information into the larger puzzle. The big piece was still missing, the one that tied Delmos in. If it existed at all. Again, I had the feeling that I already knew something of importance. I groped for it, but it continued to elude me.

"Please tell me the rest of the story," Sarah Jane said dully.

"All right," I said. "This is what it looks like to me. Lockridge used the information about John to blackmail somebody in the family. Certainly not the Colonel. Probably not John himself. Most likely Elizabeth. She was well entrenched at that point, and she had the most to lose if John ended up being disinherited and found the nerve to cut her loose. Since she was only in it for the money from the start, she couldn't afford to risk the truth coming out. So she agreed to Carter's terms, whatever they were. Cash payments possibly, but I'd be surprised if there wasn't more to it than that. Maybe some lucrative legal business through her contacts in the upper crust. And I'd venture to guess that when the Colonel dies, Lockridge is going to get himself cut in on her share. All nicely signed and notarized, I'll bet. He may even have designs on John's slice, once the Colonel is gone. Plus, Elizabeth's also been throwing sexual favors his way. That may have been part of the deal, too."

"I'd heard," she said tersely.

"So everything's going swimmingly for our boy. Then George and Alice die in a car accident, and things begin to happen. They're still carrying a policy for their long-lost grandson. The insurance company doesn't have a clue where he is, so they farm the job out to Continental Pacific Investigations. Harlow Brennerman gets the case, and he's good. He traces John back here. Somehow he discovers the setup at the Majors place. I know he talked with their chauffeur; he told me as much. Not that it would have required much inside information to learn that John is considered the Colonel's natural son. So now Brennerman stops and checks his options. What he comes up with looks like a chance to run a profitable little blackmail scam of his own. Bigger bucks than for locating a missing beneficiary. For some reason that we'll never know, he thinks I can help him pull it off. Maybe he simply wanted to buy me out of his hair, since

I was already working for the victim-to-be. In any case, the day John hires me to locate Leigh, Brennerman is trying to get his scheme in gear.

"But it doesn't work. Brennerman underestimates the opposition. He doesn't realize how much the participants have invested in their own double-dealing and how far they'll go to protect that investment. It's a costly mistake for old Harlow. It gets him very dead. Lockridge killed him, of that I'm sure, though it'd be awfully difficult to prove in court at this point."

"But why kill him? That's a pretty extreme measure. It means risking that the whole thing will come out, anyway. And besides, there'll just be another investigator to take Brennerman's place."

"What you've discovered is that I'm still missing a few of the pieces," I said. "Those are all good questions. Personally, my feeling is that Lockridge was being threatened by more than just Brennerman. He got a visit from the Colonel a few days ago, and that may have something to do with it. I need to ask the Colonel what they chatted about next chance I get."

"Do you think Brennerman might simply have been the last straw?"

"Could be. If dear Carter was on a short fuse already, he may have lashed out at Brennerman without even thinking about it."

"That wouldn't be out of character," she said coldly. "But I'm going to have to be honest with you. Carter can be cruel, and violent. Yet I don't think he has the guts to kill. Unless it was an accident."

"Well, it sure doesn't look that way. In any case, our friend Elizabeth knew for damn sure what would—or might—happen and must have foreseen that she could become a suspect one day. She's not stupid. So she set up a meeting with me to give her an alibi for the crucial hours, simultaneously readying Lockridge for his little trip to the motel. At that time she didn't know that I'd met Brennerman. I dropped the name during our conversation. She must've about had a heart attack when that happened. But she is one cool customer, that woman. She barely batted an eyelash. She almost convinced me that she'd never heard of him, and that's tough to do with someone like me. I listen to lies and half-truths every day in my job. I'm pretty good at spotting them.

"Anyway, I never let Elizabeth know that I was meeting Brennerman later that night, but it turned out to be an unexpected bonus for her. The next day she learned that I'd discovered the body.

How, I don't know. Probably through Lockridge's connections in the sheriff's office. That set her wheels turning. She decided to try and set me up for the murder. First, through Lockridge, she leaked to the sheriff that I had talked about Brennerman to her the night before and also that I had mentioned the Majors connection. A lie, of course, but a nice touch. Then she got the murder weapon from Carter and planted it in my apartment."

"What!"

"Another nice touch, eh? The sheriff and some of his boys paid me a 'surprise' visit about eleven-thirty last night. Lo and behold, they find the gun that did old Harlow in cleverly hidden under my sofa. Of course, they haven't had a chance to run ballistics tests yet, but you can count on it that it's the gun, all right. So Elizabeth's winging it at this point, but she's damn good. Once she realized that she couldn't keep Brennerman's connection to the Majors family quiet, she did a quick about-face and essentially told the sheriff herself. At the same time, she started planting evidence here and there to make them ignore that aspect of the case and concentrate on me instead. Lockridge meanwhile doesn't care who takes the rap so long as he doesn't get sucked down the tubes with them."

"This is all so hard to believe."

"Believe it, Sarah Jane. These people are totally ruthless when it comes to protecting their share of the big pie."

She stared at her cup. "I need something a little stronger in this mud. You?"

"Well, maybe just a taste. Jameson if you have it."

She fetched the whiskey.

"Bushmills okay?" she asked.

"It'll do."

We vitalized our coffee.

"So," Sarah Jane said, "why aren't you in jail?"

"My charm, of course. Also, I happen to have an airtight alibi."

"Good. I don't care what it is so long as you have it." She chewed on her lip. "Now I hope there isn't anything else."

"I'm afraid there is."

She groaned. "Are you trying to cause the death of a senior citizen?"

"Sarah Jane"—I laughed—"you're a senior citizen about as much as Alexander Haig is a great statesman."

"All right, let's have it." She smiled. "What's a couple more heart seizures among friends?"

"Lockridge tried to make Leigh have sex with him."

"The son of a bitch." Her expression was grim. Old Carter was in trouble now. "Did she get him in the balls?"

" 'Fraid not. She did, however, repulse his advances."

"The bastard'll pay for this."

"The best way we can make him pay is to pin Brennerman's murder on him. If I can get the pieces fitted together properly. Try this on: when Leigh rejected him, Lockridge got abusive." She nodded in a way that indicated she knew about his abusiveness. "He apparently called her a few nasty names, the usual stuff. But he also insinuated that he might be her natural father." I raised my eyebrows.

"I'll kill him, I—"

"What do you think? Any chance it's true?"

She deflated again. "I don't know," she said wearily. "Anything's possible. He knew about John well before Leigh was born. If we assume that he blackmailed Elizabeth for sex right from the start, then there's no reason it couldn't be true. Hell, he might not have even *had* to blackmail her. Like I told you, John and Elizabeth don't exactly add up to a sexual dynamo. It's hard to see him as my own son at times, but that's *one* thing at least that I *am* sure of."

"If it *is* true," I said, "it would give Lockridge a double hold over Elizabeth. He could bleed her dry."

"My heart goes out to her."

"I'm touched by your concern . . . So what we need to know is why the Colonel went to see Lockridge recently. You got any ideas?"

She thought it over. "Well, the thing that first occurs is that he might have wanted to rewrite part of his will. But I don't have the foggiest why, or what it might mean to Lockridge and Elizabeth."

"Yeah, that's a definite possibility. Another one that occurred to me is that Brennerman went first to the Colonel, who went immediately to his lawyer."

"Maybe," she said, "but I doubt it. The old crow would probably have shot him on the spot. He's still quite a marksman, I believe, as is Elizabeth, by the way."

"In any case, I guess the Colonel is the man to ask. Think he'd tell me?"

144

"If you let him know about Lockridge trying to make Leigh. On second thought, you'd better not. The Colonel would likely blow Carter's head off for something like that."

"Okay," I said, "the only question left is, How do we tie Delmos Venable in? Any thoughts on that?"

"Not a one. Are you sure that thing's connected? Delmos does have other enemies."

Yeah, I thought, that he does. The White Brothers.

"I'm not *sure* of anything. But I assume a connection until convinced otherwise."

"If Carter's that deep in this, I may kill him myself."

"If he is—and he may well be—the state'll do you one better, Sarah Jane. They'll lock him away someplace where he'll be humiliated and sexually abused every day of the rest of his life until he's too old for anyone to care anymore."

"Good."

"Well, it's a fate I wouldn't wish on my worst enemy, but I do sympathize with your views."

"Time to get to work now, Swift," she reminded me.

"Right you are. Next time let's do breakfast again."

"You get those two put away and you've got a month of free breakfasts coming."

"You're on," I said.

• • •

We broke up and I went outside. It was cold and overcast, with a few random snowflakes swirling about and maybe a half an inch on the ground. I realized that I needed to get some food into my battered face before I did anything else. I headed for a greasy spoon just off the downtown mall.

On my way, I had to cross Court Square. There it seemed like there was a cop on every street corner. That fit. Court Square would be the first place they'd think to protect. What good would it do to arrest the doers of wrong if you had no court to try them in?

I got to the restaurant without being challenged, although I received several suspicious eyeballings. You tend to forget that you look like hell in spite of how bad you feel and in spite of the way people react to you. But even today I could look the way I did and walk through Court Square without question. It's strange. If my skin was a little bit darker, I'm sure I never would have made it to breakfast. What a world.

While I waited for my eggs and home fries, I read through the special edition of the *Depressor*.

Jonesy and crew must have worked like maniacs all night to get the thing out. The entire front page was stories concerning the murder and/or the riot. Related stories were scattered throughout the first section. Section 2 is mostly sports and classified. I turned instinctively to the sports pages and read them through. Not much there. An analysis of how Virginia stacked up against Carolina if Delmos couldn't play was probably the highlight. Not very well, was the answer. Surprise!

In section 1, I found an assortment of the predictable, the insulting and the banal. A lead story so dry it might have been ripped off the AP wire rather than written by an eyewitness. I wondered if the *Press* news reporters had been afraid to go out into the streets. A bold headline declaring, "Black Leader Courted Disaster," followed by a disgusting story that suggested that Ward Williams might somehow have been to *blame* for his own murder without ever actually coming out and saying it. A self-righteous editorial condemning "senseless violence" with no shred of empathy for what the people involved might be feeling. I didn't know a single intelligent person who thought of the *Press* as anything but an abysmal joke, at best. Here was why. If Jonesy wanted an entrée to the *Washington Post*, he needed a better springboard than this.

It was so bad that I almost didn't make it to page 7.

There, sandwiched between the movie schedules and the social notices, I found a short article by the staff's lone black writer. He'd been assigned to do a filler piece on Delmos Venable. It figured. Take the only man you have who might understand what's going on in the streets and put him on something else.

The story was accompanied by a small photo of Delmos leaving the hospital, head bandaged, flanked by his parents. I started to read, then stopped and stared at the picture. What was it about them?

Suddenly, it came to me, the thing that I'd known all along that was so important I couldn't see it. The thing that just might tie Delmos into the whole unlikely sequence. I felt a rush like you must get if you dig needles and amphetamine is your drug of choice.

My mind started making connections, and it didn't stop until it had everything linked up. It was still just a theory, of course. But it was a hell of a theory. The biggest mystery in this case was why it had taken me so damnably long to see the light.

I wolfed down the rest of my eggs and fries and made for the nearest telephone. The Colonel was in, and he'd see me. He probably thought I'd reconsidered about spying on Elizabeth's sexual habits.

Of course, I hadn't.

What I'd seen in that photo, and what should have struck me two days earlier, was the shades of color involved. George Venable was a dark black man. Vonda was lighter, true. But Delmos was lighter still, the color of coffee with a bit of cream in it.

Okay, I know there are a lot of reasons why such things happen, but in this case one explanation made a great deal more sense than any other.

Next I called Storm Taylor's house. Delmos was in. I told them to tell him I was on my way over and not to go out until I got there. They said he wouldn't be going anywhere. He was sleeping.

Then I called down to Sikhland.

"How're you doing?" I asked Leigh.

"I'm fine," she said. "I feel much better since I talked to you. You were right about opening up to someone."

She hadn't heard.

"Good. I'm arranging things on this end. I'll be down to get you, but it may not be until tonight."

"Have you spoken to him?" she asked.

"Yes. I'll tell you about it later. I'm in kind of a rush now." No point in worrying her unnecessarily.

• • •

The Taylors lived in a quiet, upper-middle-class neighborhood a couple of blocks south of University Hall. Storm answered the door. A tall man who'd played college ball himself, known as a southern gentleman of impeccable manners off the court. Under game conditions, he was transformed: fiery, involved every second of play, a referee baiter. Also a winner.

"Mr. Swift," he said. "I owe you thanks for what you're doing in this matter."

147

"No need," I said. "I like the kid."

"As do I. I hope that your business with him won't take too long. He's had a rather trying twenty-four hours."

"It shouldn't."

"Good. Under the circumstances— Uh, how much do you know, Mr. Swift?"

"I know about the death threat, if that's what you mean."

"That's what I mean. Considering that, I think it best that we keep Delmos under wraps for a while. He can see Miss Majors after the threats are . . . dealt with. Perhaps you could keep her from rushing up here."

"I'll do what I can. I agree that the kid needs protection."

"Thank you again. Now come with me, please. We'll see if he's awake."

Taylor took me down into the basement. He maintained a small apartment there. It was tidy and had its own private entrance.

"There's a police officer on duty outside," Taylor explined. "Anyone who tried to come in through the house would have to get past me."

He said it as if he wouldn't be easy to get past. I believed him. We got Delmos up, and then Taylor left us alone.

"Swift," Delmos said.

"In the flesh. Or what's left of it."

He smiled. "For sure, you don't look so hot."

"You look kind of beat yourself."

"It was a long night. I was on the street until dawn. Maybe it wasn't the best thing to do in my condition, but I think we helped some. I been out like a light since I got back."

"Well, you helped *me* some, at least."

Sitting there, chitchatting, I realized again how fond I'd become of Delmos, and not just because he'd saved my life. This was a genuine person, someone who'd managed to avoid layering on the kind of bullshit most of us need to protect ourselves. I don't meet many people like that in my trade. Probably wouldn't meet many no matter what I did.

I also realized that I wasn't going to do what I'd set out to do. I'd intended to work Delmos around to the subject of his parentage. Maybe he could confirm what I suspected without my having to ask him directly. Well, maybe he could, but we weren't going to talk

148

about it today. I just didn't have the heart. The Colonel could tell me what I wanted to know.

"How's Leigh?" he asked. "Have you talked to her?"

"She's fine. I spoke to her a few minutes ago. She hasn't heard about anything that's going on up here."

"Not about me, either?"

I shook my head. "I figured it was best not to tell her over the phone. I'll go down there tonight and explain everything. Then she can decide if she wants to ride back here with me or what."

"That sounds good. I do miss her, though."

"I know you do. My guess is that when she finds out, she's going to want to come play nurse for you."

"Long as I get to play doctor."

I laughed. "You know," I said, "for someone your age you've got a very dirty mind."

"Count on it."

"Let me just warn you that it gets worse as you get older." I savored a quick little fantasy of my own. "But seriously, Storm thinks you ought to stay in seclusion for a while. I agree with him."

"You know about the White Brothers thing?"

"Yeah, I heard."

"You think they did this?" He pointed at his bandaged head.

"As of now, we'd better assume it, because even if they didn't, they might. They hate you enough, apparently. But there are other possibilities. I'm looking into them."

"Who?"

"I can't tell you yet. I'm still pursuing the lead, such as it is. If I'm right, though, we'll have the person soon. If not, the cops'll eventually break that White Brother down at the Security Complex. One way or the other, you'll be safe before too long. Think you and Leigh can postpone your reunion for a bit?"

"I don't know," he grumbled. "Besides, the people may need me—"

"You've done your part. More than. You got shot in the head only yesterday. Your assailant's still at large. People will understand if you need some time to rest up."

"Well . . ."

"One day, okay? I'll be in touch first thing in the morning, to let you know what Leigh and I have worked out."

149

"All right."

"Good. Now I've got to get moving. There's a lot to do."

"Thanks, Swift."

"Just remember my tickets to the game Saturday, will you? I'll need two." I thought of Patrick. "No, make it three."

He smiled. Shyly, almost. How could anyone want to kill him?

"No problem," he said.

I left by the apartment's private entrance. The plainclothes cop was leaning against the outside wall, trying to look like he wasn't freezing his buns off. We nodded to each other. Between him and Taylor they ought to be able to make Delmos stay put. Which relieved me of a worry I definitely didn't want.

Before heading for the Majors estate, I needed a phone. I drove to a nearby Seven-Eleven and put in a second call to Sikhland. Bruce answered.

"Is Leigh back in her room?" I asked.

"Yes. Why?"

"I don't want her to overhear."

"Overhear what?"

"Listen, Ali Gupta, do you all have TV or radio down there?"

"We prefer not to."

"How about the paper?"

"Once a week. On Sunday. What's going on, Swift?"

"A lot, take my word for it. Okay. Please do me a favor. If you hear any news from Charlottesville today, don't tell Leigh about it."

"What's going *on?*"

"I can't say. Not right now." I couldn't afford to take the chance, not with brother Ali. "Just trust me. Please. I'll be down there later today, and I'll make it all clear, honestly. But I need your help."

"I don't know about this."

"If you hear something, you'll understand. Believe me, it'll be better if she doesn't find out just yet."

"No promises, Swift."

"Ali."

"What?"

"Your father fired me last night. I don't think he likes me anymore. It's . . . Leigh I'm working for now."

He paused. Then he said, "I'm still not sure I have any reason to trust you. We'll see." And he hung up.

There's no trust left in the world, I thought to myself. Right, and why should there be?

I phoned my answering service.

Patricia Ryan had called and wanted me to call back. Be still, my beating heart.

"Swift Investigations, at your service, ma'am," I said when I had Lockridge & Lee on the line.

"Loren," she said in a soft voice, "what is going on?"

Must be the question of the day. Two out of three had asked it now.

"Why the whisper?" I asked. "If it's to lay some sweet nothings on me, don't bother. I've heard them all before."

"I can't talk now," she said, just as softly as before. "Can you meet me after work?"

"Sure. Your place or mine?"

"The Jefferson. Five o'clock?"

"It's a date."

"I've got to go. See you then."

I stared at the dead phone. Not a human being. Just a bunch of wires and black plastic.

" 'Bye, lover," I said to it.

· 8 ·

The Colonel received me in his library once again. Three visits to the house and I'd seen exactly three rooms. They were certainly creatures of habit, this family.

The Colonel had aged badly since I'd last seen him. He sat listlessly behind the desk and paid me only token notice when Deya showed me into the room. Whereas two days ago he'd seemed like a predator, alert and probing, today he was more like the prey. I knew then that in my roundabout way I had stumbled on the truth.

"Sit down, Switft," he said with no discernible enthusiasm.

I sat in the padded leather chair. We looked at each other for a while, but it wasn't me that he was seeing. He was near the end of the long slide, and he knew it; what he saw was the large vat of shit at the bottom.

Finally, he focused on my face.

"Jeezis," he said, "what happened to you?"

"I was in the right place, but it was definitely the wrong time."

"The riot?"

"Yeah."

"I don't want to hear about it." He brushed the possibility aside with his hand, as if that's the only thing he'd been hearing about for the previous seventeen years.

"Good. I'm not that keen on talking about it, anyway."

"If you came to take the job," he said, "I'm not sure it's open anymore. I've had kind of a rough couple of days. But thanks for finding my granddaughter."

"I don't need a job," I said. "As for finding your granddaughter,

152

that was easy. What's gonna be hard is what comes next. And I understand about the past two days."

He looked at me sharply for the first time.

"I do believe the young man has something on his mind," he said, folding hands over belly. "Please continue."

"Sure. First off, I don't need to spy on Elizabeth, and you don't need me to. The man she's been sleeping with, or one of them at least, is your very own personal lawyer."

"Lockridge."

"Well, you've just won the Name-That-Man Contest, but that's about all the information is worth. The truth is that Elizabeth is up to her neck in matters a bit more serious."

"Like what?" The Colonel was himself again. The fragile old ears were taking in every word, and the dark hawk's eyes were shining.

"Like murder."

"What!"

"It's a little complicated," I said, "but it begins with Elizabeth and Lockridge. They've been in cahoots for some time, siphoning off money from your estate. Somehow." Never tell them more than they need to know. "In addition to sleeping together, of course, so I'm sure John had nothing to do with it. The scam began to unravel when a man named Harlow Brennerman tumbled to it."

"Never heard of him."

"You wouldn't've. He was a California P.I. who was here on a different case and one way or another got wind of what they were up to. He tried to use what he'd learned to cut himself in, and they killed him."

"They?"

"Well, Lockridge actually pulled the trigger, but Elizabeth knew about it and helped plan it."

"Just like that."

"Not exactly. I have reason to believe that they might not have reacted so decisively if it hadn't been for you."

"Me?"

"I'm sorry, Colonel, like I said. But I think what set them off was the visit you paid to Lockridge last week. What did you two talk about, if I may ask?"

He stared at me without the slightest bit of affection. That really wasn't fair. Here I was, attempting to rid him of someone he couldn't stand, and he was making me feel like the messenger in those old plays who gets his head chopped off for bringing the king the rotten news.

When he continued to stare, I said, "I'm trying to put a pair of murderers away, Colonel. You're not on trial here."

"It don't have nothing to do with it," he said finally.

"I think it does."

"Ah, you wouldn't understand, anyway."

"Try me."

"It don't matter."

"Yes, it does. Colonel, you've got a murderer for a lawyer, and you've got his accomplice living under your own roof. What makes you think you aren't on their list of undesirables?"

"They wouldn't have the nerve."

"Yes, they would. They've already proven it. Now what did you and Lockridge talk about?"

"I told you it don't matter."

This was getting us exactly nowhere. I took a deep breath and said the words he didn't want to hear.

"Delmos Venable."

"You'd best explain yourself, Swift," he said with a look that would have turned even Doris Day into the original Ice Princess.

"Like I said before, I understand how rough the past two days have been for you."

"How could you?"

"Because I know how you feel about Delmos."

"You don't know nothing. That boy is like a son to me. When I heard that somebody's trying to kill him, it sickened me."

"Yes, but it's not quite that simple, is it?"

"Meaning?"

"Meaning that 'like' isn't the word we're really looking for."

"How much do you know?" he said. The cold anger was gone, replaced by resignation.

"Enough," I said. "Here's the way it looks to me. I think that twenty years ago you found yourself with a beautiful young housekeeper who happened to be black. I think you had an affair with her and that she got pregnant. Accepting paternity would have been out of the question for you. So she married someone else, then had the kid. Maybe her husband even knows who the father is. But everyone's kept their mouths shut because you've secretly arranged

154

that she be well taken care of over the years. It hasn't mattered. Until now. I think that you've begun to feel guilty about not providing for your unacknowledged son in case you should pass on. So I think you went to Carter Lockridge to write a new version of your will, cutting Delmos in. Am I on the right track?"

"Who told you all this?"

"Colonel, you forget that I'm in the investigation business. I do this every day of the world that I have a job to work on. And it's a rare day that I get any hard facts to play with. Mostly I have to make deductions. That's all I'm doing here. I don't know any of these things for certain, but they fit into the framework of what I *do* know better than any of the other possible guesses."

"You're a pretty good guesser, young Swift."

"Thanks, but it's going to be a whole lot easier if I could stop guessing now and start to deal with what really happened. I'd like for you to talk to me. Unfortunately, I can't promise you complete confidentiality. I'd like to, but if any of this becomes relevant to the sheriff's murder investigation, I'll have to tell him what I know. That's ground rule number one. All I *can* say is that I'll do my damndest to keep things quiet."

"No need. I'm not ashamed. He's a hell of a kid."

"Yes, he is."

"But I suppose it would be better for Vonda if it didn't come out."

"Probably."

"All right," he said wearily, "all right.

"You know most of the story already. Vonda Sims at twenty-four was the most beautiful girl I'd ever seen—black, white, red, or purple. She was also the best lay I've ever had. We did it every day and every whichaway, and the fact that we couldn't let anybody find out only made it more exciting. It went on for a year before she got pregnant. What a year. I was fifty at the time, understand, but it just might've been the youngest year of my whole life.

"Anyway, when she did get pregnant, I was all for saying to hell with what people think and coming out into the open. But she wouldn't hear of it. Said it would be the worst thing for everybody. Maybe she was right, but if I had it to do over, I never would of let her get away. Hell, once we got into the nineteen sixties, people were screwing across the color line everywhere, even in the Old South.

"So it didn't work out. She married George Venable, who'd been asking her forever. He knew she was pregnant, but he didn't care as long as she was with him from then on. And she was. We never laid hand nor foot on each other ever after. She told George that she was pregnant because she'd gotten drunk one night and slept with a high yella from Lynchburg, which was a smart thing to do because no way the kid was gonna be as dark as she is. She said it was a one-night stand and the guy would never be around again. George bought it. He was so happy to marry her, she could've told him anything and he would've said it didn't make any difference.

"Maybe, over the years, George guessed. I'd promised Vonda that Delmos would have the best of everything, including a good education, and it's a promise I had no trouble with. I kept her on here for a long time. Gave George a job, too. Whenever they needed anything, they got it. In cash, of course. We were very careful; no one ever found out that I know of. After a while, it didn't matter anymore. It became evident that Delmos was something special as a ballplayer and wouldn't be needing my help to get his education. He had a full scholarship anyplace he wanted to go. I was tickled that he chose to stay in Charlottesville, where I could go to every game.

"But then one day I got to thinking. Suppose something happened to him and he couldn't play ball no more. That's not so rare. They get their knees tore up, and suddenly it's all over. What then? And what if I wasn't around to help out? Maybe he'd want to go to graduate school—he's smart enough, you know—and the basketball money wouldn't be there. I couldn't let that happen, Swift.

"So, like you said, I went to Lockridge to make a few changes to my will, mostly giving Delmos his fair share."

The lengthy retelling of the story had taken it out of him. He was slumped in his chair like the Thinker after a particularly thoughtful day. But I got the feeling he was relieved, too. I decided to give him a rest.

"You have any whiskey in here?" I asked. It seemed like a safe bet. Every other room in the house had a bar. "I think we could use a drink."

"Right you are," he said.

He opened a cabinet behind him, pulled outo a bottle of Jack Daniels and a couple of glasses, and poured two stiff shots. We drank in silence.

I looked around me. Old books. Old furniture. Old people. The

156

windowless room was like a crypt. I had a sudden fear that some malevolent deity would freeze the scene exactly like it was and we'd pass eternity this way, him telling his story over and over again, me listening. It made me want out of the house as soon as possible.

I looked back at the Colonel. The whiskey had revived him.

"Thank you for telling me," I said.

"It don't matter." He did his hand-waving dismissal again. "We got more important things to talk about. Suppose I was to hire you?"

"I told you I—"

"Listen up, boy. I don't need you to spy on Elizabeth anymore, obviously. I want you to find who's after my son."

"You don't have to hire me for that. I'll do it for free. So will the cops. People care about him, you know."

"All right. But I'll still pay you if you find the bastard. Now who do you think done it?"

"I don't know."

"You think somebody like these White Brothers, the ones who killed Williams?"

Once again I had to decide whether or not to tell someone about the threatening note. This time, since I was dealing with the boy's father, the person had somewhat more of a right to know. But again I decided against it. It wouldn't serve any useful purpose. Besides, I was becoming more and more convinced that it wasn't a White Brother who had pulled the trigger early Wednesday morning.

"It's a possibility," I said.

"I thought so, too."

"People like that wouldn't think too highly of his political activities. But you've got to figure the cops are looking in that direction. They're not dumb. I'd best stay out of it until I see what they come up with."

"Okay. Say, you know any of those boys personally?"

"No."

"Well, I can probably get you a name or two if it turns out you have to go that way. You let me know."

"Thanks."

"Swift," he said, fixing me with the predator's eye, "do you think Lockridge might have did it?"

"He could have," I said. "If my theory is correct and your changing the will threatened his little game, whatever it was, then he had motive. Plus I'm certain that he killed Brennerman. That would

157

have been easy for him, and it shows that he's not afraid of taking life. But Delmos was a little close to home, a little more likely to bring suspicion down on him at some future point. And you've got to consider that the Lawn is a hard area to get in and out of without being seen by somebody. Even at that hour. He's a careful man; I doubt he would have taken the risk."

"Elizabeth, then?"

I couldn't meet his eyes. He was waiting to jump on the answer to that one.

"I think not." I lied. In fact, she was number one on my suspect list. But I didn't have the slightest bit of evidence. The Colonel was apt to make speculation into fact, and I couldn't chance his taking matters into his own hands.

"And for many of the same reasons," I went on. "In addition to which, although she's nasty enough, I just don't believe she has the guts." That'd be the day. "She usually finds someone else to do her dirty work for her."

"Are you suggesting she hired someone?"

"No, not really. I think she's up to her neck in the Brennerman thing, but not this one. Hiring a gun is not a simple matter, and the chance of it coming back to haunt you is way too great."

"Then it's someone unconnected to the family?"

"That's my best guess at the moment."

He chewed on that for a while. I think he was disappointed. He'd wanted it to be somebody he could personally lay his hands on.

"Just find the bastard," he said suddenly.

"I'll try," I said. "First thing to do is nail Elizabeth and Lockridge for the Brennerman murder. I'm a little lacking in hard evidence there, so we'll have to work on it. In the process we may turn up something that goes beyond it."

"I'll help you all I can."

"Good. I may need it. Would you be willing to talk to Ridley Campbell if it comes down to it?"

"Whatever."

"Okay. Now, there's . . . Leigh."

"What's the matter? You said she was all right."

"She is. But now, well . . . the reason she disappeared was that she and Delmos had fallen in love and she needed some time alone to sort things out."

"Oh, Jesus."

"Yeah, I know. She's going to require some taking care of."

"Has she heard yet?"

"About the shooting? I don't think so. They don't have a TV down there, and they don't get the paper. So she hadn't heard earlier today. I'll be checking with her later. Then sometime tonight I'll go down and get her. But to tell you the truth, I don't think the attempted murder is going to be as bad on her as the other thing."

"What other thing?"

"The relationship. She and Delmos are"—I did some quick figuring—"uncle and niece, or something like that."

"Jesus, Swift, do we have to tell her?"

"C'mon Colonel, these kids are in love. They may be thinking about marriage, children. Is it the sort of thing that should be kept from them?"

"I guess not." He sighed. More bad news, and yet more.

"Unless—"

"What?"

"Unless they're not really related."

"What!?"

"I have reason to believe that John may not be Leigh's father."

"My God. Where in the hell did you pick that up?"

"I can't tell you that. But I promise you, I'll do my best to find out whether it's true."

"I'm not sure I want to know." He sighed. "What difference does it make, anyway? She'll always be my granddaughter to me."

"Look on the bright side, Colonel. If it's true, none of the other need ever come out. There'd be no point in dredging it up." On the dark side, of course, it would mean that Leigh was carrying some very bad genes. But no one ever said you couldn't overcome the forces of heredity. Whoever her parents turned out to be, Leigh was already proof of that.

My last remark had failed to cheer the Colonel up. He looked beaten. No wonder. The Majors family's sexual past was a real quagmire. The trip through it must have worn him out, and he didn't even know about John yet. I held that part back. The old bigot may have richly deserved to hear the worst, but it just wasn't in me to tell him.

159

"All right," he said finally, "what happens next? You going to bring Leigh back here?"

"No. I don't think either John or Elizabeth will be able to give her what she needs."

"I agree. Elizabeth doesn't care. John does, but his understanding is . . . limited."

"That's about the way I see it."

"What do you propose?"

"I think the best place for her is with her grandmother. At least until things quiet down a little."

He nodded. "Good choice. Sarah Jane'll stand by her through anything."

"Okay. Now there's just one other thing." I paused.

"Get to it, boy." He'd had enough.

"Well . . . there *is* the possibility that you might be in some . . . danger."

"Oh, horse crap!"

"No, I mean it, Colonel. Now that everything's coming apart for Carter and Elizabeth, there's no telling what they may do. The timing would be bad for them, but you never know. The sheriff's gonna be looking in on you. Just in case."

"I can take care of myself."

"I'm sure. But it mightn't be a bad idea to stick close to John for a while. And you should definitely be on your guard if Lockridge shows up here. In fact, call me if he does. If you can't get me, call Ridley Campbell."

"Don't worry. I'm a better shot than any of these peckerwoods."

"Easy, Colonel," I said. "Let's keep the body count where it is if we can. I think it would be best if you don't talk to anybody about all of this. Can I depend on you?"

"Talk?" he snorted. "To this bunch? Fat chance."

"That's it, then." I stood up. "The next time you see me, I may have the sheriff in tow. In the meantime, just be careful."

He poured himself another tumbler of whiskey and raised the glass to me, saying, "Now go find the bastard, Swift." Then he took a long, hard swallow. I knew who he meant.

"He'll get found," I said. "Maybe not by me, but he'll get found." Or she will.

• • •

On my way out S.R. 666, I picked my way through the Majors mess.

It was intricately convoluted, and yet it wasn't. Because at the most basic level each aspect of the case boiled down to the same thing. Greed. The old bottom line. As simple and banal as that.

First came the Colonel, driven by his desire to become a land baron and, privately, by his hunger for the sexual favors of black women. A caricature of the Southern male through three centuries of history.

And Sarah Jane. Even she, much as I liked her, wasn't untouched. In return for her economic successes, she'd had to make a devil's bargain with the Colonel, one that required forty years of silent support for the initial lie on which it was based.

Then John. His affluence, too, was founded on the lie, and over the years he'd had to totally armor himself against the world in order to preserve it.

Carter Lockridge. Sucking the blood of the family for twenty years. He'd used sex, then blackmail, to consolidate his position. Eventually, it had come to murder, and he'd embraced that like a long-lost lover.

Finally, Elizabeth. Perhaps the toughest of the lot, she'd held on to what she had through a loveless marriage, the enmity of her in-laws, and twenty years of blackmail by her lover. And all of it had only served to make her more ruthless and clever than before. She'd managed in the end to manipulate even the slippery Lockridge into a less strategic position by convincing him to commit murder. True, it was information she could never use without exposing her role as an accessory, but it at least put her on an equal footing with him in the shifting power dynamics of the situation.

What a crew.

And the stigma continued on into the next generation. Son Bruce raged at his parents and dropped out to spend his time playing war games with automatic weapons. Melissa deadened the misery of her life with Quaaludes, coke, booze, and indiscriminate sex.

Only Leigh and Delmos seemed to have escaped. And now one was on the verge of a nervous breakdown, and the other was dodging bullets.

Who was after him?

That was as far as I got with the train of thought when the green

Mustang appeared in my rearview mirror. She was gunning it and closing fast. That wasn't the smartest thing to do on a narrow road slick with light snow dusted over occasional patches of ice.

But driving safety didn't appear to be one of her primary considerations at the moment.

I pulled as far to the right as I could to let her pass. Instead, Melissa settled in dead on my rear bumper, less than three feet back, and matched me move for move. When I slowed, she nudged Clementine forward again. I could see her face clearly now; it was like some deranged Halloween mask. She was stoned out of her tree on a combination of drugs that only God knew about for sure. It would be just my luck to be on the scene when she went around the final bend of the yellow brick drug road and into the perpetual darkness of terminal mind warp. She frightened me more than the six black kids with their three hundred years of pent-up anger.

I swerved suddenly to the left, but she followed me easily, giving me another friendly nudge in the process. I swerved back. The old VW was no match for her car. Whatever Melissa wanted, we were going to play by her rules.

We crested a hill and entered a long straightaway that sloped slightly downward. She whacked me once more from behind, soundly enough to snap my head back, then pulled out next to me. I looked over and wished I hadn't. Her face was as cold and remote as a distant star. Calmly, she raised the middle finger of her right hand. Her detached expression gave way to a soundless manic laughter, but it was with the mouth only; there was no humor in her eyes.

I braked, but not quickly enough. She swerved right and hit Clementine on the left fender, hard, then took off down the road. The combination of braking and being sideswiped put the VW into a nasty spin. I fought it as best I could, turning into the skid, but it was hopeless. Clementine's handling characteristics range from fair to poor in the best of times, and this was not one of them. The car slid across the shoulder into a drainage ditch, slamming against the embankment. One of the front wheels ended up off the ground, and it spun slowly to a stop.

I opened my eyes and found myself looking back the way I'd come. The road was empty.

Slowly, I unbuckled the seat belt and checked for damages. I'd hit my forearm on the steering wheel. There'd be some bruises on my shoulder and belly from the belt. My ribs ached worse than before. That was it. A few minor additions to the agony inventory. No problem.

I got out.

Things couldn't have been much worse. There was no way to extricate Clementine without a tow truck. I was still over a mile from U.S. 29, on a seldom-used secondary road. It was cold and snowing a little, with the promise of more to come any old time.

I swore up and down at the crazy little bitch.

When that didn't do any good, I started for the highway on foot.

• • •

The people at the family grocery on U.S. 29 were becoming old friends. I cashed in a buck and went out to the phone booth.

My very first call was to the sheriff's office. I was still mad as hell at Melissa Majors.

A woman answered the phone.

"Ridley, please," I said. "This is Loren Swift."

"I'm sorry, sir," she said. "Sheriff Campbell isn't in the office at the moment. Could one of the deputies help?"

"Yeah, I guess so."

"Hold a moment, please."

There was a bunch of clickings and electronic whatnots and a long pause. Then a familiar voice came on the line.

"Well, well," it said, "if it isn't the fearless detective. And what can the law do for you today?"

Christ. It was Thurman. I promised myself that I wouldn't mouth off to cops anymore. It was a promise I'd never be able to keep, but I made it, anyway, with the finest intentions, just in case the patron saint of P.I.s happened to be listening.

"Look, Thurman," I said, "I know you don't like me, but I've got something here that's serious cop business."

"What's that? One of your faggot boyfriends mark you up again?" Such a clever fellow.

"No, it's a girl this time. Her name's Melissa Majors, and she drives a green Mustang, one of the old ones." I gave him the license number. "She tried to run me into a tree with her car. She's crazy, and she shouldn't be on the road. I suggest you pick her up before she does kill someone. I'll come down and file an assault charge later."

"Aw, poor Swifty." He chuckled. "The bad little girl didn't hurt him, did she?" I think he might actually have said "wittle." Jesus.

"Thurman," I said patiently, "the girl is bonkers. Can you get that through your thick skull? She's taking who knows what drugs, and she's stoned out of her gourd. She's dangerous, I guarantee it. For Christ's sake, pick her up, will you?"

"Well, we're awfully busy this afternoon, you know, with the disturbances and all. I'll have to see."

"Just do it! Ridley will have your ass if you don't, I swear he will."

"Oooooh, I'm afraid. I better get right on that little old thing. See you real soon, Swifty." His voice dripped with anticipation of our first meeting alone in a dark alley.

"Thurman—"

He hung up.

I cursed and banged the receiver against the coin box, then remembered that I didn't want to break my only means of communication with the outside world.

The nearest towing service that I knew of operated out of a small station on the southern edge of town, about ten miles away. I called them. The man told me he'd be out in a half hour or so. Sure.

Then I called my answering service. Nothing there.

Next I called Patricia.

"Something's come up," I said. "I may be a little late."

"What is it?" She sounded worried.

"Not much. Somebody just tried to kill me, is all."

"Loren!"

"Easy, kid." I laughed. I really shouldn't say such things. "They didn't succeed, as you can hear. Just a drunken hit-and-run driver. I'm fine, but my car will take some getting back on the road."

"Does this have anything to do with that crazy Majors family?"

"How'd you guess?"

"It's not funny. They're *insane*, Loren!"

"My God, I never would have suspected. Crazy people masquerading as normal? Right here in our very own Charlottesville? There's something terribly wrong with the world if that's the case."

"Jesus," she said, "you're incorrigible."

"Take it slow on the compliments, please; they go to my head. Anyway, I don't know *what* time I'm going to make it into town. Depends on what happens with Clementine."

"Who's Clementine?"

164

"Oh. My car."

"Clementine?"

"It's a long story. I'll tell you sometime. So how about if I drop by your place when I can?"

"Sure, that's fine. See you then."

"Ah, Patricia."

"Yes."

"Well, where do you live, or should I just follow the scent of smoldering passion?"

She laughed and gave me an address in the northern part of Charlottesville. A nice neighborhood but not too fancy.

"I'd been hoping for Belmont," I said.

"That where you live?"

"Yup."

"Alas, we're not all so choosy. 'Bye."

I made my last call.

"Jonesy," I said when I got him on the line, "this is Swift. Anything new on the Venable case?"

"A little. I heard a rumor that the cops turned up a witness, some student who couldn't sleep and was looking out her window about two in the morning. She saw someone around Delmos's window but was looking away when she heard the shot. Couldn't say much more than that, except that the visitor seemed to be a woman. It doesn't help a whole lot, since we still have half the human race to suspect, but it considerably diminishes the chances the White Brothers were in on it. I've asked around. Everyone seems to agree that this particular group isn't too keen on women. As their name implies."

"I'd had trouble believing it, anyway."

"Do tell. What else you got?"

"Not yet, Jonesy. It's still a lot of speculation. Nothing more."

"Okay, pal. Just don't forget me."

"I won't. Thanks."

So it was Elizabeth, after all. True, there was no guarantee the White Brothers wouldn't take a shot at Delmos at some future point. But they hadn't taken this one. It was up to the cops to see that they never had a follow-up chance.

I examined the puzzle, carefully fitting the pieces.

If everything goes according to plan, Elizabeth kills Delmos, while

165

Lockridge knocks off Brennerman. Pretty extreme measures. But then there's a lot of money at stake. The Delmos killing is the most sensible from their point of view. With Delmos out of the way the Colonel's will change becomes meaningless no matter how long he lives. The portions of the eventual pie become substantially enlarged.

The other killing makes less sense. The best explanation is that it buys them some time before the next investigator heads out looking for John Grimsley. Maybe the new guy won't be as good as Brennerman, and he won't have the benefit of Harlow's notes to start with. Even if he's top notch, the Colonel may die, one way or another, in the interim.

There were some strong motivations there, to be sure. Yet it was difficult to believe that they'd actually planned to commit two murders in one night. And on such short notice. The Delmos complication they'd known about for several days—time to plan things. But Brennerman had walked into their lives the same day he was killed. Maybe Lockridge had only intended to scare him off, but things had gotten out of hand. Maybe he didn't know what Elizabeth had in store for Delmos; she might have been doing that on her own. Maybe Lockridge *still* didn't know she'd fired the shot.

That could be. Because most likely she had a patsy set up for the Delmos shooting, the way she had tried to pin Brennerman on me. Maybe, somehow, the fall guy was Lockridge. But then she'd missed. And then the Williams/White Brothers thing had exploded on the scene. That was a godsend. With Delmos alive and the cops beating the bushes for racists, she could relax.

But for how long? She still had to dump Lockridge, if that was her intent. And there was still the problem with the will. She'd have to move on that at some point. Which meant both Delmos and the Colonel remained targets. She wouldn't miss twice.

I whacked the side of the phone booth.

God damn her! Her and her greasy boyfriend. I'd see both of them in the slammer if it was the last thing I did. And her maniac daughter committed to a home for hopeless druggies.

I went back into the grocery store and chewed the fat with the people who ran the place while I waited for the man with the tow truck to show up. We talked about the riot and the murder, the stuff you would expect to be on people's minds.

The truck was two hours getting there. When it finally arrived, the redneck mama driving it pulled my car out of the ditch in a jiffy and hauled her to town.

At the garage they shoved Clementine into a service bay, and I did some more waiting. I felt like someone watching an operation on his hand after the arm's been numbed by a local anesthetic. How, I wondered, did we ever get so attached to our vehicles that we think of them as living extensions of our bodies?

· 9 ·

It had been dark for an hour by the time I got Clementine back on the road. They'd pounded away at her, fixing the fender so it wasn't crushed up against the tire. I'd told them it was important for me to have transportation today and had paid them accordingly.

She ran, but with a bit of a limp.

The last thing the mechanic said to me was "She'll be okay for short hops, but the frame is bent, and that's gonna make for some funky handling. I wouldn't advise doing much driving in this kind of weather before you get it straightened out."

I had no choice but to ignore his advice.

The sky around Charlottesville was red again tonight. More fires. I didn't like how that felt, so I drove over to Belmont. This time I parked within spitting distance of my apartment.

When I got inside, I called Jonesy again.

"Nothing new on the investigation," he said, "but that's no surprise."

"The rioting's gotten worse?"

"Boy, you sure don't keep up with the news, do you? It's not worse, only about the same. But that's bad enough. They've torched two more University buildings. Every state trooper that can be spared is in town. Everyone's praying for a big snowstorm. I think the mayor's on the verge of asking the governor to call out the guard if we don't get it soon. But I don't know what they're gonna do if they arrest anyone else. The slammer's full as it is."

"Jesus, Jonesy, I moved here from Boston to get away from this kind of stuff."

"Welcome to the U.S. of A., old buddy. Or as one of my fellow scribblers once put it, every place in the world is exactly like every other place."

"Truman Capote?" I guessed.

"John MacDonald."

"Oh, well. I'm not very literate, as you know."

"Neither is Truman Capote, and it hasn't hurt him none."

"I wouldn't know about that."

"No, you wouldn't. Anyway, the troopers have set up roadblocks here and there. They're stopping anyone who looks suspicious and searching for guns and gasoline and whatnot. I guess it's a necessary step, but the First Amendment people around here are pretty blown away by it all."

"You know the spots?" I was going to have to be able to get around unimpeded.

He ticked them off. "Let's see, there's one at University and Emmet. One on East High, by Martha Jefferson Hospital. One on West Main, at Ridge. One at JPA and Maury. One on Avon headed in." That one was in Belmont. I must've just missed it driving home. "And a couple more near exits off the By-pass. I think that's the lot. But they could be moving them around, of course."

"Thanks again, Jonesy. I won't forget what I owe you."

"The meter's still running."

"I know. Soon. See you."

I called the sheriff's office.

"The sheriff isn't in," the lady said. "Could one—"

"No, they couldn't. Where is he?"

"I believe he's out in one of the cars, sir."

"All right. This is Loren Swift. Get him on the radio and tell him I have something for him on the Brennerman case. You got that?"

"The Brennerman case."

"Right. Get it to him right away. I guarantee you he'll want to know. Tell him to call me at home." I gave her the number.

"I'll try to reach him, sir."

"Thanks."

Ridley called me back in five minutes.

"Swift," he said, "I told you to stay out of this."

"I'm already in it, Rid. Look, I've turned up some stuff on the Brennerman thing."

"So have I. I paid a little visit to Colonel Majors this afternoon. Seems I didn't miss you by much. Funny thing, on the way out 666 I passed an orange VW in the ditch. Wouldn't've been yours, would it?"

"Of course it was mine. Did you manage to find Melissa?"

"Who?"

"Melissa Majors, for God's sake! Did you pick her up?"

"No. Why should I?"

"Jesus Christ, Ridley, didn't Thurman tell you?"

"Tell me what?" He pronounced each word distinctly.

I got a very bad feeling in my stomach. It just wouldn't do to have that drugged-out maniac running around loose at a time like this. Quickly, I recapped the story for him.

"I see," he said. The way he said them, those two words meant that my pal Thurman was about to catch some very serious hell. "I'll put out an alert."

"Good. How about Elizabeth? Did you question her?"

"She wasn't there this afternoon. I'll try again tonight. I think the Colonel will be safe until then."

"And of course you haven't talked to Lockridge."

"Let me do the sheriff's job, will you, Swift? There are a few more things happening right now than just this case, if you hadn't noticed. I'll get with Lockridge when the time is right.

"Now, what have *you* got for *me*?"

I told him what I'd learned from Sarah Jane.

"Interesting," he said. "But you're still guessing. I need more hard evidence."

"I don't have any yet. Just give me a little time—"

"Swift, I told you once to keep your nose out of this. Now don't jerk me off! Do you have anything else for me or don't you?"

"Tonight, Rid. You'll have the whole thing tonight, as soon as—"

"Goddamit! Where are you, at home?"

"Yeah."

"Stay there."

"I'm sorry, I can't. Where are you gonna be in an hour?"

I could hear him inhaling and exhaling deeply to control his anger. I was very glad that he wasn't currently in the same room with me.

"Get me through the radio," he said finally. "I'll tell them to expect your call."

170

"Okay."

"And Swift, if you screw up, so help me I will personally nail your posterior to the nearest wall."

He rang off.

· · ·

I didn't waste any time. Ridley just might swing by on the off chance of catching me still at home if he was anywhere nearby. I stuck the Police Positive in my jacket pocket. This time it would be different if I was accosted. I didn't plan on shooting anybody, but I sure didn't have any energy to waste fooling around with street punks. One look at the Police Positive and they'd be gone.

Out the door and into the street. No sign of any roving gangs. Or of Sheriff Campbell.

I drove parallel to Avon until I was sure I'd be clear of the road-block; then I rode it on in. I circled around to avoid East High, drove brazenly past Court Square, where there were a couple of cruisers idling, and turned onto Park. I was white, and I was alone. They let me be.

I hurried down Park. Some intuitive sense of urgency was pushing me, though I couldn't have said what for. When I rounded the last bend before the street slopes down to the By-pass, I was going much too fast. I probably wouldn't have spotted the roadblock in time, anyway. As it was, there was nothing to do but come to as graceful a stop as possible.

The trooper looked my car over as he sidled up to the window. I rolled it down. He was carrying a nasty-looking nightstick that he tapped rhythmically into his hand.

When he saw my battered face up close, he said evenly, "Okay, brother, get out nice and slow, will you?" One of his buddies joined him when he said that. The second man's right hand rested on the revolver at his hip. I did as I was told.

They spread-eagled me against the side of the car and patted me down. Naturally, they took away my Police Positive. Then they searched the rest of the car, but there was nothing there they were interested in.

"You got a license for this?" the first trooper said. He held up my gun in case I didn't know what he was talking about.

I reached for my inside jacket pocket.

"May I?" I asked. You never knew with these guys.

171

He nodded.

I got out my credentials and handed them over. He examined them.

"P.I., eh?" he said, proving he could read. The second trooper was looking bored now, idly scratching at his crotch. It's those tight pants they make the smokies wear.

"Only one in town," I said. "You could look it up." I tried to sound like Casey Stengel. It was wasted on this clown. Too young.

"Well, I tell you what . . ." He consulted my license again. Memory wasn't his secret weapon. "I tell you what, Mr. Loren Swift. We got ourselves a situation here that I'm sure you're familiar with. Now I know you got you a right to carry the gun and all, but our orders are to confiscate any firearms not belonging to a state, county, or city police officer, which you ain't either of."

"I'd appreciate it if you didn't do that, sir. I'm on kind of a dangerous case at the moment."

He ignored me. He went over to the cruiser, took out a clipboard, and wrote something down. Then he came back to me, tearing off a sheet of paper.

"Here's a receipt," he said. "You can reclaim your gun at the state police barracks when this is all over."

"Ah, look officer—"

"Sorry. Our orders don't say nothing about the private sector."

"My point exactly. If—"

"Beat it, Swift," he said, flipping my wallet back to me, "before you get on my nerves and I stick you in the can on general principles."

Once again, I did as I was told. My spending the night in jail wasn't an acceptable part of the general scenario.

I drove back to my apartment, avoiding the roadblocks. I circled around, looking for any Ridley Campbells that might be lurking thereabouts. No sign of any. I parked with the motor running, sprinted to the apartment, grabbed the Walther, and sprinted back to the car. When they held the next Olympic trials for the one-hundred-yard gun-retrieval dash, I'd be ready.

This time out I was very, very careful, and I got to Patricia's without incident.

She lived in a small white frame house in a mixed neighborhood of ranches, bungalows, and unpretentious two-story brick jobs. There was a double wide driveway along the side of the house with a

172

narrow paved path leading off it. This turned into a long, gently sloping ramp that you could roll up right to the front door. The door itself was flush with the stoop.

I knocked.

A young man in a wheelchair opened the door. Same eyes, hair about the same color, but lighter. A good bit broader in the shoulders.

"You would be Patrick, then," I said.

"Aye. And you would be Mr. Swift. Patricia said to expect you. Please come in."

He wheeled ahead of me into a small living room. The furniture was secondhand but quality stuff. All wood; not a piece of plastic in sight. My kind of woman. I sat on a sturdy oak chair with foam cushion and back. Comfy and probably better for your spine than the sink-in-up-to-your-waist models I'd gotten used to lately.

"Patricia just got in the shower," Patrick said. "Can I get you something to drink?"

"A beer would be fine."

He went off to the kitchen. I looked around. The house was effectively modified for someone in a wheelchair, but so subtly you might not notice if you didn't know. There were no steps up or down between rooms. No clutter on the floor. The furniture arranged so that movement from here to there was unobstructed. Important items within reach of a seated person. She'd done a masterful job. I was glad she didn't remind me of Marilyn anymore.

Patrick returned with a cold Stroh's and one of those tall V-shaped beer glasses. Pilsener, I think they're called. The beer really hit the spot. I hadn't realized until that moment how burned out I was. I'd had a long, hard day on top of a very bad night, and there was no telling how long it would be before I got any sleep. I stretched my body against the chair and let the alcohol go to work. It was only beer, but almost immediately my muscles began to relax, and the bruises didn't hurt so much. Power of suggestion.

"Tough day?" Patrick said.

"Yeah," I heard myself saying.

"You look it."

"Thanks, kid." I laughed. "You should see the other guys."

" 'Guys?' Hey . . . Macho Man." He said it like Richard Pryor says it in his stage act.

"That's me, all right. One guy, I broke his knuckle with my nose.

173

He was jumping up and down all over the place, what with the pain. He even started crying. Then he went and got his mama, and she beat the living hell out of me."

He laughed at that.

"I understand you're into computer programming," I said. I find fighting a very boring thing to talk about for long.

"Yeah. It's a good field for someone with my . . . limitations."

"From what Patricia tells me, you don't recognize very many of those."

"Well, I do the best I can. My latest project is to get back on the ski slopes. I'm working with a guy up at Wintergreen, designing some special equipment." Wintergreen was the nearest ski resort. "There's no reason why I shouldn't be able to. Some French guy's already done it. Course he was world class before his accident, whereas I was what you might call Albemarle County class before mine." He grinned. "But we'll make it."

"I'll bet you will. I was also admiring the way your sister's got the house set up. She's done quite a job."

"Hasn't she, though? You should see my room. C'mon."

"Okay."

I followed him into the nearest of what would be the two bedrooms. It was an amazing space. Nothing was farther from the floor than mid-thigh height on me. Along one whole wall was a long, very narrow work space, every inch of it accessible to Patrick's hands. On it was an assortment of electronic devices. I recognized an Apple II computer. Attached was a printer marked Epson. There was also a nice-looking hi-fi system, a couple of oscilloscopes, and a lot of stuff that I didn't recognize.

"Wow," I said.

He shrugged. "My insurance money. They give you a lot when you end up like me."

The bathroom must have been between the two bedrooms. I could hear water running behind a door in the far wall. Without much success, I tried not to have lascivious thoughts.

"Hey, let me show you something," he said. "What day were you born?"

"Ah, I don't believe in that astrology stuff."

"This isn't astrology. What day?"

I told him.

"And what year?

I told him that, too. Grudgingly.

His floppies were stored in boxes racked up against the wall. He selected a box, removed the disk, and slotted it into the console. He punched some keys, and the screen came to life. Words appeared. He punched some more keys, and the words were replaced by some others. This continued for a while. They came and went so fast that I couldn't follow what was happening.

Finally, Patrick said, "Ta da," and gestured at the screen.

On it were three broad sine waves of different frequencies that intersected each other here and there. Along the horizontal axis were numbers from one to thirty-one. The vertical axis had a zero at mid-screen, with plus one and two above it and minus one and two below.

"What the hell is that?" I said.

"Your biorhythms for this month," Patrick said. "This first curve is your mental state. This one's emotional, and that's physical. Each one gets stronger as it approaches the top of the screen and weaker in the other direction. The numbers at the bottom are the days of the month. Look, here's yesterday, for example. Your mental state's low, which means you probably got into the fight for a stupid reason. But your physical's high, so the outcome could have been a lot worse."

I couldn't argue with any of that.

"You figure all of this out yourself?" I asked.

"Nah. The parameters are well established. You just take the person's day of birth and progress the cycles forward in twenty-three-, twenty-eight-, and thirty-three-day blocks, depending on which one it is. It was a pretty simple program to write. All I did was to work up some nice graphics for it."

I shook my head slowly. "Whatever happened to baseball and girlie magazines?" I asked.

"Nothing. I like both of them, too. You want to see my program for predicting next year's pennant winners?"

"Talk to me in April. If you can handicap baseball games better than my bookie, I'll buy you a hundred shares of IBM."

"You got a deal."

He switched off the computer, and we went back into the living room. Behind us, the water in the shower had stopped running.

175

Patricia came out a couple of minutes later. She was barefoot and had her hair wrapped in a towel. As she entered the room, she was cinching a green velour robe around herself. Before she got it snug, I glimpsed a triangle of pale winter flesh that included her throat and upper belly, as well as the softly rounded edges of her breasts. My hands started to sweat. Now this is silly, I thought. I'm a grown man, not some virginal schoolboy whose best lady friend is Mary Fivefingers.

Right. Keep talking.

"Patrick—" she said, then spotted me. "Oh, Loren, I'm glad you're here, I— Good Lord, you look ghastly. What happened?" She came over and sat next to me. I tried not to drool.

"Nothing much," I said. "There were a couple of guys molesting a little old lady, and when I went to her aid, she hit me with her—"

"Loren."

"Yes, ma'am."

"Don't trivialize rape, okay?" The look in her eye said that she meant it.

"Sorry."

"Besides, I want to know— Patrick, get the man a drink or something."

I grabbed the beer glass off the floor where I'd set it and held it up to her.

"He already has," I said, "and he did my biological rhythms for me. He says if my physical curve hadn't of been up, I'd look a whole lot worse. That right?"

"Yeah," Patrick said. "I think your emotional curve is up, too." With a slight leer. Smartass kid.

I turned back to Patricia.

"But my intellectual curve is down. Actually, mine spends more time near the bottom than most people's. That's how come I'm in the line of work I am. Also why I get beat up."

"Will you two please knock it off?" Patricia said. "I asked you a serious question."

"All right. I got in a fight last night. I lost."

"The riot?"

"Yup. Right place, wrong time." If you've got a good line, don't hesitate to recycle it.

176

"How bad is it?"

"You see the worst. The rest of my body is like a Technicolor dream. Want a peek?"

She smiled. "Not at the moment. And then what happened? You said something this afternoon about an accident."

"Oh, yeah, there was that." Truthfully, I'd almost put it out of my mind. "But it wasn't any accident. Melissa Majors tried to kill me."

"She what!"

"Tried to kill me. With her car. Forced me off the road, you know?"

"Melissa is John's daughter?"

"Yeah, the youngest."

"I've never met her—"

"No loss."

"But why was she out to get you? Or is that something I shouldn't ask?"

"You can ask." I grinned. "It's not an unwanted pregnancy or anything like that. She's a very crazy girl who's intensified her craziness with booze and Quaaludes and who knows whatall until she barely knows what planet she's on anymore. I don't think she had any awareness at all of what she was doing."

"God."

"No, just a child of her time."

"Very funny. You survived, I see, much to our delight."

"Yeah, a bruise on top of a bruise still only makes one bruise. The car didn't fare as well, though. I only just got her back on the road about an hour ago."

"Loren, what's going on with the Majors family?"

"It's sort of coming apart."

"And you're right in the middle of things."

"Not really. John fired me last night. Or rather, I finished the job he hired me to do. I must admit that it was the most complex simple case I've ever had."

"If you're out of it now, why does Elizabeth Majors still have to deal with you?"

She had me there. I'd been under the impression that I was the one who was going to deal with Elizabeth.

"Beats me. I hope I never run across the woman again," I said guardedly. The last thing on earth I wanted to do was involve Patricia Ryan in this miserable mess. Or maybe the next to last. Dead last currently belonged to being caught out walking on a deserted country road when Melissa Majors drove by.

"Well, she hopes to run across *you*," Patricia said.

"Say what?"

"That's why I wanted to see you tonight. She stormed into the office first thing this morning, and she was hopping mad."

I'll bet. After what I told her last night, she probably had her sights set on Carter's *cojones*, at the least. They truly deserved each other, those two. Perhaps we could arrange for adjacent burial plots.

"She just barged right into Carter's office," Patricia went on. "He had a client in there, but she didn't care. She commenced yelling at him as if they were alone. The client had the good sense to step into the outer office for the duration, but not before I heard your name mentioned. They screamed back and forth for about ten minutes, but I couldn't make out what was going on with the door closed. Finally, she came storming out again. He called something to her as she was leaving. It was a question, and I heard your name again. She said, 'I'll deal with him.' I tell you, Loren, that woman's face—she's a nasty one. I wouldn't have wanted to be in her way for any reason. Luckily, she didn't even notice I was there. The poor client was in shock. But the point is, What's going on and what do they want with you?"

I certainly couldn't blame Patricia for not caring to get in Elizabeth's way.

"Can I take a rain check on answering that one?" I asked.

"No."

"Look, Patricia, I appreciate your being concerned enough to tell me what you have. But there's no reason for you to get sucked into this thing. A couple of days at the most, it'll be over. Then we can go about the business of getting better acquainted. In the meantime, the farther away you stay from the Majors family, the better it'll be for your health."

"You forgot maybe that I work for Carter Lockridge?"

"No, I didn't forget."

"Well?"

"I don't know. Use some sick leave for a day or two."

"Thanks a lot."

178

I shrugged. "I'm in a thankless job. I guarantee you, you wouldn't want to be more mixed up with these people than you already are. But if I advise you to just stay away for a while, then I'm denying you things that you think you need to know. I catch it coming and going. That's a bit of a no-win situation."

She thought that over.

"You want another beer?" Patrick asked.

I shook my head. "Thanks. This one hit the spot. Another and I might fall asleep in this chair. And I've got a lot more to do tonight before I can let that happen." The prospect didn't exactly cheer me.

"Okay," Patrick said. "Then if you'all will excuse me, I've got some serious work to do."

"You're excused," I said. "But maybe next time you'll show me how one of those infernal machines works. I've been curious."

He grinned. "Even *you* can predict the outcome of this summer's pennant races."

"That I'd like to see, just as long as the thing doesn't do a Tommy Lasorda imitation."

He laughed, raised his chair into a full wheelie, spun it a hundred and eighty degrees, and made the grand exit.

"Will you at least call me tomorrow?" Patricia asked when his door had closed. She was more subdued now.

"If not before," I said.

"What's it like out there now?"

"It's cold, it's beginning to snow, and there's more cops cruising around than I ever saw in one place before. I think the riot will probably burn itself out by morning."

"What are you going to do next? Or is that another state secret?" She wasn't giving up without getting in the last jab. I liked that.

"Glad you asked," I said. "Me and Carter are gonna try and get a couple of things straight between us." In truth, I hadn't known what I was going to do immediately after I left Patricia's. But those were the words that came out. When they did, I knew my chat with Lockridge was long overdue. "Could you tell me where to find him?"

She gave me his home address. "If not there, try the office. Other than that, your guess is as good as mine."

"Thanks."

179

I got up. Unenthusiastically.

"I'll be in touch," I said. "And by the way, I was serious about calling in sick. Lockridge is in big trouble. People in that kind of spot are rather unpredictable."

"Consider me warned," she said.

·10·

I drove by Lockridge's house. It was dark. Just to be certain, I knocked on the door. Nobody came.

Next I cruised by Court Square, taking great care to avoid the roadblocks along the way. I didn't want to lose the Walther at this point. The thought of confronting Lockridge amidst all those guns without one of my own gave me the chills.

There was a light on in his office.

I parked and thought about what I ought to say, if he really was there. The question was: Since I no longer needed to quiz him about Ward Williams and the White Brothers, what did I hope to accomplish?

I ordered my priorities. The first was just to confront the man. To sit across from him and feel what a slime lord he actually was. To deal with him forearmed with a knowledge of the things he'd done.

Test him and let him test me.

Now that I had a few things on him, perhaps I could provoke him. Maybe not on the spot, although the thought of his trying to take me then and there brought on a sweet flush of anticipation. No, probably not that, but if he knew that I knew, it would have to stir him to action in the long run. I'd be setting myself up as the Judas goat—a spot I don't normally like to be in—but in this case I didn't mind. Because it meant that somewhere along the line he was going to screw up, and when he did, I'd feed him to Campbell faster than the Earl of the same name hits the off-tackle hole. Besides, I wanted to watch his cool come apart as he learned that he hadn't covered his tracks quite well enough.

Beyond this, there was something else I could do that might prove extremely valuable. That was to drive a wedge between Lockridge and Elizabeth Majors. From what Patricia had said, it looked like I'd already made some significant progress toward that goal. I could now come at it from the other direction, egging Carter on with the revelation of what I knew about Elizabeth and some sly intimations that she just might be thinking about cutting him loose at this point. If I raised his paranoia to a high enough pitch, any one of a number of interesting things could happen.

Carter and Elizabeth might kill each other off, thereby making the world a nicer place in which to live.

Or one might end up dead and the other in the slammer. Same net result.

Or he might turn her in. If I'd figured out that Elizabeth had made the attempt on Delmos, chances were he had, too, if he didn't know already. He might even have the proof that I lacked. If so, he might be able to strike a very good deal with the cops. Of course, she could turn around and go state's evidence in the Brennerman case. He could then try for a self-defense plea, with Brennerman unable to contradict him. The possibilities were endless. Eventually, they'd both get nailed for something; of that I was sure.

Any way it worked out, if I played my part right, they were both getting pulled out of circulation real soon.

So why was I hesitating?

I was, and I knew it. It wasn't fear. Lockridge was a dangerous man, no question, but I had him where I could put the leash on anytime I felt like it. And it wasn't lack of motivation. I wanted him and his girlfriend locked away somewhere ugly. Forever. And I wanted it badly.

But I was having trouble getting out of the car. What was it?

Something that Marilyn had told me in the last days of our disintegrating marriage came back to me then.

"Loren," she'd said, "It's really hopeless, and you know why?" She went on without waiting for an answer. She was always doing that. "Because you don't *do* anything. You're not engaged with life."

I'd protested feebly.

"No, it's true, Loren. Look at what you do for a living. You choose a job where the important thing is what's happening in someone

182

else's life, not yours. You get to stand on the sidelines and watch, which is exactly the position you're most comfortable in. Do you know what I'm saying to you?"

I didn't, but I pretended I did. She always saw through me.

"No, you don't," she'd countered. "You're so blind to the reality of your existence that you don't even know when you're not getting anything out of life anymore. Or when you're making those closest to you miserable. And I can't see where you're ever going to change."

I asked her what I could do. It was the wrong question, of course.

"Loren!" she'd screamed. "If you don't know, how can I *possibly* tell you? I don't want to be married to a *spectator* anymore. I want to be with someone who's in*volved!*"

Involved in what? I'd asked. It probably sounded like a stupid question. She certainly treated it like one, throwing up her hands and making a grand exit from the room. But I'd meant it. I hadn't felt like I was uninvolved in what I did, and I'd never particularly seen it as a more or less noble line of work than any other. My belief had always been, I do what I do, someone else does what they do, and eventually we end up covered with the very same earth. So what's the big difference? I guess what Marilyn meant was that she wanted a guy who was involved in fighting corruption in government or the spread of nuclear weapons or something of that nature, because that's the type she seemed to go for when she left me. Which I suppose answers the question by example.

Anyway, back then I hadn't known what Marilyn was talking about, but sitting in my car on Court Square with the snow slowly building up on the windshield, I finally did. The reason that I couldn't get out of the car was that I had become involved in a case. I cared about the outcome. That was a major kind of commitment for me to make. Ultimately, the confrontation with Lockridge represented a confrontation with myself. And that scared me. I had no idea how I'd handle myself in such a novel situation.

Nevertheless, I was going to find out. I opened the door and stepped into the snow-filled night. Marilyn would have been proud of me.

Not that I much cared what Marilyn thought anymore. No, right now I was more concerned that Patricia Ryan be able to bear with me until this vile business was over.

• • •

183

The door to the building was open, as was the outer door to Lockridge's office. As soon as I pushed through it, I knew something was wrong.

A light was on, but the office was too quiet. When someone's around, there are always little noises that you hear. Or if not that, there's a quality to the air that announces the presence of another human being. There was none of that here. The place was deathly still.

Why would he go out and leave his door unlocked? Lockridge was not that kind of man.

I moved across the room, the thick-pile carpeting swallowing up the sound of my passage. The door to Carter's inner sanctum was ajar. I went in, my fingers curled around the Walther.

His office was much as it had been when I was last there. The walls still glowed with the soft radiance of understated wealth. The photos and trophies and certificates were all in their appointed places. Likewise the guns, except for one of the matched set of Colt Woodsmans. No doubt it was the gun on the floor next to Lockridge's leather chair.

The hand was hanging in the air, above and to the left of the gun. Attached to the hand was the body that had formerly contained the soul of Carter Lockridge. He was slumped in his chair, feet on the floor and arms sticking straight out to the sides. His head rested on the chair back, with open eyes directed at the ceiling. His mouth was open also, forming a small "o," as if he'd been surprised upon discovering what the big sleep was really all about.

The once-noble gray hair was disfigured by the blood that had exited from the single bullet wound to the temple.

I wish I could say, like the poet, that every man's death diminishes me, but I can't. I'm just not the type. This man's passing didn't diminish me in the slightest.

Being careful not to touch anything, I poked around a little. There was nothing to indicate what might have happened. I hadn't expected that there would be, but you never knew. Pretty soon, the paranoia began to creep up on me. There were, after all, about a hundred cops within spitting distance of this office, and I couldn't afford to have one of them find me there. It was time to split.

I found the note on the way out. It had been left in Patricia Ryan's typewriter, right where it was typed.

It said: "I can no longer live with the things that I've done." There was no signature, of course.

So this was a suicide?

In a horse's ass, it was. I had no doubts as to who had knocked off brother Lockridge.

I recalled one of my previous conversations with him. I'd asked if any of the guns were loaded, and he'd said yes, some. For protection. When I'd pointed out that they could just as easily be used against *him*, he replied that his edge was in knowing which ones were loaded and which not, whereas a potential killer wouldn't. Sorry, Carter. The edge obviously didn't apply when the assailant knew all your little habits.

Elizabeth had made one large mistake, though, and that definitely came as a surprise.

She'd shot him in the right temple and tucked the gun away under his right hand. But Carter had been a lefty. If a guy is going to take the big plunge, he's not going to entrust the job to his weak hand. Nor will he reach all the way around his face in order to shoot himself in the opposite side of the head. So she'd blundered there. It wasn't the sort of error she'd make if she could help it. Probably a shot from the right side was all she'd been able to manage, given the layout of the room, and she was trying to make the best of a bad situation, hoping no one would notice.

There were other flaws, too. An unsigned suicide note. Bound to raise suspicions. Also, a paraffin test on Lockridge's hand would reveal that he hadn't fired a gun recently, unless she'd put the gun in his hand and fired another shot after he was dead. If she'd done that, a half-competent police search would turn up the other slug. Finally, the coroner would determine from the absence of powder burns on the head that the trigger hadn't been pulled from only a few inches away. Unless he'd let her get that close with a gun in her hand. Given Lockridge, that was highly unlikely.

I left the office as I'd found it.

I walked out the front door, figuring that if I was going to be seen, I'd be seen, and there was nothing I could do about it. I didn't think I had been. The arrival of the snow had substantially reduced activity in the area, and that was good news. It would give me a greater freedom of movement for the rest of the evening. That was something I could use.

I got into Clementine, closing the door gingerly. The driver's side window was a spiderweb of cracks but still holding together, despite all the car had been through. The next door slam could well cause it to shatter. Cold as it was, I didn't want that.

I sat still for a moment, pondering the changed situation. Elizabeth was the only one left now. If we could nail her, it would be over. The problem was how best to go about accomplishing that, since the evidence against her was still pretty circumstantial.

The first thing to do, I decided, was to get Lockridge's death reported. That was something I couldn't do myself, at least not openly. The last thing I wanted now was to spend the rest of the night answering the same questions over and over. An anonymous tip didn't seem like the way to go, either. That could come back to haunt me later. The only alternative was to have someone respectable discover the body soon, as the result of some routine activity. And there was only one way I knew of to ensure that.

Feeling extremely guilty, I drove back to Patricia Ryan's.

This time she answered the door herself.

"Loren," she said, "what is it?"

"Lockridge's dead."

"What?"

"He's dead. Can I come in?"

She just sort of gawked at me, so I went on inside. She closed the door and followed.

"What happened?" she said. "You didn't—"

"Where's Patrick?" I cut in.

"He's gone out," she said mechanically. "For the night. A friend . . ."

"Okay," I said. "It wasn't me. I found Lockridge in his office. He's been dead for a while."

"How . . ."

"Somebody shot him, with one of his own guns. Once. In the head. Look, why don't you get yourself a drink?"

She nodded numbly and went into the kitchen.

"You?" she called from in there.

There was nothing I wanted more at the moment than a good

186

stiff shot of Irish whiskey. But I knew I couldn't afford it. The night was getting old, and there was a lot left to do.

"No," I called back.

She came in, gulping at a small glassful of something, looking like she was standing witness at an electrocution and the man in charge had just pulled the big switch.

"You gonna be okay?" I asked.

"I . . . I guess so. Wh— what happened?"

"He wasn't home, so I cruised by his office, and the light was on. He was slouched in the chair in his office, very dead. The gun was on the floor next to him. It was one of that matched set of Colt Woodsmans that he has. In your typewriter I found a suicide note. It said he couldn't live with what he'd done, whatever that's supposed to mean. But if he was a suicide, I'm Muammar Khadafy."

"Somebody . . . killed him?"

I nodded.

"Who?"

"I don't know for sure," I said. "But if I were a betting man, which I am, I'd lay my life savings on Elizabeth Majors. Any odds you like."

"Elizabeth . . . but why?"

"The way I see it, Lockridge didn't know it, but he was playing out of his league. He thought he had her on the spot, and in a way he did, all these years. She even shared his bed. But all along she knew that some day she'd have to get rid of him. I'll say this for her: when the right moment came along, she didn't waste any time. She's as tough as they come."

"What happens now?"

"Good question," I said. "Do you think you can pull yourself together?"

"Me? I don't know. What do you mean?"

I took a deep breath. I hated to say what I was going to, but there wasn't much choice. Forgive me, Lord.

"Patricia, someone has got to discover the body."

"Someone will. I mean, in the morning— Oh, no, that's not what you're getting at, is it? Oh, no— Loren, I *can't!*"

"I'm hoping that you can."

"Why *me?*"

"Because I can't do it and it needs to be done as soon as possible

187

so the sheriff can get the news. If I did it, I'd become a prime suspect. The cops wouldn't let me go until next week sometime. That can't happen. There's too much at stake."

"What?"

"Other lives, for example."

"I don't understand."

"Patricia, this woman is crazy. She's killed, and she may kill again. Some people, once they get a taste of it, they can't stop. We've got to get her put away as soon as we can. Tonight, if possible. There's no way I can help make it happen if I'm stuck in some windowless room with a homicide detective all night. Do you see?"

"But why me? You haven't answered that."

"Because you're someone who would have a plausible reason for going back to the office at night. You could be retrieving something you forgot, or whatever. You're not an instant suspect. And because . . . because you're one of the few people that I trust."

"Should I be flattered?"

"Yeah, but it doesn't matter if you're not. All that matters is whether you'll do it."

She looked inside herself for a long moment. I let her alone.

"It's important?" she said finally.

"It's important."

"You really think she might kill somebody else?"

"Absolutely."

"Then I'll do it."

I wanted to jump up and down and give her a very large number of kisses. That would have to wait.

Instead, I said, "Thanks. I owe you one. Or two or three."

I smiled, and she smiled, and that was that.

"Okay," Patricia said, "but what do I do?"

A reasonable question. I tried to gather together all the wild tangles inside my head.

"What you do," I said, "is pretend you had some reason to return to the office tonight. Maybe you need to pick up some work that has to be done over the weekend. Whatever. You go there. If you don't want to look at him, you don't have to. I've told you enough that you'll be convincing. All you have to do is call the cops and wait until they get there. After that, they'll tell you exactly what they want. As long as you have a halfway reasonable story, they won't hassle you very much.

188

"Now about me. If the cops don't ask you if you've seen me tonight, don't volunteer the information. They probably won't. There's nothing to connect the three of us at this point. If they do ask, though, don't lie. You can tell my first visit just the way it happened, minus my saying that Lockridge's was the next stop. Say I never told you where I was going. Then you'll have to mention this visit, as well. What'll we do about that?"

I thought. C'mon, Swift, we need something plausible, and we need it now.

"Okay. Tell them that at the end of the first visit I left a package for you to hold for me. Tell them that I came back, made a couple of phone calls, then grabbed the package and left in a hurry. Without telling you anything. That'll throw it all onto me."

"What's in the package?"

"Tell them that you didn't open it but that it was small and heavy and could have been a gun. When they cross-check, I'll say that I left my gun here until I needed it, because I didn't want to risk having it confiscated at a roadblock. It'll hold water."

"Oh, and one other thing. This might sound obvious, too, but if you're going back to the office to pick up some work, it needs to be there. You know what I mean? If you've already brought it home, be sure to take it to the office and plant it before you call the cops."

She nodded.

"You don't make this sound very easy," she said.

"It won't be. The hardest part may be having to spend some time alone in the office with a dead man while you wait for the cops to arrive. But they're only two blocks away, so it shouldn't be that long. Think you're up to it?"

"I really don't know. I might run screaming out into the street."

"Well, that's okay, too. As long as you can convince the cops that you were the first one on the scene, almost anything will do. All I need is for the sheriff to get wind of Lockridge's murder. That'll get him on my side."

"What do you mean?"

"I'm sorry," I said. "But like I told you, Campbell kind of has it in for me at the moment. At the same time, I'm trying to show him what's really going on. When he finds out Lockridge is dead, he's going to pay more attention to what I have to say."

"God, this is confusing," she said.

"I know, and I'm sorry."

"Quit apologizing, will you?"

We looked at each other in silence for a moment. In that moment we were as good as naked. A relationship of some kind was established.

"I'll make it up to you," I said.

I would, too. If such a thing were possible. She gave me a weak smile.

"Now, I *do* need to use the phone," I said. She nodded and pointed it out to me.

I really did. During all of this I'd almost lost track of Leigh. She still needed care, and I'd promised myself that I was going to be there. I called Sikh City. Gupta Bruce himself answered.

"Ali," I said. "It's Swift. I need to talk to Leigh."

"Sorry," he said, "you can't."

"C'mon, it's important. She's expecting me to call."

"You can't because she's not here."

That was not what I wanted to hear. My bowels started crawling slowly toward my belly.

"What do you mean, not there?" I said as evenly as I could.

"Just what I said. She ain't here. She left about an hour ago."

"Where did she go, Bruce?"

"I can't tell you. And my name's not Bruce." There was a trace of amusement in his voice that, had he been in front of me, I'd have rearranged his face for.

"Goddamit, Br— Ali, look. It's important that I get in touch with her. Her life may be in danger."

"Oh, come off it, Swift. She's with friends."

"How do you know that?"

"Somebody called and said that a friend of hers wanted to see her. It must've been someone who meant a lot to her. She was very excited about going."

Bad. Very bad.

"Who was the caller?"

"I don't know. Someone else took the call. He said it was a female voice. Somebody she knew well from what he heard before he left the room."

Jesus.

"Where'd they go, Ali?"

"Sorry. She asked me not to tell anyone."

"I need to know." Control.

190

"Sorry. She said anyone, and you're anyone. Don't worry about it."

"Look, you little twerp! You don't have an idea in hell what's going on! I tell you your sister's life happens to be in danger and you're giving me some song and dance about a half-ass promise!"

"Swift," he said coldly, "stay out of my face, will you? And hers, too."

Then he hung up.

I called back. Someone else answered, told me that Hassan was not available to speak with me, and rang off.

I don't know what I looked like, but Patricia was gaping at me like I was the bottomless pit of horrors.

"Loren," she said, "what *is* it? What's *wrong?*"

I held up my hand.

My eyes were on her, but she might as well have been in the next town. I was seeing in my mind the last conversation I'd had with the Colonel. There was something there of importance. What was it?

Something about the will.

That was it. The Colonel said he'd gone to Lockridge's office to make some changes to his will. *Some* changes. And that they were mostly concerned with cutting Delmos in. *Mostly.* It had passed right over my head at the time, and we'd switched to another subject. Now it was critically important. What other changes had he proposed making? I wasn't sure I wanted to know.

"Sorry," I said to Patricia, "I had to think something through."

"It doesn't look like you came to a good conclusion."

"I didn't."

"Can you tell me?"

"Not this minute. Hang on."

I got the Colonel on the line.

"You remember that conversation we had about your will," I said.

"Right," he said.

"Well, I need to know something. My recollection is that you said you went to Lockridge to make some changes, mostly concerning Delmos. Correct?"

"Sounds about right."

"Does that mean that the changes concerning Delmos weren't the only ones that you were making?"

"There were a couple of others. What are you getting at?"

191

"What others?"

"Is this important?"

"Yes, it's important. What others, Colonel?"

"I decided to leave a bit more to Sarah Jane. And to Leigh. Less to John and the mistake he married. And Melissa. They're changes I should have made long ago, too. Why?"

"Are we talking substantial changes here, Colonel, all told?"

"I don't know. Depends on who you are. Some people might think so. Why, boy?"

My heart was beating hard, down around my knees somewhere.

"Just trying to make some connections," I forced myself to say. "There are a few things I still don't understand."

"Like what?"

"I'll have to explain later, Colonel. Right now I need to speak to Elizabeth."

"Don't think she's here. You want me to check?"

"Please. It's important."

Several minutes passed, aging me a couple of years. Then the Colonel came back on.

"She ain't here, Swift. Nor John, either. I don't know where they might be."

"Did they give any—"

"Nope, but that's not unusual around here. Anyway, I was conked out for a good while earlier on. I don't know who's come and gone. I asked Deya for you. She wasn't sure, either. She'd been working in the guest wing, though she thought John and Elizabeth were headed somewhere together. But I doubt it. I looked outside, and the cars are gone, the Aston and Mercedes both. Mustang's the only one in there."

It was an answer I'd been expecting, but I still felt my legs beginning to go wobbly.

"All right," I said. "I'll be back in touch later tonight. Until then, keep yourself well protected."

"I don't suppose you're going to tell me what this is all about?"

"I will later. There are some things I've got to do as quickly as possible right now."

"Don't keep me in the dark too long, boy."

I hung up. There was a small chair next to the telephone. I sat down before I fell down.

"Bad," Patricia said.

"Bad."

Or maybe not. The thing was to avoid panic. There might be a simple explanation for everything. I needed to continue to be logical.

If a woman had called Leigh, it might have been Sarah Jane. I called Sarah Jane. It wasn't her.

That left only Delmos. He hadn't been the one to call her, of course. But someone might have on his behalf. Very farfetched. Still, it was conceivable. Much more likely was that she might have tracked him down and spoken to him since I last saw him. Even if she hadn't, I was feeling a little guilty keeping him in the dark any longer. He was one of the few people who cared about her. He had a right to know what was going on.

On the other hand, what good would it do to set him worrying, too? I agonized over the decision. Another couple of hours would have helped, to think things through properly. I didn't have another couple of hours or even a couple of extra minutes. I decided to call him. The off chance that he might have some information tipped the scales.

I told Delmos what little I knew. He hadn't been behind the call to her. Nor had she contacted him.

"Any idea who might have phoned her?" I said.

"I don't know," he said. "None of her friends know where she is. And no one in the family cares that much about her. Except her father. I can't think of a reason he'd have someone do it for him, though."

"It could've been him. He's not at home, I checked. But I doubt it. The thing is, we don't really know anything for sure. I see three possibilities. First off, Bruce may be telling the truth. In that case, it could have been anyone, and she might be anywhere, and only Bruce will be able to help us. Then again, Bruce might have lied, which he wouldn't hesitate to do to me. She could still be at the ashram. Or she could have gone off somewhere on her own. If so, forget the why. The important question is where. What about that family cabin?"

"What about it? Why would she go there?"

"I don't know," I said, trying not to let the exasperation show through. "Maybe she needed to be even farther away from people.

Maybe anything, for Christ's sake. The point is, she *could* have gone there. She even mentioned it when I talked with her."

"Swift, let's don't get angry with each other. Remember, I want her safe and well even more than you do."

"I'm sorry. Let's start over. Have you thought about how to get to the place?"

"Yes. It might take a while, but I'd find it."

"Does it have a phone?"

"I don't think so. The Colonel liked the idea of having a place where he could get away from it all."

"Okay. I'll probably have to go to the ashram, then. Bruce has the key to this whole thing, and if I have to beat it out of him, I will. That's assuming he's there. He may have skipped out for all I know. If he has, we might as well check out the cabin together. I'll call you from the ashram. We can meet somewhere, and you can take me there."

"If you do get something out of him, call me, anyway, all right?"

"Sure. Now just sit tight, okay?"

After a long pause, he sighed and said, "Okay, I'll try."

When I'd hung up, I thought briefly about calling in the cops. I decided there was no sense in it. They'd need about five hours to establish probable cause. I couldn't wait. Not when I didn't know what was happening out there. Even if I got the cops moving sooner, Bruce would clam up the minute he saw them, the way he reacted to authority. And they wouldn't be able to do a thing about it, because they wouldn't be able to go at him the same way I was going to. No, I had to do it alone. It might already be too late, but I had to try.

"Can I help?" Patricia asked.

God, I'd almost forgotten about the part she still had to play. I put my arms around her and kissed her gently.

"I've got to go," I said. "I'll get back to you just as soon as I can. You might want to get some coffee in you before you go over there. It's apt to be a long night, and there's no rush. Give it half an hour after I leave. That'll make it look less like there's a connection between me and your going there, just in case anyone asks. And . . . look, I'm sorry you got sucked into this mess."

I hugged her again.

"But thanks."

She shrugged. "I would have been, sooner or later." Pause. "There
. . . there's not going to be any more killing, is there?"
"I hope not."
"Be careful. Please."
I nodded.

· 11 ·

Outside, it was snowing steadily. There was maybe an inch on the
ground already. That'd slow me down some. But it would put everyone else in the same boat.

Heading back down U.S. 29 South, I gave myself a nasty talking-
to. So far, I'd done about everything wrong that you could do. Up
to a point, you could keep on blundering and it wouldn't make any
difference. Past that point, bad things had a way of happening.

In this case, bad things meant people dying.

I hadn't been able to prevent Harlow Brennerman from dying,
or Carter Lockridge, but I didn't really care about them. They were
no loss to the world. I did care about Delmos Venable, but I probably
wouldn't have been able to prevent him from dying, either, if it
had been in the cards.

Two deaths and one near miss. Figuring Delmos to be safe for
the time being, that narrowed the field of potential remaining vic-
tims quite a bit. To two, I would say.

Leigh Majors and the Colonel.

I wasn't worried about the Colonel. He was tough, and he already
distrusted his daughter-in-law. He wouldn't be taken by surprise.
I *was* worried about Leigh. She was much too vulnerable to be
mixed up with people like this.

Of course, the woman who had called and lured Leigh out with
some lie or other didn't have to be Elizabeth. Even if it was, it
didn't have to mean something sinister. Maybe she just wanted to
talk things over with her daughter. There could be a dozen innocent
explanations.

Somehow, that wasn't very convincing.

I pushed Clementine a little harder down the slickening highway.

I thought about Gupta Bruce. Goddam smug little pseudo-Hindu. It was his fault that I was driving my mangled car faster than I should through a steadily worsening snowstorm. If anything happened to his sister, he'd have to stand a lot of the blame for that, too. I wondered how he'd make it, trying to catch his breath with half a silk turban jammed down his throat.

I had to cool down. It had been a long time since I was this angry at anyone. Usually I just write off stupid behavior to inevitable human perversity. But this was different. An innocent person's life could be at stake here. There was no room for perversity. If I went in to see Bruce Majors in this frame of mind, I might kill him before I found out what I needed to know.

The snow'd been heavier in Nelson County. A couple of inches on the ground and more on the way. I watched it settle on the mountains. That calmed me some.

The big Sikh was on the porch to greet me once again. They must have had some sort of alarm at the base of the driveway that went off when a car pulled in. A bell would ring in the house, and the big Sikh would come out onto the porch, like Pavlov's dog, to scare away the unwanted.

I was sure to be on the unwanted list.

So what?

The big guy stood with arms folded across his chest. "What do you want here, Mr. Investi—" was what he got out.

I never broke stride. Went straight up the steps and gave him a shove the way I'd learned to do it in aikido class, not physically forceful but with the strength of my will behind it. He hadn't been well balanced and went down hard on his butt. He was very surprised.

Before he had a chance to figure out what had happened, I was through the door and down the hall.

I barged into Bruce's room.

He was sitting on his sleeping mat, cross-legged, with his hands resting on his knees. The thumb and forefinger of each hand made a small circle. His eyes were closed, and he was breathing deeply. Some sort of meditation posture. I really hated to interrupt him. Sure I did.

His eyes came open, and he stared at me blankly, as if I were

197

some incomprehensible creature he'd dreamed up in his meditative state. I strode across the room fast, grabbed him by the shirt front, and yanked him to his feet. The physical strength generated by my anger surprised even me, but I didn't stop to dwell on it. I propelled Bruce in front of me and banged him against the wall. Then I slapped his face good and hard, once with the forehand, once with the backhand. The second blow split his lower lip, and blood began to trickle onto his chin. He raised his hands in front of his face and tried to squirm away, but I had him pinned to the spot, and I wasn't letting go. I balled my fist and made as if to punch his lights out. He cowered and tried to say something. No words came out.

I didn't yell at him.

Instead, I said, "Where is she?" in a voice that was supposed to represent cold fury, an emotion I can't sustain in real life.

He burbled something or other.

"Bruce," I said in the same voice, "you tell me where she is, or you're going to need a very competent plastic surgeon." Mr. tough guy. I'm terrific in confrontations with helpless little wimps.

"The family cabin," he spluttered. "Over near Howardsville."

"She really got a call?"

He hesitated.

"C'mon, Bruce," I said, raising my fist again.

"It was—was like I told you. I swear it."

I jerked him away from the wall. "Let's go," I said. No letup on the professional muscle act. We had a twenty-mile drive in front of us. I didn't like that.

There was a sound behind me, and I froze. No other sound in the world like it. Someone ramming home the bolt on a bolt-action rifle.

I turned slowly.

Dorjé Khan was standing there with the big Sikh. The big fellow was the one with the gun. I searched his face for some sign of reluctance to use it and didn't find any. I decided I'd better speak with the boss man, but he went first.

"What's going on here?" he said. Sensible question.

"I find it easier to talk," I said, "when I'm not trying to guess the bore on a rifle."

Khan motioned with his hand, and the big guy lowered his gun. Perhaps a trifle disappointedly.

"Thanks, Khan," I said. "Now this is what's happening. Ali's sister

Leigh is in serious trouble. From what I understand, she got a phone call, and then she left. Who took the call?"

Khan looked at Bruce. "Singh," Bruce said.

"Where is he?"

"Gone," Khan said. "Won't be back until Monday."

"Damn."

"What kind of trouble are we talking about?" Khan asked. No matter what we were discussing, he maintained the same steady tone of voice. A leader, no doubt about it.

"The worst kind," I said. "The kind that gets people dead."

Khan raised his eyebrows but didn't say anything.

"It's a long story," I went on, "and we don't have the time right now. You've got to trust me. Two people are dead already, and it could easily have been three. I think Leigh may be next on the list. Ali knows where she is. He has to take me to her before it's too late."

He turned to Bruce. "What do you know of this, Gupta Hassan?"

Bruce just looked at him dumbly, his bleeding mouth slightly ajar.

"For God's sake, Khan," I said, "we're wasting precious time!"

I could see him groping for the right decision, but he wasn't going to hurry it.

"All right," he said finally. And to Bruce, "Go with him."

I didn't give him a chance to reconsider. I thanked him and hustled brother Ali on out of there as soon as I got a jacket thrown over his scrawny frame.

• • •

On the way to the cabin, Bruce mumbled directions, and I drove. We didn't say much. There wasn't much to say. And I was preoccupied with getting there as quickly as I could, at the same time dreading what I'd find. There weren't but so many possibilities. Most of them bad.

If anything had happened to Leigh, I would be to blame. Me and the skinny cretin riding in the passenger's seat.

At least he had an excuse; he was a dumb kid. What did I have? An overtaxed brain? Mid-life crisis? Incompetent biological rhythms? No, I'd screwed up, pure and simple. I was supposed to be good in situations like this, and I hadn't been.

What I should have done was make Leigh's safety my first concern. Of course, by the time I found out she was in danger, it was a little late. But I should have guessed. I should have. It's what I do for a living, and now, when it really counted for something, I hadn't done it.

All that was left was hope.

It was in short supply.

Just before we reached Howardsville, I realized I hadn't checked in with Delmos. He'd understand, I knew. Things had been a bit touch-and-go back at the ashram. I'd call him as soon as I could.

Then we were turning toward the river. We drove a mile or two on a succession of gravel roads and pulled up at the end of a long driveway. By that time my stomach was wound as tightly as the inside of a golf ball.

"This is it," Bruce said.

With the snow giving the land a ghostly luminescence, I could see fairly well. The drive sloped gently downward, with open fields on both sides. It was lined with dogwood. Eventually, it disappeared into the trees. In the distance I could just make out a dark mass that would be the James River. The cabin was hidden from the road. It would be.

Cautiously, I turned in, testing the depth of the snow. I judged that I could make it in and out if we didn't stay long. One way or the other, we wouldn't.

I followed the tracks leading in. There were two sets of them. One had been there for a while; the other was more recent.

We drove through a small patch of woods. The cabin was in a clearing on the far side. It was a cabin like the Majors place on 666 was a house. Two-story wood contemporary with the windows on the second floor cantilevered out. Redwood deck all around. And so on. I wasn't looking for details.

There was a Dodge Dart parked near it. I stopped the VW.

"Leigh's?" I asked Bruce.

He nodded. It was the only other car in sight. That chilled my blood.

"Wait here," I said. He didn't mind. He hunched down into his jacket and stared blankly at the floor.

I got out, leaving the motor running and the headlights on. I knelt down and studied the tire tracks. The ones belonging to the Dart were the oldest. There were two sets of the others. Coming and going. In addition, they were sickeningly familiar. The Aston Martin.

My hand tightened around the gun in my coat pocket. If she'd been there at that moment, I'd have killed her.

I forced myself to walk to the cabin, holding the Walther in front of me. You never knew for sure.

The front door creaked, but only slightly. Inside it was warm. A large cast-iron Lange stove in the center of the room was putting out enough heat to keep things comfy even though the ceiling was twenty feet up. A railed balcony ran around the three-sided upper landing.

The room was peaceful, as if its occupant were out for a walk in the snow. There were no signs of violence except for the slender blonde form lying face down on the floor near the stove. I went over and knelt next to her.

There was no point in checking for a pulse. You see death a few times, and you get to recognize it instantly.

Her skull had been caved in from behind, and she lay where she had fallen, in a thickened pool of blood. Next to her was a bloody fireplace poker.

Fleetingly, I wondered why Elizabeth had left the murder weapon lying there. It wasn't like her, unless she was too far gone to care anymore.

I stood up.

There wasn't anything that could be done here. There was plenty to do elsewhere.

I went over to the stove. It was set on an arrangement of un-mortared bricks. I grabbed a couple of loose ones and a small stack of newspaper.

Outside, I carefully spread some newspaper over the freshest tire tracks I could find and weighted down the ends with bricks. Not a professional job, but it should ensure that the impressions were preserved until the cops arrived. I marked the spot with a stick.

Then I got back in my car.

"Wh— wh—" Bruce said between chattering teeth.

"Your sister's dead, Bruce," I said.

He made some kind of high, wailing sound and tried to open the door on his side. I grabbed the shoulder of his jacket and yanked him back.

"There's nothing to see," I said. "Pull yourself together. I need you."

He continued shrieking, so I slapped him. Once. Not hard, but it did the trick, returning our relationship to an earlier level. He put his face in his hands and quieted down. His body shook with an occasional sob.

"Who?" he said from behind his hands.

I wanted to tell him just about everyone in his family, when you came down to it. "It doesn't matter," I said. "But I need your help to get them. Can you help me?"

He didn't speak for a long time. Finally, he just nodded.

"Good," I said, and started back up the drive.

About halfway to the top, another car turned in. I froze. Jesus, now what? Bruce began whimpering again and tried to bury himself in his seat.

If it was the killer returning to the scene of her crime for some reason, she probably would have driven on by when she saw Clementine's lights and realized the crime had been discovered. On the other hand, she was a crack shot.

Well, if it was my day to buy the farm, then it was my day. There wasn't anything to do but start forward. When I did, the other car did, too. We stopped when we were ten yards from one another. No bullets came through the windshield.

Then the driver's door of the other car popped open and a back-lighted figure began coming toward me. I'd nearly pulled my gun when he spoke.

"Swift," he cried. "Swift, it's me!"

Oh, God. My body went numb all over. I released the death grip I'd had on the Walther and got out.

"Delmos," I managed to say, "what in the living hell are you doing here?"

"I couldn't just sit there, Swift. I tried, but I couldn't. I thought she might have come here, since she mentioned it to you. It was better than sitting. I got lost on the way. Did you find her?"

"No. She's not here."

"Well, did you search the place? Do you think she's been here?"

"I did. There's no sign."

"Let me look, too. I might find something you missed."

"Delmos, I'm a detective. I don't miss things. Where's your body-guard?"

"I went out the bathroom window. This isn't cop business."

He had gone out the window. He was standing there without a coat on, waiting for me to say something good. Bruce chose that moment to up the volume of his moaning.

"Who's with you?" Delmos said.

"It's Bruce," I said. "He led me here."

"What's he doing? What's going on, Swift?"

I could hear the fear in his voice, but there was nothing to be done. It was time to end the charade.

"Delmos," I said, taking his arm. He tore it away from me.

"You bastard," he said. "You lied to me. Didn't you?"

I couldn't say anything. Lies and death. It was all there, hanging motionless in the falling snow. For a moment all I could see of Delmos's face was the whites of his eyes. He started for the cabin. I jumped in front of him.

"Don't go in there," I said.

"Swift, get out of my way."

I put my hand on his chest.

"Don't do it," I repeated. "She's dead. You won't want to remember her this way."

He brushed my hand aside and took one step forward.

I hit him. In the face. I used the open palm, but I cupped it. I wanted him to feel the blow. He did. It staggered him. Then he was on me, and we both went down. We rolled over and over in the snow, with him pummeling me. I protected myself as best I could. I didn't fight back. It wouldn't have done much good, anyway. He was younger and quicker and stronger, a lot of each. He could have killed me with his bare hands if he wanted.

At one point I thought he was going to. He had me by the throat and had started choking. Then, abruptly, it was over. His grip relaxed, and my head fell back into the snow. My breathing was labored, but I was getting the air in.

We got up.

"It's bad?" he asked.

"Yes."

He began to tremble. I put my arms around him and held him as he cried. He held me back, and I cried, too.

203

When we were finished, he said, "You're right. It's not the way I want to remember her." And we walked back to the car.

"I've got to get the cops down here," I said. "You'll drive straight home?"

"You can trust me," he said.

He backed out and turned down the road, heading east. I trusted him.

I drove into Howardsville, found an outside phone at a service station, and put in an immediate call to Ridley Campbell. He got back to me in less than two minutes. I told him what I'd found, and he wasn't pleased.

"You should of took me along, Swift," he said. The anger in his voice was palpable.

"There wasn't time. Bruce wouldn't have talked if you were around. I thought I could save her if I went alone. For Christ's sake, Rid, I liked the girl. You think I *wanted* her to die?"

"Swift," I don't know nothing about you anymore. The only thing I'm interested in is, What are we gonna do now?" His tone clearly implied that whatever I had in mind, it'd better be good.

"I want to help you catch a murderer. Maybe two murderers."

"If you're thinking of Carter Lockridge, forget it. He's dead."

"What? When?" Academy Award time.

"Couple of hours ago. His secretary found him in his office when she went back to pick up some stuff. Looks like suicide."

"You believe that?"

"Why shouldn't I? There was a note."

"Ridley, if Lockridge is dead, there's a hundred percent chance Elizabeth Majors had a hand in it. Hasn't that got through to you yet?"

"Don't push me, Swift."

"All right. I don't care about Lockridge, anyway."

"Meaning what?"

"I'll tell you later. Can you meet me at the grocery on 29, near 666?"

"When?"

"Half an hour."

"Why shouldn't I bust you right now?"

"You probably should, as much as I've screwed up. But I can help you nail Elizabeth."

"How?"

"She might talk to me where she wouldn't talk to you."

"How does that help me?"

"You can listen in."

That shut him up for a bit. When he spoke again, it sounded like he'd gathered his anger in the interim.

"I'm still not saying I ain't gonna bust you, Swift," he said.

"Rid, the way I feel right now, I wouldn't care if you did. But I'd rather help you get this woman put away. Just meet me in a half hour, will you, please? I think we can wrap it all up tonight. I— I've got something else for you, too."

"Jesus H. Christ, what is it now?"

"I've got Venable's assailant, as well."

"Goddam you, Swift! If you've been holding back evidence on *that*, the city boys'll fry your ass in cottonseed oil!"

"I haven't been holding anything back," I said wearily. "I wasn't sure who pulled the trigger until fifteen minutes ago. Now I am. She's yours. Need I say that your department won't exactly look bad if you make the collar?"

"What're you suggesting?"

"C'mon, Sheriff. It's been a tough three days. Not counting the riot, we've had four murders and an attempt on the area's leading sports figure. Up to now, the only murderer anyone's got is Ward Williams's. I can wrap up Lockridge, Brennerman, Leigh Majors, and Venable for you. You'll be a hero. The public will see the county out doing a helluva job, while the city'll still be taking flak over the Williams thing. You know what that'll mean for the department."

"You want some kind of deal?"

"Jesus, Rid, what I *want* is for Leigh Majors to still be alive. But she's not. So let's bury our differences, all right? If we cooperate, we can nail her killer tonight."

"I don't know. . . . I suppose it's worth a try."

"It's all we've got left."

"You know I can't make you any promises. About what happens after."

"Your word's good enough for me. Off the record, of course."

"Done."

"Thanks."

"Now give me a murderer, Swift."

"Okay. Here's what I need. Send someone down to Howardsville to take care of the evidence here. There's a fireplace poker with bloody hair all over it and some very important tire tracks in the snow. I've covered them with newspaper and marked them so they won't get obliterated by what's coming down, but it's a stopgap measure. How soon can you get the experts out?"

"The first car'll be there in fifteen minutes. Maybe forty-five for the experts. You know how they are."

"Right. I'll leave Bruce Majors here to take them to the cabin. He's pretty shaken up, but he should do. He's not involved in any of the murders."

"What about on my end?"

"Just meet me at the grocery with two good men. Better not bring Thurm. If I saw him tonight, I'd probably go for him."

"You won't see him. When my men let their personal feelings interfere with the job, they're gone."

"That's it, then. I'll set our visit up."

"Good. Let's move on it."

I hung up and called the Majors place. Deya answered. I arranged with her to let us in and told her to tell John and Elizabeth I was coming—alone, of course—and to have them ready to meet me. I also asked her to see that the Colonel was tucked away somewhere safe. Since we would be needing her cooperation, I told her about the sheriff's being secretly with me and gave her a few brief details of the plan. She seemed eager to help. I wasn't surprised.

I gave my overcoat to Bruce and left him on the street corner. If Ridley said there'd be a car there in fifteen minutes, there would. Bruce'd survive.

Then I climbed into Clementine and headed north.

·12·

I rode out to the Majors place in one of Ridley's unmarked cruisers. Clementine had made it to the rendezvous, but that was about all I wanted to ask of her. There were four or five inches of snow on the ground now, and the back roads demanded more in the way of tires than I was carrying. I surely didn't want to end up in the ditch along 666 once again. The old VW had suffered enough abuse the past couple of days as it was.

There were four of us. One of the deputies was driving, with Campbell next to him in front. I was in the back with another deputy. Neither of the deputies was Thurman. The sheriff was a man of his word.

I'd just finished my reconstruction of the events leading to three murders and a near miss. We were getting close to the estate.

Ridley leaned over the seat and asked if I had a gun on me.

"Yeah," I said.

He held out his hand.

"Aw, c'mon, Rid," I said. "I might need it."

"You'll get it back," he said. "Let's leave the cop stuff to us from here on out."

I forked it over.

"Only one thing about your story," he said. "We tried to run the pistol that killed Brennerman to ground, but it was cold, like you guessed. And Lockridge was the one told us about you and Brennerman. It was the day after, and he'd already heard that you'd shown up at the motel the night of the murder. He passed along the info as something he'd picked up during his job as family lawyer.

Friend of the police and all that. But that's not the reason we came to search your apartment."

"It isn't?"

"Nope. We got a tip."

"From who?"

"Don't know. The switchboard lady took the call. She said it sounded like a woman holding something over the phone to disguise her voice. Whoever it was said that if we tossed your apartment we might find something of interest in the Brennerman case."

"Elizabeth," I said. "But why?"

"It is strange."

It was. She wouldn't have wanted to alert the cops that someone besides me knew about the gun unless it was Lockridge. She'd have had him do it. I didn't understand.

Then we were at the Majors driveway.

"Anything else you want to cover before we go in there?" Campbell asked.

"Just stay close by," I said. "Once I get started on Elizabeth, she's apt to do anything. Since you've seen fit to confiscate my protection, I'd prefer it if you put in an appearance *before* she has a chance to add any extraneous holes to my body."

"We'll do our best, sir."

I buzzed Deya, and she opened the gate for us. We circled the dormant fountain and parked near the garage, setting up an obstruction to any quick exits. The Majorses' cars were all lined up in their little stalls.

We left one of the deputies to watch the house from outside and went in.

Deya escorted us to the big room. Ridley and the other deputy stayed near the door, which we left slightly ajar. Like they do it in the movies.

John and Elizabeth were waiting in their usual spots. I took a good deep breath and went over to them. John was visibly angry, Elizabeth wary.

"Mr. Swift," he said, "what is the meaning of this? Do you realize what time it is?"

"It's late," I said.

"It certainly is. Besides which, I was under the impression that we'd had our final dealings with you."

"You paid me for three days. I just wanted you to get your money's worth." I walked to the bar. "Mind if I have a drink?" I called over my shoulder. There was no answer, so I looked back at them. John was staring at me as if he were about to start spluttering like one of those long-suffering dads on the old TV family sitcoms. I poured myself a small Irish whiskey straight.

"Anybody else want anything?" I called cheerily. No reply. Considering how I felt, this kind of behavior was a pretty heavy act for me, but I needed to get things started and didn't know how to go about doing it. Plus I badly wanted the drink.

I went back over to the unsmiling Majorses and sank into the couch.

"There," I said, taking a healthy swallow. "That's better."

"Mr. Swift," John said icily, "will you kindly state the nature of your business with us?"

"In good time. Let me catch my breath first. I've had kind of a rough day, as you can see."

"Our vision's fine, Swift," Elizabeth said. "What is it that you want?"

"Oh, just a little talk. That's all."

"And what do you want to talk about?"

"Murder."

"I'm not following you," John said. "You mean this business with Ward Williams? What does that have to do with us?"

"No, not Williams's murder. Harlow Brennerman's."

"Harlow Brennerman? I've never heard of him."

"You might not have. His death wasn't big news after the rioting in Charlottesville started. But he was here two days ago."

"He was? Oh, was that the insurance man who came out to see you, Elizabeth?"

I chuckled. "Yeah, he was selling insurance, all right. Only it wasn't the kind you buy from Mutual of Omaha."

"What do you mean?"

"I mean blackmail."

"Elizabeth, what is this man talking about?"

"I haven't the slightest—"

I banged my whiskey glass down on the table.

"All right, you two," I said, "let's cut the crap, shall we? Elizabeth knows exactly what I'm talking about, and if you gave it a little thought, so would you."

John got to his feet. "Mr. Swift, I really don't feel like being insulted in my own house!"

"Sit down, John," I said calmly, "sit down. We've got a lot to talk about tonight, and you'd best relax as much as you can. C'mon, sit." He sat. He was still angry, but he did it.

"Good," I said. "Now, let's begin at the beginning, okay? Which would be your birth, wouldn't it, John?"

"My birth?" he said stonily. "What in hell does that have to do with anything?" The way he said the word "hell," it was evident that he didn't use it much.

"It shouldn't, but it does. In fact, if you had told the Colonel a long time ago that you weren't his child, chances are we wouldn't be in such a mess today."

"How did you—"

"Knock it off, John. In three days I've dug up all the family secrets. That means they aren't so very secret. I'll bet that the only person who *doesn't* know about you is the man who should have been told first. I think he's fond enough of you that he wouldn't have cared much."

John chewed on his lip. He was badly agitated. I thought I could also detect the beginning of some nervousness on Elizabeth's part, but with her it was impossible to tell for sure. In any case, she made no move to speak. I got a crawly feeling that she was silently stalking me, that she was waiting to learn everything I knew before committing herself to action. When she did act, I hoped that Ridley would be quick through the door.

"But again," I went on, "it probably wouldn't have made that much difference if the wrong people hadn't found out. Unfortunately, one of the wrong people turned out to be your wife. How many times did she use it against you over the years?" He looked down at his knees. "Once or twice, eh? But she wasn't even the worst offender. We'll have to award that dubious distinction to your lawyer."

John's head snapped erect. "Lockridge knew? How—" He looked back and forth and confusedly between the two of us.

"It doesn't matter," I said. No use naming Sarah Jane. She and John were among the few who were going to survive all this, and if she wanted to tell him, she could. "Like I told you, if I found out, anyone could've. Lockridge did. Ever since, he's been putting the screws to Elizabeth." John gaped at his wife. "Yeah, twenty years of blackmail. Nice fellow, your lawyer. Gouge you up front for his legal work, then gouge you behind your back through your wife. But don't start feeling sorry for the little lady just yet. She gets her revenge in a later chapter, as we shall see."

Without a word, John got up and fetched himself a glass of whiskey. While he was gone, Elizabeth and I engaged in a staring contest. She won handily. I didn't care; it was still the early rounds.

And then I thought: this woman has murdered her lover and her own daughter, all in the past few hours, yet she's not even as shaky as her husband. How can she be so cool?

I watched John pour his drink. He spilled some on the counter top.

"That was the way of things for a long time," I continued after John had returned. "Then, enter Harlow Brennerman, who threw an incredible monkey wrench into the works. You see, John, he was working for an insurance company in California. It appears that your grandparents, the ones on your real father's side, kept an insurance policy in your name all these years. Several months ago they were killed in an auto accident. Nobody knew where you were, so the insurance company hired an investigator. Brennerman. He tracked you here. Then, somehow, he tumbled to the game you've been playing with the Colonel. That suggested a little easy blackmail money to him. So he put the bite on Elizabeth. Wrong person. She tipped *her* blackmailer, Lockridge, and he did the rest. He couldn't afford to have Brennerman horning in on things any more than she could."

"Carter actually *killed* this Brennerman!?"

"Yeah, with darling Elizabeth directing traffic. She even set me up as her alibi in case she came under suspicion later. I think she may have been planning to throw Lockridge to the cops someday, now that she had something on him. It must have been hell being under his thumb all those years. What was it like, Elizabeth?"

My opening shot. It just glanced off her like a rubber bullet off a wild boar. She wasn't going to rattle easily, but then I hadn't expected her to.

"You're talking through your hat, Swift," was all she said, cool as

211

the fifth of November. Her husband appeared to be in shock at this point. He drained his whiskey in one very large gulp. I waited while he poured another. We had as long as it took.

This time I avoided Elizabeth's gaze, though I could still feel it on me.

"Anyway," I said when we were all settled again, "when Elizabeth originally decided to use me as her alibi, she didn't realize that I'd already met Brennerman. The next day she learned that I'd discovered the body. That gave her an even better idea. She had Lockridge tell the cops that I'd been talking to him about the guy earlier in the day and that I'd said he was connected to the Majors family. Then she planted the murder weapon in my apartment. How'd you get in, Elizabeth?"

She rolled her eyes heavenward, as if there'd be any help coming from that direction.

"You're really out of your mind, Swift," she said, and she looked perplexed. Genuinely.

"Quite the contrary, my dear, and the sheriff has been *very* interested in my theories. You see, you had a pretty good idea there, setting me up to take the fall for Brennerman's murder. Except for one little detail that you didn't know about. I stopped for a drink on the way to the motel. It's an airtight alibi. Once the sheriff confirmed that I'd been framed, he became extremely interested in whoever had been feeding him information. Because, of course, that person—or persons, in this case—would necessarily have a good reason for wanting the blame put on someone else. That reason would naturally be their own involvement. I hope you don't think that Ridley Campbell didn't see that right away. He's quite an intelligent man, you know." Might as well earn a few extra points with the sheriff while I was at it. They could come in handy.

"You don't know what you're talking about," she said, crossing her arms under her breasts. "Where's the evidence to go with all these wild stories, if I may ask?" There was a trace of amusement there. That wasn't right, not right at all. But John apparently hadn't seen it.

"Elizabeth!" John said. "What do you mean, where's the evidence? You're acting like it's all— Oh, my God, it's true, isn't it? Every—"

She turned to him and said, "Shut up!" with such menace that his face turned nearly inside out in its haste to obey. Then she

212

returned her attention to me. She was something. At this hour, the makeup was gone, and the honey hair framing her face was a bit tangled. She looked human. Beautifully human. As long as you didn't know what went on under the surface.

"Do you have any more fairy tales for us, Mr. Swift?" she asked. "Because I'm getting a little tired, if you want to know the truth. It's been a long day."

A long day? Jesus, she *wasn't* human. My own anger began to rise. I held it down.

"Of course there's more. You certain you don't want to take over?" I said as evenly as I could.

"Get on with it, will you?"

"If you insist. All right, the next thing that happened was that Delmos Venable almost got his head blown off. Wouldn't happen to know anything about that one, would you?"

"I barely knew the kid," she said. "What in hell would I want to—"

"Nice try, Elizabeth. But no go. Shall we talk a little about your motive?"

"Motive?" John said. He'd got his voice back, but it didn't make complete sentences yet.

"Yes, indeed. The oldest one in the book. You see, above all things, Elizabeth wanted to maintain herself in the style to which she'd become accustomed. Which meant staying tapped in to the Colonel's money. The only potential obstacle to this seemed to be the secret of your parentage. Typically, she was able to turn that to her own advantage. You went along because you thought you had to. But there was another threat that neither you nor she knew about. Delmos Venable."

"Delmos?" John mouthed the word without actually speaking it.

"Not directly, of course. The poor kid wouldn't be able to find his way around a blackmail plot if you led him by the hand. No, it was something beyond his control. The fact that he was the Colonel's illegitimate child."

"The Colonel's . . . son?" He was getting there. Three words that time. Elizabeth had leaned back in her chair and was looking confused. This wasn't the way it was supposed to go. Not at all. By this time, she should have begun to come unglued. A tiny seed of doubt settled into the back of my mind. Still, I kept at it.

"Yes. So he was a threat if the Colonel decided to alter his will.

And he was even more of a threat if the Colonel ever found out about you. That's why she tried to kill him. She failed there, so let's move on, shall we?"

Elizabeth groaned and muttered, "Jesus Christ deliver us."

"But—" John said.

"Don't worry, John, we'll get back to Delmos in good time. Now, this morning she went to Lockridge's office, and they had a knock-down, drag-out fight. Which might've had something to do with what I told her last night. That right, ma'am?"

As I said it, it didn't sound right even to me. How could she be concerned with who Leigh slept with, then later in the day calmly bludgeon the kid to death? It was crazy. Unless . . . I forced myself to look at what I didn't want to see. Unless . . . unless her pride had been offended, and that meant more to her than her daughter's life.

"You're disgusting," Elizabeth said, bringing me back.

"That so? *How* disgusting, Elizabeth? As disgusting as the man who tried to rape your daughter?"

John's eyes bugged out. Conflicting emotions raced across his face, one after the other. It was like watching high, fast-moving clouds pass in front of the moon.

"Even *you* didn't go for that one, did you?"

This was it, but it was beginning to scare me. The tension in the room had palpably thickened the air, and it felt about ten degrees hotter. There was no stopping now; I had to keep at it if I was going to make Elizabeth crack. It was fifty-fifty whether that would happen before John had a stroke. I silently implored him to hang in there.

Elizabeth was holding on to her cool, but it was fraying at the edges.

"Swift, I don't have to listen to your stupid fantasies—"

"What'd he say when you confronted him, that he figured she'd be better than you?"

Saying it, I felt ugly.

"You bastard," she said in a low growl. It was a dare. She was ready for the fight now.

"Elizabeth," John whimpered, "what is he talking—"

"Shut *up!*" she hissed.

"That what you said to Carter, lady? What'd he do then, laugh in your face?"

"He's scum," she said between clenched teeth. I didn't note the tense. I should have.

"Well, now, that may be the first true thing you've ever said to me, Elizabeth. When'd you realize that, after he tried to put the make on your daughter? That must be it. Yes, behold the devoted mother. Standing up for the child she's hated ever since the kid was old enough to make her look like a barrel of rusty nails by comparison."

She glared at me, close to striking out. I turned casually to John then, as if I could care less.

"But she didn't kill him then. Too many witnesses around. She got him to stay late at the office and went back for him. The suicide note was a mistake, my dear. No one leaves notes like that. Plus he was left-handed, and you shot him in the right temple. Blunders, Elizabeth. You would have done better to make it look like an intruder. What happened, you panic? That's not like you."

I'd been watching Elizabeth through all this, and I couldn't believe what I was seeing. She'd been completely turned around. The rage was gone. She was stunned. There was no faking it; she didn't know. She really *didn't know!*

"Carter is . . . dead?" she said.

"Of course he is. You know that." I was so confused, the words were out before I knew what I was saying.

"How would *I* know? John and I had to go to Greene County this evening. Nobody there told us. We only got back a little over an hour ago."

"But—" I stammered, grasping for something to make sense out of the turn of events, "—but you were in Howardsville . . ."

"Howardsville? What are you *talk*ing about? How could I have been in *Howards*ville?"

"Your car . . ."

"Swift, my *car* may have been in Howardsville, but *I* was in Greene County. As John will tell you." She gestured in his direction. "Maybe Melissa had it. What does Howardsville have to do with anything, anyway?"

Then John spoke.

"Where's Leigh?" he said without the trace of a quiver in his voice.

The question made my blood run cold. I didn't want to tell him.

Not here, not now. I looked over at him. His emotions had done another about-face. He was staring at Elizabeth, and there was an icy fury in his eye. I remembered the story of how his son had blown up after years of keeping it in and Sarah Jane's observation that John was much like Bruce. I needed to head him off but couldn't think of a thing to say. I watched helplessly.

Elizabeth didn't look at him. She was fixed on me; John didn't count.

Oh, but he did.

He repeated the question, this time in an understated snarl that carried a menace no one could miss.

"For God's sake," she said, turning to him, "who cares where that little ninny is?"

Then she saw the expression on his face, and I doubt she'd ever seen it before. It stopped her dead.

The moment hung there, somewhere beyond normal time.

In that moment, I understood. Maybe my comprehension finally caught up with my doubts. Or maybe it was when she said, "that little ninny," in a way that no one who knew the truth ever could have. Whatever.

Elizabeth had a lot to answer for. Like blackmail. Like the demise of Harlow Brennerman, in which she'd almost certainly conspired. Like maybe even the attempt on Delmos, though I was beginning to doubt it.

But she hadn't killed Lockridge. I wasn't sure who had, but it wasn't her. And she hadn't murdered Leigh, either.

It was Melissa.

"John," I said, "hold on a minute—"

Too little, too late. I had ceased to exist. Now there was only the two of them.

John's body began to shake. It was almost imperceptible at first but rapidly progressed to a raw, violent vibration. A living Mt. Saint Helens. He focused on Elizabeth. There was silence for the longest two seconds of my life; then he blew.

"Where's my daughter?" he bellowed. *"Where is Leigh?"*

It must have unnerved her. She rose from her chair, terrified. She shouldn't have done that.

John roared something unintelligible and shot out of his chair with a speed astonishing for a man of his bulk. Elizabeth lunged for a handbag that was sitting on the coffee table, but she never reached it. He crashed into her, and they fell to the floor together, her nails slashing at his face.

"John!" I yelled. *"No!"*

But he was completely out of reach, oblivious even to the wounds she'd opened near his eyes. He'd grabbed her by the throat and was in the process of choking her to death, all the while chanting his question over and over. I jumped onto his back and screamed for Ridley.

I tried to pull his hands away from her, but it was sheer futility. He had the superhuman strength of the possessed. She would have been dead if Campbell and the deputy hadn't come running in to help out. It was all the three of us could do just to haul him off her. Even after we'd pried him loose, he continued to kick and flail for several minutes, and it took all of us to hold him down. Finally, the fit subsided.

After that, the first voice was Elizabeth's. It was raspy from the throttling she'd just received but intelligible.

"Let him go," she said.

We looked up to see her standing over us. She'd made it to the handbag and was holding a small revolver, a .32 caliber at the most, but at this range perfectly lethal. The gun was twitching slightly, but not enough.

Campbell started to make a move, but I laid a hand on his arm.

"She's good, Rid," I said.

That got a half smile and a nod of affirmation from her.

We let John go. He just sat there, looking bewildered, all of the fight gone out of him. I'd have wagered he didn't remember a thing from the previous five minutes.

"Now," Elizabeth said, "back off."

We got to our feet slowly and followed instructions.

When she was satisfied with where we were, she directed her attention to her husband.

"You animal," she rasped. "How dare you do that to me?"

She aimed the gun at his head.

"Elizabeth, wait!" I said.

"For what? If I'm going down, the least I can do is take this miserable dog with me."

"I don't think that would be wise, Mrs. Majors," Ridley began.

217

"I was wrong," I said. "I know you didn't—"

Out of the corner of my eye, I caught a slight movement. Without turning my head, I looked toward the opposite end of the room. It was the Colonel. He must have heard all the screaming and come to investigate, entering the room by the far door without anyone noticing. Who knows how long he'd been there, watching. In one hand was his cane; in the other, a .45 service automatic.

Elizabeth thumbed back the hammer on her revolver.

At the same moment, the Colonel's voice boomed across the room. "Drop it, Elizabeth!"

But she didn't drop it. She turned toward him with the gun still in her hand. That was aggressive enough for the Colonel. He fired. The sound of the .45 was monstrous, like a thunderclap at the gates of hell.

Whatever else age might have done to the Colonel, it hadn't ruined his aim. The slug entered her body right over the heart, tearing open a massive, sickening hole. Blood geysered into the air, and the force of the impact knocked her flat. She was probably dead before she hit the parquet floor, but the blood continued to pour out of her body, forming an ugly, steadily widening pool.

The Colonel stood there, motionless, the smoking gun still held in front of him, his eyes fixed uncomprehendingly on the wreckage of his family.

For a long moment none of us moved. We just stared.

Campbell was the first to speak. "Jesus fucking Christ," he said in a low, bone-weary voice.

Things started happening after that as Ridley fell into his natural role of director of the action.

First he disarmed the Colonel, who hadn't the vaguest idea what was going on anymore. Then he sent out for his other deputy and put the two of them to work, phoning for ambulances and more cops, bagging evidence, starting in on the paper work.

I slumped into the nearest chair. All the tension, pain, and fatigue of the past three days seemed to fall on me at once with the collective weight of a wrecking ball. I felt as if I had witnessed about ten years of bloody civil warfare.

I was drifting off right there, having almost forgotten that the real murderess was still loose somewhere, when Ridley came over and stared down at me.

"Did Elizabeth kill her daughter?" he asked. He wasn't pleased, but he wasn't as angry as he'd been earlier in the evening. He seemed more resigned than anything else. The thing had become such an elemental bloodletting that I think he realized it was impossible to blame someone like me. You might as well blame Lockridge for starting it twenty years earlier. Or Brennerman for being a crooked P.I. Or Thurm for not doing his job. Or the Lord for creating these people in the first place.

I shook my head. "It was Melissa."

"You're sure?"

"I'm sure."

"You think she's here?"

"Probably. All the cars are in the garage."

"Let's go find her, then."

"One minute," I said, and went over to John.

He looked at me. I could tell that he knew who I was, but he didn't care.

"John . . ." I said.

"Is she . . ." he said, but he didn't really want to know. Not now. And I didn't want to tell him.

I rested my hand on his shoulder, then turned away and straggled after the sheriff. Before we left the scene, I forced myself to take a final look at Elizabeth's body. Five minutes earlier she'd been a living being, and now she was an inert form lying in a congealing puddle of blood. I hadn't expected to feel anything for her, and yet I did. Remorse, with a good measure of guilt mixed in. She'd been a rotten person, but she hadn't killed anybody, and she hadn't deserved to die as she did. That she had was partially due to what I'd told the Colonel. Maybe. Which placed a little of the blame for all this squarely on my head. For a moment I thought I was going to be sick.

Then I pulled it together and followed Ridley into the hall.

Deya led us to Melissa's room. On the way I cursed myself for having tried to fit all aspects of this case into one neat little box. For having mistakenly seen each event as the logical outgrowth of its predecessor. For having been unable to prevent even one of the killings. In the end, I was truly my own worst enemy. And everybody else's.

The door was locked. Ridley pounded on it. When there was no response, he threw himself against it.

The smell hit us first as the door splintered open.

I nearly threw up.

Ridley looked at me with the question that didn't need to be asked. I shrugged. It wasn't the stench of final decay, but it wasn't far from it. I didn't know what it meant, and I didn't really want to. But I followed him into the room.

Melissa was lying on the bed, naked, curled up into the fetal position. She was alive, in a manner of speaking. The beautiful young body was smeared with its own waste. The lips were drawn back, and the teeth bared in a mirthless rictus that mimicked death. The eyes were fixed on something that wasn't visible to another soul.

She'd gone far, far beyond the bottom of the long slide.

Cain and Abel, I thought. Move the story up a few thousand years, change the gender, add in some modern wonders like Quaaludes and PCP, and this is what you get.

"Jesus fucking Christ," Campbell said again.

"Rid," I said, "I can't handle any more of this," and I walked out. Out of the room. Out of the house. Out of the broken lives of the remaining Majorses. My only regret was that I couldn't walk out of a world where such things threaten to become commonplace.

The snow was still coming down, falling equally on those who'd deserved their premature ends and those who hadn't.

I leaned against the fabulous fountain and began to retch.

· 13 ·

"My God, that's ugly," Patricia Ryan said.

We were sitting around the table at her house, sipping coffee with a touch of Irish whiskey and a little hand-whipped cream on the top. Dinner was over, and I'd just finished recounting the events at the Majors mansion Thursday night.

"Yeah," I said. "This is the first time in my life I've been involved in something this bad. Charlottesville will never be quite the same for me."

No, it wouldn't. Thursday was two days in the past now. It had snowed and snowed, eventually accumulating eight or ten inches. The riot over Ward Williams's death had petered out. His killer was awaiting trial. Angry people had gone home. A bipartisan group had been appointed by the city/county governments to look into the matter. Bruce had gone back to the Sikhs. The Colonel and Melissa had been locked up, leaving John to rattle around in the mansion by himself. Leigh would be buried on Sunday. A peculiar calm had descended on the town, with even the night's basketball game failing to generate the normal enthusiasm.

Life went on. As usual for most folks, perhaps. For those who hadn't seen one teenager lying in her own blood and another lying in her own filth.

I was seriously considering chucking my chosen profession. Although what I could be retrained to do at my age was beyond me.

"What kind of person *was* she?" Patricia said.

"Well," I said, "Melissa wanted to be loved, like any adolescent. I did, you did, she did. She didn't get any at home, so she looked elsewhere. She got a fast car, started drinking and using drugs, turned on the sex charm for anyone who'd stay in one place long enough. None of it worked. At the same time, her sister was favored by her father and had the affection of the one person they'd both been crazy about since childhood. Delmos. She was eaten up with jealousy. A lot of teenagers go through nearly identical circumstances. Given a society to grow up in that's drug dependent and obsessed with guns, it's a wonder that the Melissas of America are relatively rare."

She sighed. "That's a pretty cynical view."

"If you wish, though I prefer realistic. If I didn't have that perspective, I'd most likely be dead by now."

"I suppose so. And I do see what you're driving at. There's her greed, too. All kids are greedy until they bang against the world for a while. I guess if you're rich all your life, if you've never known anything else, then you might not *have* to face up to not getting everything you want. Which was Melissa. Having everything and wanting more."

"And look at her role models."

"Right. Greed must have seemed as natural to her as breathing in and out. But that's not uncommon, either. A lot of people, most people, never push it as far as she did. I imagine it was the drugs."

"Well," I said, "who can say? It's a convenient answer, but who knows exactly what it is that pushes someone so far out they can't get back? I've never heard any kind of head-shrink explanation that told me anything. But there's no denying that drugs can help, and when you start mixing them, watch out. You can't imagine what kind of pharmacy Melissa kept stashed away in that room. Coke, 'ludes, crystal meth, the works. Plus about every room in the house has a wet bar. She could have strung herself halfway to the moon every day of her life if she wanted to. A few months of that and somebody's bound to get hurt."

"Too often the innocent."

She looked over at Patrick, who'd been listening quietly. There was an awkward silence.

Finally, Patrick said, "Drunk driver. He walked away from it."

"I'm sorry," I said.

"It's done. Just treat me like anyone else, and life will still be worth living."

"You're something else," Patricia said.

"Ah, cut the crap," Patrick said. "Let's change the subject. How much do you know about what led up to Thursday night?"

"As it turns out," I said, "we know quite a lot. But I warn you that it's just more ugliness. You sure you want to hear it?"

"We will anyway, eventually," Patricia said.

"Okay. It begins and ends with Melissa, of course. She's a seriously disturbed person, everyone agrees on that. But you have to remember that while she was downed out half her life, the other half she was hatching some heavy schemes to gain control of the family money.

"The money, that's the key to everything. Melissa wanted it. So did Elizabeth. Lockridge wanted to cut himself in. It was a delicate balance on the best of days—with each of the participants conniving to come out with the biggest slice of the pie in the end—but it held for a long while.

"Then three things happened. First, the Colonel decided to change his will, acknowledging Delmos and upping Leigh's share, cutting back Melissa's, John's, and Elizabeth's. Second, Leigh took off and John hired me to find her. And third, Brennerman showed up. He put the bite on Elizabeth, threatening to use what he knew about John's parentage to destroy the whole elaborate setup. That was intolerable.

"Elizabeth moved fast. She got Lockridge to agree to pay Brennerman a visit, while she tried to get me off the case. But fast as Elizabeth was moving, so was Melissa. She went to see Brennerman on her own."

"Melissa?" Patrick said. "How'd she know about Brennerman?"

"She listened at the door while Brennerman was putting the screws to her mother. The Majors's maid, Deya, found her out there, but she figured it wasn't a maid's business so she didn't say anything to anybody. Later, after the shootout, it seemed like it might be important and she told the cops.

"Whatever Melissa overheard, it was enough to convince her that Brennerman was a real threat. She decided to have a chat with him. Just in case, she took a gun along, but she was hedging her bets. It wasn't *her* gun, the one she normally kept in her car. It was Lockridge's gun."

"Lockridge's?" Patricia said. "How did Melissa—"

223

"I'll get to that. For now, just realize that she went to the motel with a pistol in her coat pocket that wasn't her own. She tried to reason with Brennerman. It didn't work. He thought he was holding all the good cards, and he wasn't afraid of a teenage girl. That was a mistake. It got him quickly dead."

"Melissa shot Brennerman?" Patrick said. "I thought that Lockridge . . ."

I nodded. "He was there, too."

"Grand Central Station."

"Just about. The three of us went there independently, none knowing the plans of any of the others. It's a wonder we didn't all end up in Room 14 at the same time. Pure chance.

"Anyway, when Lockridge arrived at the motel, he must have been awfully surprised. But I doubt he spent much time grieving. Someone had just saved him a lot of trouble. He's the one who stripped the room, in order to delay identification of the body while he and Elizabeth carried out whatever plan they had to prevent the Colonel from altering his will. They had to have devised *some* kind of plan, because the Colonel isn't the sort who would have tolerated much inaction when he wanted something done. Whatever the plan was, you can be sure it wasn't in anyone's best interests but their own.

"On his way back to Charlottesville, I saw Lockridge's car. That was bad news for him, but it also turned out badly for me, since it misdirected my attention right at the beginning. Consequently, it was a big break for Melissa. I never saw what she was doing, even though there was plenty to see if I'd been intelligent enough to give it some impartial thought."

"C'mon Loren," Patricia said. "You couldn't have known. Don't blame yourself." She put a hand on my arm.

"I try not to. But when you start making the kind of mistakes that get people killed, maybe it's time to get out of the business."

"Perhaps," she said, and left it at that.

"So Melissa got her first taste of blood," I continued. "Maybe she liked it. At the least it seems to have whetted her appetite for sex, because the next place she showed up was in my bed. I guess that's no surprise, considering how wrapped together sex and violence are these days.

"I turned her down, of course, and she stalked out of the room.

224

I was still sitting on the bed when she left. On the way out, she screamed from the living room that I was a faggot. That's when she must have slid Lockridge's gun under my sofa."

"So she hadn't intended to frame you," Patrick said.

"No. She did it in the heat of her anger. Whatever frame she'd originally had in mind involved Lockridge, since it was his gun. That would have been somewhere further down the road."

"I don't understand," Patricia said. "Why would it even occur to Melissa to try to frame you? She didn't know there was any connection between you and Brennerman, did she?"

"Actually, she did. When she pulled the gun on Brennerman in the motel room, and he realized she was serious, he tried to get her to put it away by saying that he was expecting me momentarily, and that she couldn't risk shooting him for that reason. Obviously, it didn't work. All it did was tip Melissa that I'd probably be the one to discover the body."

"Are you going to tell us how you know all this?" Patricia asked.

"Bear with me," I said. "Now, Melissa left my apartment in a rage. She'd killed one man that night and then been sexually rejected by another. She'd been doing a lot of uppers, coke or speed; she had to have, considering how downed she'd been earlier in the day. What she most wanted to do was to vent her anger and frustration on me, I suppose. But I was armed. Leigh would have been a good second choice, but Melissa didn't know where she was at that point. So she struck out at the next most likely target."

"Delmos," Patricia whispered.

"I'm afraid so. It was probably only half thought out, but it makes a certain warped sense given the state she was in. Delmos was someone she wanted desperately and he'd rejected her advances. In addition, by hurting him she would be hurting Leigh. And there was a third factor, which I'll get to in a minute."

"But she'd left the gun in your apartment," Patrick pointed out.

"Right. An impulsive act that she probably regretted. Though not for long, I suspect. It was Lockridge's gun. As such, it might be used against him in the Brennerman murder, but that was about it.

"Anyway, there was a second gun. John confirmed that. It seems that a year or so ago Melissa had some trouble with a hitchhiker she picked up. Since then, John told the cops, she'd always kept a loaded pistol in the glove compartment of the Mustang. That's the

225

one she used on Delmos, wherever it is now. They haven't found it yet."

"Jesus," Patrick said.

"Yeah, it was quite a night. With the attempt on Delmos, it was over. After that, she ditched the gun someplace and went home and crashed. It must have been a pretty steep drop, what with the drugs and all the adrenalin she would have generated.

"The next day she lay low. Leaving the Brennerman gun at my place, though unpremeditated, wouldn't have looked like such a bad idea. Provided the cops found it. So she tipped them. It was risky. By so doing, she was exposing herself. But she obviously decided it was worth it.

"From her point of view, not much else happened that day. Except for one very important thing. She found out where her sister was."

"I've been wondering how she knew that," Patrick said.

"Her father told her," I said. "It came out when the cops talked to him.

"After I met with John and Elizabeth Wednesday night, and gave them my report, Melissa asked them what I'd found out. It probably seemed like an innocent question. John had no reason not to tell her, so he did. It's a gruesome twist to the story."

There was a long pause then. We drank our Irish coffee and thought our own peculiar thoughts.

"Now we do Thursday?" Patrick said finally.

"Now we do Thursday," I said. "Melissa had probably already decided to murder her sister. Maybe it was years earlier, who knows? But first she made a date to see Lockridge, after hours."

"Oh no," Patricia groaned. "Melissa killed . . . Carter, too?"

"Yes. And it's only because of that that we know all the things we do. You see, Lockridge's office was wired."

"*Wired?*"

"Wired. There was a voice-activated recording system in there. Whatever was said in the office, it's all on tape."

"Oh come on, Loren. I *worked* for the man. How could I not have known about it?"

"Why on earth should Lockridge tell *you* what he was doing?"

"I don't know. I thought . . . I don't know."

"It's a moot point," I said. "He taped his conversations. The city

226

cops told Campbell about it and he called today to tell me. That's something he probably shouldn't have done, technically. But I guess Rid felt I deserved to know for sure who had killed whom. It won't matter in the long run. They'll never try Melissa for anything; all of the bloodshed apparently sent her completely around the bend. They've got her in the hospital now, and the prognosis is pretty bleak. She's still comatose."

"Well, what's on the tapes?" Patrick asked.

"Tape, actually," I said. "Lockridge was too crafty to leave them lying around. So the only one the cops found was the one that had been running when he died. That's the important one, of course. Where he stashed the others we may never know, and perhaps it's just as well.

"In any case, one thing the tape makes clear is that Melissa and Lockridge had a prior, ah, relationship."

"Oh God," Patricia said.

"Uh huh. Leigh was the only family holdout, I'm afraid. But with Melissa it wasn't exactly true love. They argued for quite a while. During the course of events, Melissa revealed the things I've told you about so far. How she knew about Brennerman. What happened at the motel. She thought he'd be pleased. I'm sure he was, though he certainly wasn't about to admit it. She was trying to talk him into some kind of partnership, offering sex and the prospect of lots of money. But he didn't need her for that. He had her over a barrel now and he realized it. There was no reason to be anything but cool to her proposals.

"Then they talked about Delmos. She admitted having taken the shot at him. She thought that would please Lockridge too, especially since he'd told her about the will change."

"He *told* her!" Patricia said.

"Yes. Lockridge had been intimate with Melissa. He realized she was a human time bomb waiting for the right match. And he knew of her mixed feelings about Delmos. So he manipulated her. Judging from the conversation, he hadn't told her about the part of the change that favored Leigh. Even Lockridge wasn't *that* nasty. He just planted the seeds against Delmos. It couldn't have done him much harm, and there was the off chance it would do him a lot of good. It was worth it."

"Loren," Patricia pleaded. She was hurt, badly hurt. But better she got it from me than the papers. "Loren, I can't believe all this. How could I have . . ."

"Patricia, you work for someone for years and you think you have a handle on who he is. Yet in many ways it's an artificial relationship, based solely on money given for services received. You never really *know* the person. It's not a failing of yours; it's built into the situation. You couldn't see more than he chose for you to see."

She didn't say anything. She wouldn't let this rest easily, just as I wouldn't Leigh's death. But if things worked out we could at least help each other.

"I guess that's about it," Patrick said.

"Yeah, that's about it. Melissa's final ploy was to tell Lockridge that it was his gun she'd used on Brennerman—one she'd stolen from his house after one of their trysts. She thought that might make him susceptible to a little blackmail of her own. Instead he just laughed at her. The gun was dead cold. No way the cops could ever trace it to him. And if she went to the cops with her story, well, who would you believe: a respected lawyer or some teenage druggie? He owned her.

"That's when she threatened him with one of the Colts off the wall. Carter was cool to the very end. He just told her to stop playing games. He really didn't believe she'd do it, even when she walked right up to him and pointed the thing at his head. The man's self-confidence was astonishing.

"Afterward, Melissa typed that ridiculous suicide note. Then she drove home. Judging from when Lockridge was killed and when she contacted Leigh from the mansion, she moved directly from shooting him into the plan to kill her sister. All it took was a phony message from Delmos, asking Leigh to meet him at the family cabin. She stayed in the house a minimum of time, then took off in her mother's car. Why, we'll never know. Maybe it was a drug-fuzzied scheme to try and implicate Elizabeth, which she hoped to flesh out with other 'evidence.' Whatever. I think it's safe to say Melissa was beginning to come unstuck at this point.

"Leigh never had a chance. The poor kid had been an unwitting emotional thorn in Melissa's side for a long time. Plus she was bound to inherit at least her share of the Majors money. Plus Delmos favored her over her sister.

"So Melissa killed her, then drove back to the estate, clinging to whatever shreds of sanity were left. Eventually, she must have realized that John and Elizabeth had been off somewhere together and that her half-baked frame wasn't going to work. In any case, something pushed her all the way over the edge, and she locked herself in her room. I've told you how she was when we found her."

There was another long silence.

"What's going to happen to you?" Patrick said eventually.

I sighed. "Good question. Mainly, I've got to find a way to live with it all. Elizabeth is dead, in part due to what I did. Leigh is dead, in part because of what I didn't do."

Patricia started to interrupt, but I held up my hand.

"Please," I said. "Don't try to be my conscience. I'll get it worked out, but with myself and by myself. It's just going to hurt for a while. It has to. Leigh didn't deserve to die. And while Elizabeth was a thoroughly rotten human being, she didn't deserve her fate, either. Do you understand what I'm feeling?"

Patricia nodded. I don't believe she could have spoken at that moment if she'd wanted to. Patrick did instead.

"How do you stand legally?" he asked.

"Ah," I said, "there is that. Well, I suppose they might have enough to arrest me. Lacking that, they could certainly pull my license if they wanted to. But I don't think any of that will happen. All the killings are solved, and I didn't have a direct hand in any of them. That's the most important item. And I didn't mislead the sheriff. Plus there's Deputy Thurman's screw-up. If he'd done his job Leigh might still be alive. Any trial or hearing involving me would bring that right out into the open. Campbell's a good man, and a realist. He'll prefer to handle that aspect of things quietly. And you can be sure that Thurm will never do police work again."

Again there was a lull. The subject was about talked out.

"Loren," Patricia said finally, "let's get the bloody hell out of here and not discuss all this ever again."

"How about a ball game," I said. "It's Saturday night, and I hear there's a good one in town."

She smiled for the first time in a while. "You're on."

Delmos had gotten us three seats for the North Carolina game. Actually, two seats and a spot for Patrick's chair. In the president's box, no less. When the president of the University learned I'd helped put Delmos's would-be killer away, I imagine he was only too happy to set us up.

Before the game, Delmos had come over. I'd phoned him on Friday, but this was the first time I'd seen him since—well, since everything. His head was still bandaged.

We didn't talk about the past. There was nothing more to say. We'd shared a moment that was about as intimate as two people who aren't lovers can share.

Instead, I introduced him to Patricia. And to Patrick, who was thrilled.

"You don't look like you're ready to play tonight," I said.

"I'm not going to start," he said. "But I'll go in if they need me."

"Don't take chances. There's the whole rest of the season, y'know. The NCAAs, stuff like that."

"I was aware."

"Okay. Good luck. And . . . let's beat the bastards."

He'd grinned and trotted off to warm up.

The game was a typical Carolina/Virginia matchup. Carolina was loaded with high school all-Americans and was ranked in the top five, as they inevitably are. Virginia had gotten a couple of the players that Carolina hadn't had room on the roster for. But they had only one legitimate superstar, Delmos. The rest were decent if not great players who simply played well together. Give the credit to Storm Taylor for making them number one.

The game began. I loved it. Taylor and Dean Smith paced along their respective ends of the sideline, working the referees, trying to get the calls going their way. Smith had the most success. He usually does. For years, rival ACC coaches have been trying to figure out his secret. They haven't yet, and he's not telling.

Carolina broke on top early, as is their custom, and by halftime they were up twelve. Dean's justly famous trap press was giving Virginia's guards fits. Without Delmos in there, they couldn't match the Tar Heels' quickness. When Virginia did manage to get into their half-court game, Carolina packed themselves back into a tight zone, effectively denying the Cavalier forward line the ball. The guards were allowed the outside shot. Again, without Delmos there wasn't much of a threat.

The first five minutes of the second half, the Heels went to work on a blowout. The lead rose to eighteen. Then, abruptly, inex-

230

plicably, the momentum shifted. I'm always amazed that that can happen, but I don't argue with it. It's what makes college basketball the most exciting sport around.

The tide reversed. Carolina started turning the ball over. Virginia's guards started hitting, loosening the zone and creating a few layups. The Tar Heel shooting touch turned to stone. Slowly but surely, the big lead evaporated, the way it usually seems to do in these contests.

In desperation, Carolina went to the four corners. Unfortunately for them, Phil Ford graduated many years ago, and no one has been able to run it quite as well since. The Cavs broke it and kept whittling away.

Now, with eight seconds left, Virginia had the ball under its own basket, down two. Time was out.

"Del-*mos*! Del-*mos*!" the crowd chanted.

He took off his warm-up shirt. The crowd went berserk. Number 32, Delmos Venable, was in the game.

On the court, the Carolina players fell back, guarding against a long pass that would move Virginia up without using any time. The inbounder chose to go to Delmos, right at the end line. The clock started.

Delmos took off, straight down the center of the court. No one contested him until he crossed into Carolina's defensive end. Then the Tar Heel point guard moved out to the perimeter to block Delmos from pulling up and taking a foul-line jumper. At the top of the key, Delmos put a move on him. He planted his lead foot, spun completely around, switched the dribble to his left hand, and accelerated toward the basket like he hadn't missed a step. The crowd screamed. The Carolina defender was so stunned that he just kind of waved at Delmos going by, catching his upper arm. Whistle. Foul. One-and-one. Two seconds left.

Delmos walked to the line and took the ball. He didn't like to waste a lot of time when it came to freebies. The idea was to shoot. He bounced the ball once and put it up. Nothing but net.

Back came the ball. He bounced it once and lofted the final foul shot. It hit the back of the rim, ricocheted forward and back a couple of times, then rolled off. A Virginia player grabbed the rebound, threw up an off-balance shot, missed. North Carolina pulled down the second rebound as the buzzer went off.

The game was over.